Sojourn Volume 1: What Dreams Await

Steven Gamella

Prologue: The Legend of Uehara:

Initiation

"Many eons ago, when humanity was still a young, virile species, long

before the knowledge of the Elders had been passed down through the

Talisman that bore his name, the hero known only as Uehara set out on a

grand journey across the stars, bound for parts unknown. In his Avatar

body, he carried a great and wondrous power within him, one that

granted him a God-like radiance that shined down upon all those who saw

him. For hundreds of years he traveled across the Republic into wild

space, settling and colonizing many worlds in the name of humankind and

its allies; the Elohim, the Astari and many other species of sentient organisms. He traveled this way, until he encountered, by pure chance, an ancient civilization long-since forgotten by humanity at large.

In eons past, a group of rogue colonists had broken away from the Republic and had formed their own Empire in wild space, completely cut off from the Republic and in control of more than 150 colony worlds. These colonists had interbred with a native humanoid species and had discarded their Avatar bodies in exchange for biological immortality, rather than cybernetic. Uehara landed on this lost Empire's capital world and was immediately viewed with suspicion by these people, who promptly imprisoned him on their world. These people, calling themselves the Sunangels, believed in the philosophies of heroism, strength, and dominating one's enemies. Based on this belief system, the Sunangels turned Uehara loose, but followed his ship back to Republic space...the Great Sunangel War had begun. Uehara, leading his band of Lightbringer followers, rallied the Republic Senate and the fleet to engage the Sunangels in open warfare, and using the almighty power contained within his Avatar body, the Sunangels were eventually defeated, but only after the Republic capital worlds of Earth and Stronghold were razed to the ground by the Sunangels. The Sunangels eventually faded into obscurity and were absorbed by the Republic, and the Republic, paranoid beyond all belief, razed all forms of life on their planets to the ground. In one of the darkest moments of Republic history, the Republic fleet demolished thousands of innocent civilians' homes, at the protest of the Lightbringers...However, after this war, the Lightbringers became Republic heroes, and began establishing a presence throughout the Republic, eventually settling on a small colony world more than 600 million light years away from Earth. This satellite was called Oumi, and the Lightbringers still worship and practice on this world even today, in the Fourteenth Age of humanity, a time of great peace and prosperity.

The Order of Lightbringers was tasked with carrying on the legendary hero and explorer's values and traditions, including the beliefs in self-sufficiency and self-betterment. Social justice became central to the Lightbringers' philosophy, as did bettering the lives of all Mankind by making the difficult decisions that no one else could make. Uehara's consciousness merged with the energy of the Universe, and became imbued within the Talisman that bears his name. On Oumi, this Talisman is held within the inner sanctum of Heiei Castle, where it waits to be awakened once again...Now, Koda, please step forward..." Elder Master Iori said, his face illuminated by a sacred flame. Surrounding him, deep within the Inner Sanctum of Heiei Castle were the Lightbringers, clad in white hoods with a crimson emblem emblazoned upon their outfits. In the center of the circle, a nervous young man sat, listening to the Lightbringers chanting eerily all around him.

"The ancient values of our Order have been preserved in the Talisman of our Founder, our Light, our power and our Godly essence. Young Koda, do you understand what makes us so powerful?" Elder Master Iori asked.

"I believe so," Koda replied.

"Master Munraito...step forward to begin the process..." Elder Master Iori instructed. Another hooded Lightbringer stood up and sat in front of Koda.

"Every traditional society is characterized by the presence of entities, be they gods, spirits, mortals or traditions that, by virtue of their natural superiority, whether acquired or innate, embody a power beyond mortal comprehension," Munraito began, while Koda listened intently.

"One of these beings is known as 'Light,' referred to in many human cultures with such names as Lucifer, Kalki, Vajra, Radiant, or simply 'The One.' What we choose to call it, however, is irrelevant; it simply IS. According to the original meaning of the term, 'Light' did not refer to any personification, anthropomorphic deity or actual being, but the overarching force of knowledge. This force, in Greek mythology, was written as 'demos,' from which the English word 'Demon' is derived. Therefore, Light represents knowledge and free will, so crucial to human existence, but so vilified by the Church; hence 'demons' are entities of evil. This is not so in many Eastern cultures. As you doubtlessly know, demons are creatures bearing knowledge beyond human comprehension, which did not have to be supernatural in nature, but could be very real. Light's power was felt everywhere the force of humans traveled; they brought enlightenment and justice to the deprived lands of the Earth and the vastness of the Universe, and will continue to do so as long as the human race exists, ad infinitum. Though Light has never been personified in a human form, its manifestation is often in any society's leader," Munraito explained.

"One such leader is the Pontifex, according to the original meaning of the word and the society he oversaw. Pontifex by itself means 'builder of bridges,' or 'path-maker.' In ancient times, the word 'pons' also meant 'path.' Moreover, the Pontifex was usually associated with an Emperor, or a 'rex,' in Latin. Servius, a late-fourth century Roman commentator on the works of Virgil, reported that in traditional times, the Pontifex would also be the king and priest of Rome. Likewise, a saying in the Nordic and

Germanic traditions states that 'the leaders will build our bridges.' The Japanese also had a saying that 'the Emperor is the Light-' Munraito explained further.

"Thus, Light is most often personified in the form of an emperor, or a 'Pontifex,' which, in modern times, is applied to the Pope or a high level of clergy in whatever faith he belongs to. Thus, true monarchs and leaders are the personification of Light and Knowledge, as the philosopher Julius Evola wrote, 'beyond ordinary life.' The presence of such individuals has a profound effect on the world in which they live. Entire spiritual existences of civilizations are lifted by the mere presence of such men and women, from their god-like authority and their 'pontifical' meditation.

These influences permeate people's thoughts, intentions, actions and lives, ordering every aspect of their existence, while at the same time encouraging strong-minded individuals to exercise their 'inner God' and to seek their own prosperity, using their wits and reason to find their way in the world, this our Pantheon Doctrine exemplifies," Munraito continued.

"These influences also make fortune to the general health, prosperity and well-being of the Pontifex's society. However, given the infrequency of Pontifex-type personalities in history, one must ask, where does this power come from, and how do these 'Light' individuals stay in power? In the world of ancient societies, the most important foundations for kings, chiefs and Emperors, was their transcendent and inhuman qualities. These qualities were very real to those who witnessed them firsthand, and were widely feared by the lesser minds. This reverence and respect assured the Pontifex an eternal position of power and respect among those intelligent enough to see his genius, as the Egyptian Pharaohs, the Roman Emperors and the leaders of Nazi Germany and Napoleonic Europe proved.

Traditional societies, unlike those of decadent and later times, completely ignored the mere politics and rhetoric of authority. They trusted the roots of the Pontifex's power to lay solely in the leader's strength, violence, wisdom, physical appearance, and minimal concern for the collective. These early manifestations of Light were solely self-serving, sociopathic entities that had one goal: to attain ultimate, everlasting power over a realm, long after the individual Pontifex passed away. The Pontifex was a divine presence in human form, a God among Men. In the modern world, however, the Pontifex still exists, yet he hides, afraid to assert his dominance, for a new force, the force of democracy, has taken the Pontifex's place. This democracy, the United Human Republic, will eventually destroy our society by casting it into the pit of decadence and despair. We see this problem, and that is what motivated us to start this process more than 85 years ago with the War of Light. The fact that we 'won' the war is irrelevant. The Republic's own political devices will destroy our society by allowing criminals and foul beings to erode its foundations. It is inefficient, slow and broken, since the Senate cannot agree on anything. A new system is needed, under a new Pontifex, to lead the human race out of the darkness and into the Light. Long have we awaited this time, and this pattern has repeated itself more times than you can fathom," Munraito continued to explain.

"In our tradition, our leaders are not called merely 'Lords,' but 'fighting Lords,' to designate the victorious and glorious character of the Light present in all of us. We are each a civilization unto ourselves, free of all weakness. Organic life cannot even begin to grasp the nature of our existence. I am a direct Starseed of the Universe itself, and I have reclaimed my role as Holy Light of Salvation through rituals that reproduced the victory of Naruhol Ihr Lord Horak over the previous Universal society of organics, the Sylpheed, many millions of years ago. These rites have such a power that they evoke the very force, life and power of the Universe itself within me, granting me divine providence.

The divine flame, the Hvareno, shines upon the deprived organic condition like a beacon in the night, something that you, as a Lightbringer, will come reasonably close to understanding," Munraito continued.

"In the traditional formulation of our being, the Lightbringers mix various elements inside our radiating bodies to create a non-terrestrial power, a fluid energy called 'sa,' which consecrates and gives witness to our solar, triumphant nature. It gushes forth as pure energy from one of us to another, thus guaranteeing our uninterrupted, golden sequence of divine immortality, legitimately imposed as 'regere.' Christian traditions interpret this 'glory' as a divine attribute of God, or as the beatific vision of a halo around a figure's head, or as the Christian concept of Lucifer in the sense that Light impersonates God. When viewed from different traditions, Light can also be seen as the Egyptian Uraeus, the Persian and Roman solar helixes, or the Norwegian Black Sun. In Chinese and Japanese traditions, the Emperor, as a 'son of heaven,' whom their respective societies once believed had non-human origins, enjoyed the 'mandate of heaven' in Chinese society, which implied the force we embody. The Japanese believed something similar, in that Light would embody all that is just in a ruler and king, and that the Emperor would act as a 'gardener,' growing the seeds of justice while weeding the unjust from your world.

The connection is simple. Every organic society that has ever existed has acknowledged the force of Light. It is all referencing the same overarching force of regality, and we are that force personified in a species. We are the ultimate gardeners, organic societies exist because we allow them to, and they end because we demand them to. Every creature in this universe bows to our will, from the largest animal to the smallest bacterium...and you will soon learn to harness that power. May the Light of the Divine Flame shine upon us all, the holy star which walks with us and lights up from the depths of darkness..."

Chapter 1: A Sixth Moon

Oumi, Outer Territories. Fourteenth Age of Humanity, United Human Republic.

The sun was setting. Its radiant rays of red stained the skies of Oumi with a wondrous pallet of late-winter glory. Nestled in the shadow of the snow-capped Panarin Mountains, Heiei Castle was awash with color in the evening sun -- so beautiful, and the inspiration for many an artist from all over the United Human Republic that spanned half the Milky Way Galaxy, and many points beyond. Standing in his bedroom chamber was Master Sukui no Munraito Hikari-sama, dressed in his evening regalia, making sure that his hair looked presentable and that his robe's obi, a ceremonial sash, was tied to his liking. His name meant "Most Honorable Light of the Moon," for his pale white face, blue eyes and black hair and his title, "Sukui no," denoted him as a young man of great faith. He was the youngest Grand Master of the Lightbringer Inheritors, a group of high priests who represented the Oumi Sector in the Republic Senate on Earth and Stronghold, more than 600 million light years away. Having founded the colony as a commune many centuries before, they watched as their society grew around them. They were well respected for their powerful will and belief that humanity could accomplish anything if sufficient effort were dedicated to achieving a goal. The Senate had granted them representation alongside non-Lightbringers, even though they were from a religious organization.

At only 25 years old, Munraito was a tall, handsome, slender specimen of Japanese descent, much like everyone else on Oumi, one of the few permanent planetary settlements throughout the vast Republic. Most of the inhabitants of the Republic lived in enormous planet-sized space colonies, endlessly traveling through the vast abyss of space. The planets that humans occupied on a permanent basis were always quite special. Oumi was one of those worlds, a world of beautiful landscapes, endless red twilight, and climatic extremes. The planet orbited a red dwarf star that emitted less than 10 percent of the light of Earth's sun. The planet orbited so close to the star, Amaterasu, that the planet was tidally locked with the star. Those tidal forces ensured that one side of the planet was trapped in a perpetual, blazing-red twilight, while the other side was in a completely frozen darkness.

As Munraito prepared to give the invocation, he noticed something outside the castle that caught his attention. The vast biodiversity found on

Oumi was becoming deeply disturbed by something. Something was coming. Something very, very large. Oumi itself was one of the most complex worlds in the entire Local Group of galaxies, with hundreds of unique ecosystems that were keenly in tune with any disturbance to the environment; At the planet's perihelion, a gigantic cyclonic storm, known as the White Eye, raged endlessly, drenching vast areas of Oumi's equatorial region with constant rain and wind; the vast rainfall generated colossal rivers, which flowed across vast deltas in the southern continents. These areas were dotted with crystal-clear springs and misty mountains, whose highest peaks were capped with a layer of ethereal snow. Shrines constructed by human colonists fit into the natural beauty of the region. All life on Oumi depended on the White Eye producing rain and wind.

These lush river deltas formed Oumi's habitable zone, located in the equatorial region between the storm zone and the dark zone.

Also in Oumi's habitable zone was the "Doki-Doki" Forest, which consisted of crawling, terrestrial 10-meter high anemones, so-named for their loud heartbeats, which echoed for miles. These creatures had developed a symbiotic relationship with the local algae, allowing them to photosynthesize in the everlasting tropical sunlight from Amaterasu. The Doki-Doki Forest supported a colossal ecosystem on the river deltas. The ecosystem included both amphibious herbivores called Mudfrogs, which had six legs and their own social colony system, and predators such as the Slitherstinger, a huge, stinging slime mold that acted as the top consumer of life in the Doki-Doki Forest.

The enormous tropical forests, teeming with red or burgundy-colored plants to absorb the red wavelength from the star were awash with life, ranging from the tiny brightly-colored Bat Swallows pollinating the verdant Ookazi Roses and other native flowers, to the 4.5-meter-high Shinigami Birds. These birds were colossal, carnivorous, flightless ostrich-like creatures that hunted in packs like wolves. They had gigantic shearing beaks and tusks on either side of their naked, gray, vulture-like heads, and were covered in silky black-brown hair-like feathers, and had razor-sharp claws on the end of their shaggy wings. These claws complemented the huge sickle claws on the larger of their two toes, which they used to slash and gore their prey, much like a raptor dinosaur. Their sallow, bloodshot eyes were perfectly adapted for seeing in low-light conditions, as most of their hunting was done at night or in the depths of the tropical forests, where little sunlight penetrated. These terrifying predators were as heavy as buffaloes on Earth, and stalked the gloomy forests for prey; they were

Oumi's largest terrestrial carnivore, and very dangerous animals to meet on a jungle hike...they stayed far away from human settlements, though. The huge males, each with an enormous, handsome black ruff around the base of its neck, were occasionally seen near Heiei Castle during their spring mating season. There they would squawk loudly to establish dominance for the drab-brown females, whose necks lacked the males-only ruff and inflatable wattle.

Soaring high over the Ookazi Fields at the foot of the Panarin Mountains were ferocious aerial hunters, the incredible Velvet Impalers: huge, reptilian predators the size of small aircraft, they possessed two glowing, bioluminescent patches on their spade-shaped tails that glowed like shining eyeballs staring skyward. Zooming like living fighter-jets with rigid, 50-foot wingspans through the atmosphere, these sleek, black creatures looked almost artificial; with their fixed wings and jet-like shape, several Republic drone craft looked nearly identical to an Impaler.

Impalers were truly horrific predators, however, soaring at heights of close to 60,000 feet in the dense, warm atmosphere of Oumi, which contained 30% more oxygen than Earth. They usually hunted in pairs, but were occasionally observed in large flocks, called "Squadrons" by wildlife watchers on Oumi. Impalers were blind; they possessed no eyes, but located their prey with sonar pings. When they detected a prey animal, they would use the four methane bladder organs on their tailwings like jet engines. The special bladder organs enabled them to zoom forward at nearly 500 miles per hour, swooping down on their prey and impaling it on a gigantic lance, similar to a narwhal's tusk but as hard as titanium.

A long, spiked tongue running through the lethal lance would then drain the prey of its bodily fluids, similar to the manner in which a spider could kill an insect. Unlike the Shinigami Birds, the Impalers were indiscriminate feeders, and many an unsuspecting human had been killed and eaten by these fearsome animals.

Their native prey, however, came from the vast herds of grazing animals that populated the Ookazi Fields, as it had been for untold millions of years before the arrival of the human colonists in the era of the Republic. One such prey animal was the bizarre Zephyrsprinter, a hairless, eyeless animal covered in bioluminescent flecks on its back. It navigated by sonar, and it used a long, insect-like proboscis to feed on nectar. If threatened by a predator, these animals could run at speeds of up to 60 miles per hour, and corner on a dime. Their fore and hind legs fused into two massive, muscular limbs, primarily to avoid the Impalers and another fearsome predator of the plains, the Whiprex. This creature was about the size of a Tyrannosaurus, but jet-black and scaly, with huge, sail-like fins on its back for display, and bioluminescent patches on its back. Like the Impaler, it was a liquivore, impaling its prey on a long tongue, or radula, and draining it of bodily fluids. The Whiprexes fed upon the Zephyrsprinters and other herbivores, such as Bellow Bison, named for the sound they made when exhaling from their dorsal air-intake organs. Much like bison or elephants on Earth, these reptilian animals traveled in close-knit herds, and were highly intelligent, much like elephants. Like their earthbound counterparts, they had huge, curling tusks, which they used to clear brush and knock trees over when browsing for food.

In the high Panarin Mountains, there were Trumpethorns: bipedal, blue, horned animals with glowing patches of bioluminescence on their horns. They used these horns and loud trumpeting calls to ward off enemies and fight for territory and mates in their high upland homes. There were also antelope-like creatures, herbivores called "Hammerheads," so named for their hammer-shaped head, which functioned the same way that a hammerhead shark's cephalofoil did in Earth's oceans, aiding in finding food. All of these animals, however, were at the mercy of the Velvet Impalers, the gigantic titans of the skies.

In the forests, small, trunk-sucking Sap Sippers glided from tree trunk to tree trunk, drilling into the thick bark and drinking sap. They in turn were prey for lethal, vampiric Blade Gliders, which were large, praying-mantis like creatures that glided through the canopy as if they were flying squirrels, striking their prey down with their sharp claws and draining them of blood.

In forest clearings were huge colonies of Stinger Quills, these highly-evolved, colonial flatworms lived as ambush predators, waiting for some large animal to blunder into their territory, before leaping out of the ground and drilling into the animal's flesh as one massive tidal wave of toxic barbs, injecting a lethal neurotoxin, which killed the prey instantaneously. The Quills would then consume the animal by dissolving it. Even the largest animals on Oumi, the five-story tall Shaker Tortoise, a gigantic life-form which lived for more than 10,000 years by photosynthesizing sunlight from Amaterasu by burying themselves in the ground and allowing trees to grow on their backs, were no match for the Quills' poison.

These colossal tortoise-like creatures had an extremely low body density, allowing them to grow to truly massive sizes. They had two huge legs, and an enormous, blade-like keel which tilled the soil for new growth as the creature lumbered along. The tortoises formed a symbiotic relationship with the trees that grew on their backs, providing the trees with water, and the trees providing the tortoises with sugars, as a result of photosynthesis. Watching a gigantic tortoise-like animal howl in pain and crumple dead to the ground was an awe-inspiring experience. The Quills, after consuming a large prey item, would metamorphose into the next phase of their life cycle, the Stinger Flower, where they assumed a beautiful, but lethal, sessile lifestyle in which they resembled a bright pink blossom, much like a Japanese sakura, but still fired poisonous barbs at prey items passing by.

Jet-propelled scavengers, called Gliders, scavenged the remains of kills made by the top predators, recycling nutrients and continuing the cycle of life.

Humans, far from being the dominant forms of life in this alien Serengeti, were more often the hapless prey to these majestic creatures. Oumi was not an easy planet for a human to forge a life on, so far from the bustle of the Inner Colonies and teeming with hostile predators, but for Munraito, it was the only home he had ever known. He knew the planet inside and out, had seen almost every life form native to his world, and had lived in an ancient, lordly castle at the foot of the planet's largest mountain range, the volcanic Panarin Mountains. He saw the creatures of his world as sacred: even when they killed a human being, he did not seek revenge, for the animal was only doing what it needed to do to survive. However, on this night, something did not seem right. He could sense the arrival of something, or someone. Just the night before, Munraito had performed an initiation on his new apprentice, Koda, and for him to sense something like this at that moment was ominous, to say the least. For hundreds of years, this castle had served as the home of the esoteric Lightbringer Order and the over watch for Oumi, Mankind's most distant of colony worlds, deep in the Heaven's Gate Galaxy, more than 600 million light-years from Earth. Sensing the imbalance in the environment, Munraito stepped out of his bedroom for a moment.

"Master Iori…the animals outside the castle…they're acting strangely," Munraito said, curiously.

"Oh, that…they're just anxiously awaiting the arrival of our guests…they should be here momentarily,"

Master Iori said.

"Guests?" Munraito asked.

"Yes…this year, we've invited others," Master Iori responded.

On this particular evening, marked only by the momentary dip in the sun's position to just above the horizon, Munraito was preparing to give the annual Sakura Matsuri sermon to herald the coming of spring on Oumi, which began in the month of June, thanks the very slight axial tilt of the planet. Oumi was not completely locked to its star, but the world's axial tilt was so slight that it was barely noticeable, except towards the hours of 6:00 A.M. and 9:00 P.M, when the sunrise and sunset allowed for just 15 minutes of darkness in a 24-hour period.

Munraito's congregation gathered in the square at the foot of Heiei Castle, where the Lightbringer Inheritors lived and practiced Pantheon Doctrine. It was a great honor to give a sermon on any holiday, but to be selected by the Elder Master to give the sermon on Sakura Matsuri at sundown was immensely prestigious, and showed just how strongly Munraito valued his faith in the Pantheon Doctrine; the universal religion of the human race. Encompassing all beliefs, creeds and faiths as one unit, with a focus on progress and innovation for a brighter tomorrow, this faith attempted to explain the Universe through a blend of esotericism and scientific philosophy.

Content with his appearance, he donned the ceremonial black cap of a Lightbringer, took a deep breath, and walked out onto the famous Pontiff's Balcony, where the Lightbringers had given speeches for hundreds of years. He held the ceremonial haraeguchi over the crowd, each one holding a paper lantern with a prayer inscribed on it, painted with an elegant calligraphy pen. Master Munraito looked at his congregation and saw the usual faces. There was the man who had lost his leg fighting in the War of Light, which saw the Republic defeat an inorganic form of life known as the Naruhol Ihr; the young mother with her two children, taking them to see the magic of an early-spring sunset; and a young man who sought enlightenment in the sciences, but kept an open mind to the faiths. Munraito smiled at his congregation and gave the customary invocation for the Sakura Matsuri Festival, just as the sun dipped below the horizon:

"Come one, come all, and celebrate the ephemeral coming of spring on this glorious night, our world is alive with spirits and magic, but only if one chooses to see. Come and look, come and see, for there is much to learn about this world, about our lives, and that for which we yearn."

A beautiful sound of wind chimes echoed across the square, as the other Lightbringers rang the ceremonial bells in the Great Shrine, at the center of Heiei Castle. The paper lanterns were lit with Immersion energy, a form of Planck field energy tapped by the Republic to provide human civilization with a limitless supply of fuel for its massive machines and space-going civilizations. Relaxing music began playing as a band took a small stage, playing pan pipes, a koto, drums and wood block instruments to create a beautiful, ambient atmosphere, with Oumi's indigenous Firefly Cicadas flashing in the trees, singing their sultry tunes. It was a night that simply felt so right to say, "We are alive."

Master Munraito kneeled on the Pontiff's Balcony, with his hands held in prayer, slowly chanting in Japanese, the Holy Writs of Pantheon Doctrine:

"One...there is only self, the Universe, and all that exists. Two...all things change constantly, one cannot know anything without knowing change. Three...The only certainty is uncertainty. Four...There are no equals in the Universe, only equal ideals. Our diversity and differences makes us invincible...Five...I am a man of faith, an elite sovereign of the human race. I am above corruption. I have seen the light. I have seen the true path. I comprehend the meaning of life."

These were very strong statements to come from a man so young. However, Munraito was so brilliant, knowledgeable, and well-respected by those who knew him, that his words were almost universally seen on Oumi as the gospel truth.

As Munraito stood and looked up at Oumi's 5 silver moons, shimmering in the night sky, he noticed a small static crackle in the Northern sky. Munraito immediately recognized the leading edge of a Quantum Jump for what it was: there was a ship coming in, exiting "otherspace" back into real space. Munraito was amazed by how these Quantum Jump drives worked, and was actually able to perform the jump without a starship, thanks to his Lightbringer training and teachings. Munraito was able to synchronize the speed of his own thoughts to exactly the speed of light, and then burst through the time-space barrier in an instant, meditating in a world beyond time and space. He could, in this way, teleport anywhere in the Universe, or to any period in time as an observer, as could every Lightbringer.

For a starship to perform the same maneuver, it would use a powerful warp drive to distort space-time to such an extent that distances between two points in the Universe would become tiny. Almost instantaneously, the ship would arrive at the exit point, and by the size of the static bow wake, this was a huge ship.

The warp exit opened, and out flew an enormous, gleaming silver ship, the size of a large moon, slowly rotating to generate a gravitational force. Two enormous warp rings surrounded the ship, enabling it to reach speeds of up to one million times the speed of light. It appeared as if there was now a sixth moon in the sky, this one inching ever closer to Oumi, becoming larger and larger until it dominated the horizon. Lightning danced around the bow as the space-time continuum stabilized around the ship, high in orbit. Munraito stood on the Pontiff's Balcony looking up in awe of the traveling space colony, which was illuminated in the shining moonlight against the backdrop of the Panarin Mountains. Its many lights and Republic insignias blended in perfectly with the dazzling array of stars in the night sky.

"Ever seen one of these colony ships so close, Master Munraito? It's a real treat, I've never been off-world yet, because I haven't mastered Quantum Jumping, but I will someday," said Munraito's apprentice, a young, eager man named Koda, who was looking up at the ship in the sky.

"Yes, Koda, it's a beautiful piece of engineering. I don't understand why a colony would visit us all the way out here, though. These things are colossal, intergalactic hubs of human life all over the known Universe. Why anyone would come to our little planet out here, off of any main Republic trade routes is unknown to me. These must be the guests Master Iori was talking about, and their presence is the reason the animals were acting so strangely," Munraito said, equally puzzled by the ship's appearance.

"Maybe they're just here to enjoy the festival, or maybe they heard your speech and were so enamored by it that they came to congratulate you," Koda joked, smiling.

"Ha...I doubt it," Munraito chuckled to his apprentice.

"What would they want with me? I'm just a priest, not a saint...but I can do THIS!"

Munraito, like all humans living in the Fourteenth Age, possessed an artificial avatar body with superhuman abilities, a true transhuman. Standing atop the Pontiff's Balcony, Munraito leaped off, immediately shrouding his body in a shimmering golden-orange light. Six massive, angelic wings sprouted from his back as Munraito wheeled and spun through the night sky, until he reached the zenith of his flight.

"Munraito, what do you see up there?!" Koda yelled.

"The shuttles from the colony appear to be landing in the Ookazi Fields!" Munraito yelled back.

Alighting on the Pontiff's Balcony again, Munraito was greeted with applause from his congregation.

"Your earlier modesty speaks volumes about your faith. You are an inspiration to us all, Master Munraito, High Priest of the Light," Koda said.

"Thank you, Koda. Now, let us enjoy the festival, shall we?" Munraito invited, with a grand wave of his arm.

Munraito and Koda walked back into Heiei Castle's interior, towards the central staircase spiraling around a slowly-swaying pendulum, meant to brace the Castle against the occasional earthquakes that rattled Oumi.

"Master Munraito that was a truly inspiring invocation, your congregation is inspired every time they see you speak. You truly are worthy of the title 'Sukui no.' By the way, have you seen my datapads?" an older man said, looking for his documents.

"Did you try looking where you last left them, Master Iori?" Munraito asked.

"Oh dear, I forgot again...thank you," the Elder Master, Iori Nomato, said, his age showing in his absentmindedness. During the Fourteenth Age, human beings had developed a method of stopping the aging process automatically, thanks to various corporations' research into letting humans evolve agelessly. However, once people reached a certain age, their minds began to wander, simply because they had learned so much over the years.

He sauntered back into his chamber as Munraito and Koda walked down the elegant spiral staircase, winding around the slowly-swaying central lattice. It hummed in an even rhythm as it swayed in cadence with Oumi's weak rotation. Even though the rotation was rather weak, it was still strong enough to make the planet nearly tidally-locked to its star.

"Master Munraito, did you ever once think that there could be more to life?" Koda asked, curious about the arrival of the giant space colony in orbit.

"What could be more than this, Koda? You have a beautiful old castle, the kind every young child dreams about, as your home. You are surrounded by those who care about you and value your words and opinions. You have a beautiful world to call home, free will to think and do as you see fit, and a great future as a Lightbringer ahead of you. That ship arriving in orbit has tempted you with the promise of grand adventures, Koda, but, be patient. Once you master the art of Quantum Jumping, you can go anywhere and to any point in time in an instant. This planet, Oumi, is our sanctuary from the chaos and disorder of existence. For my entire quarter-century of existence, I have studied the Universe and everything in it, from the ideologies of the Naruhol Ihr to the sciences, faiths and histories of every world and every culture. There is but one constant: disorder. The Naruhol Ihr attempted to impose order on the chaos of organic evolution through the extermination of organic life, but they were defeated after a long and brutal conflict with the Republic, the Elohim, the Astari and the Sangresaara. There can be no order in this Universe, except for right here, on this planet and its five silver moons...and I am the sixth moon," Munraito said, very confidently.

"Alright then...forgive me for my impatience," Koda said, sheepishly.

"It is of no consequence, Koda. You have much to learn, and I will be the one to teach that to you. Elder Master Iori has asked me to take you on as my personal apprentice. He has deemed me ready to take on a learner of my own," Munraito said, placing his hand on Koda's shoulder.

"I'd be honored, Master Munraito," Koda said, kneeling in reverence.

"Rise...the training resumes tomorrow. For now, let us enjoy the festival while we can."

Munraito and Koda stepped out of the castle and into the bustling square, where Munraito's congregation danced to the music, dressed in their ceremonial kimonos and spring robes for the festival. As Munraito and Koda stepped into the square, a young woman, dressed in a flower-patterned, sky-blue kimono with a sakura fan in her right hand walked over to greet them.

She gave the traditional bow of respect to Master Munraito, and rang a ceremonial chime in her left hand.

"Would you care to dance with me, Master?" the young woman asked timidly.

"I would be honored to; such a beautiful young lady needs a dance partner," Munraito responded, with a smile on his face.

 The young woman and Munraito took each other's hands, and began a slow, rhythmic dance to the Zen music emanating from the bandstand. Koda, not to be outdone by his Master, asked another young woman to dance, and she happily obliged. Soon, both couples danced to traditional gagaku music in the castle square, with groups of Lightbringers watching from the balconies on Heiei Castle. Spectators on the ground, standing in the warm light of the Immersion lanterns under the black-velvet spring sky illuminated by Oumi's 5 moons looked up at the balconies, lit by the dim glow from the star Amaterasu low on the horizon. The space colony was orbiting high overhead, its shadow casting a huge umbra across the land far below. A group of airships, sailing on the midnight breeze, passed silently overhead, the low hum of their engines just audible over the wind in the trees and the nocturnal Firefly Cicadas. The warm spring breeze blew through the pink and white sakura blossoms on the cherry trees lining the courtyard. Introduced from Earth, they created a blizzard of cherry petals showering Master Munraito, Koda, and their two dance partners.

Everyone was so immersed in the Festival that no one noticed the fleet of white lights in the sky, flying in formation away from the space colony, directly towards the Festival. There must have been hundreds of them, each one of them a Republic starship, rocketing away from the space colony and making a westward turn towards the Panarin Mountains.

Just then, Master Munraito noticed the inbound fleet, as did the rest of the crowd and the Lightbringers. "It looks like we've got some company," Koda announced.

"So it would seem...but something is out of place. Why would they come all the way out here?" Munraito thought.

The fleet of ships made a sickening turn towards the festival, as if performing aerial acrobatics for the crowd. The ships - glowing, silver, egg-shaped craft designed by the legendary Althea Shipyard Corporation on the planet of the same name - came in for a landing. Silently and effortlessly, they landed in the Ookazi Fields, in the shadow of Heiei Castle. Wildlife scattered everywhere as they did so.

The ships' antigravity generators were deactivated, allowing them to land on the soft, dew-covered carpet of flowers and leaves. The ships' white, collective ethereal glow subsided as their engines cooled off, their plasma beam drives falling silent against the backdrop of the stars. Many of Munraito's congregation ran about 300 yards through the wet grass to greet the visitors from the stars. The starships' gangplanks opened, and their passengers stepped onto the surface to greet the citizens of Oumi.

"Greetings, people of this world..." a radiant being of divine light said, upon stepping into the warm spring air. He was surrounded by his followers, elaborately-dressed aristocrats wearing fantastical costumes and outfits, makeup and masks.

He was an incredible sight, standing 12 feet tall and glowing in the dark of the night with the hvareno, the Holy Light of Victory and Purity. He wore a shimmering, immensely gaudy and elaborate outfit, and had a chalk-white face, soothing blue eyes, and a handsome, calm, peaceful smile. His shining white hair partially covered his left eye, and he held a silver scepter in his right hand with a crown of shining laurels atop his head. His cape shimmered with the glowing red light of the sunset as the wind blew it about.

"I am Annunaki Hvarean, Holy Light of Victory and Purity, and the Baron-Administrator of the New Berlin Space Colony of the United Human Republic," the huge, radiant, humanoid creature said, his body resembling more of a hologram than a physical being.

"He's Naruhol Ihr...That's Annunaki!! Master Munraito, that creature is a war criminal!! Remember me, you freak?! But why would you, there were so many of us!!" the veteran with one leg screamed, remembering very well what this being's civilization did to his more than 80 years ago.

"Yes...I am the one, the only, Lord Annunaki. Does this trouble you? I assure you, our civilization has learned from its past mistakes...we are deeply regretful for the suffering we have caused for untold millions of years."

"Your warriors cost me my leg, my family and my youth...I cannot forgive you or any of your kind. The fact that the Republic has welcomed you with open arms is disgraceful. I cannot be in this monster's presence. Master Munraito, please tell him to leave, and take his gaudy entourage with him," the man yelled.

"Our Empire has sought to sustain itself through the farming of organic life; for millions of years we waited for organic civilizations to rise, advance, evolve, and colonize the stars, so that we would harvest them for ourselves. We imposed order on the chaos of organic evolution, but your society has taught us the error of our ways, in that one cannot consume all without consuming oneself. We lost the war for that reason; our inability to preserve resources for later generations, and our necessary 3-million-year hibernation after we consumed a society eventually doomed our war effort. We broke the cycle by learning to coexist with humans. I have left the past where it belongs, what yesterday was. Your organic mind has apparently not kept pace with mine. But then again, I never expected it would. I am conscious Light, the pinnacle of existence. You are but a genetic mutation, an accident. I have no beginning. I have no end. I am infinite. Our Legions still wait for the day when they are called into battle once more; this time as allies of the Republic. I suggest you reassess the times you live in, old man."

"You are an unimaginable MONSTER!! I shall destroy you, you war criminal!!" the 105-year old war veteran yelled.

"ENOUGH," Munraito yelled back, stepping in between Lord Annunaki and the Republic war veteran. "This is a time of peace...let us not reopen old wounds," Munraito said, sternly.

"Master Munraito...so at long last we meet again. The last time I saw you, you were but a small child," Annunaki said.

"It's been too long, Lord Annunaki," Munraito said, giving Lord Annunaki his utmost respect, much to the old veteran's chagrin.

"Yes... You are the youngest Lightbringer Master ever, an inspiration to your people wherever you go. We have much in common, Master Munraito. I command respect of my race, the Naruhol Ihr Legions bow in reverence at my very appearance. I radiate what your race calls 'Hvareno,' a solar divinity that cannot be imitated. Long have we observed your species as it rose and colonized the stars. We attacked it 85 years ago, and have accepted defeat, but our regality is unquestioned and unchallenged. Do you understand what makes us so powerful, Master Munraito?"

"Yes, but please enlighten these people," Munraito said.

"It is our free will and our Light. Free will is the only thing that can truly be called "God." It is the inner God, the Light, the Life-Force, the Radiating Body, the Augorides, the Hvareno, the Vajra, and the Dorjic. These are all different names in various human cultures referring to our reality. Naruhol Ihr are in charge of our own destiny. We alone control where we end up. However, there is always one that guides us. Every traditional society is characterized by the presence of entities, be they gods, spirits, mortals or traditions that, by virtue of their natural superiority, whether acquired or innate, embody a power beyond mortal comprehension. Our assault on your society 85 years ago began with the creation of the Lodges of the Grand Orient, a society of Republic intellectuals led by one Baron Artur Gunderstendorf. We were secretly controlling the Lodges, undermining the Republic Senate on Earth with subversive literature and subliminal messaging, too subtle for you to detect on a conscious level. This was achieved by the Grand Lodges through sexual and violent psychological manipulation, rituals in secluded, isolated locations, and psychological control of those in positions of power and in prominent positions of society. Once an influential person had fallen under our spell, he or she was held in bondage by humiliation, political pandering, financial ruin, physical harm, public exposure or other forms of blackmail, even death by execution of themselves or loved ones to ensure the loyalty of the Grand Lodges to the Naruhol Ihr agenda. Secondly, we enforced that all members of the Grand Lodges use whatever powers necessary to have candidates chosen for office in the Republic that would be obedient to our demands and loyal to our agenda, to be used as pawns by our shadow government, lurking just out of sight. Our Disciples were bred in laboratories, reared and trained from artificial conception to manage the new Universe once we took power and eventually consumed all organic life in the Universe. The methods that we used to achieve our ends were through acts of extreme violence and unexplainable phenomena, to create a sense of dread amongst the Republic citizens, so that no one knew the truth.

After more than 25 horrific acts of terror by followers of our agenda, Gunderstendorf embraced what he called the 'Luciferan Ideology,' called himself a savior and with our manipulation, was able to win the High Chancellery and become the leader of the Republic, unexpectedly engineering a civil war on a colossal scale when documents implicating the cover-up were uncovered by independent hacker groups. When the time was right, we made our presence known, albeit that we were forced into the war on your terms. Nevertheless, our arrival was the return of the Gods. You have earned the right to exist in our eyes...we see the Light your species radiates as an equal to ours, and you, Master Munraito, tower over all. This exchange is over."

Lord Annunaki glared menacingly at the one-legged Republic war veteran, with the man responding in kind. Master Munraito simply closed his eyes and sighed, realizing that the war veteran and Lord Annunaki could never get along.

"Lord Annunaki, are you and your followers here for the Festival? In that case, we welcome you to the Sakura Matsuri Festival this night."

"Yes, indeed. Come, my citizens, it is time to rejoice in the light of the moon, celebrating the coming of spring with these good people, here in the shadow of Heiei Castle," Lord Annunaki said.

"Well, Master Munraito, you are certainly a saint among men. For you to forgive him for what he did to us, you have no hate, no flaws, and live a blessed existence. May the Gods eternally bless you with a lovely wife, a beautiful home, and a lifetime of good health," the war veteran, whose name was Miyagi, said.

"One can only hope, Honorable Veteran Miyagi. I do not claim to know what the forces of nature have planned for me, nor do I claim to be flawless. I am but a man, a simple organic life form; I am not a god, nor even a Naruhol Ihr. I will eventually die, as will you and all of us. If you calculate the odds of something happening to any one of us, the odds of death are still 100%, even if you take age-related issues out of the equation. It is simply the nature of things. I must do what I must with the time I have been given," Munraito said.

Suddenly, one of Lord Annunaki's elaborately-dressed followers stepped forward, wearing a lovely Inferna Bacchanalia Ignis dress, a radiant orange, black and red gown doused in crimson fire, with a medieval-style hood over long, silky red-orange hair. She wore an elaborate masquerade mask, covering her entire face, and held a small scepter in her left hand, as ceremonially carried by persons of very high standing in the Republic on formal occasions. She approached Master Munraito and extended her elegant, red-lace gloved hand, which Master Munraito took delicately in his hand. He immediately felt an awkward sensation, like needles and pins all over his body, feeling her hand in his. It was one that he, as a Lightbringer, was trained to block and resist, for it clouded good judgment and made many a wise man into a fool. He quickly purged the sensation and asked the young woman to remove her mask, hoping to see her true face from behind her shimmering blue facade, dazzling with jewelry and feathers. Without a word, the woman placed her hands on her mask and removed it.

"Hello Master Munraito. Lord Annunaki tells me great things about you. He says you were born to do God's wonders," the woman said, very quietly.

Master Munraito looked transfixed into her stunning, sparkling blue eyes. She was utterly gorgeous, her long red hair flowing down her shoulders like a waterfall. She removed her hood to show the full length of her hair, also flowing tantalizingly down her back. Her skin was very pale, and her lips were an inviting crimson, though Master Munraito knew that their touch would be a venomous poison to his soul. Still, the temptation was overwhelming.

"By what name do you call yourself?" Master Munraito asked.

"My name is Haruna Otohime. I do believe we've met already, Hikari Munraito. How could you have forgotten me?"

At that moment, the realization of who this young woman was struck Munraito with the force of a comet impact. He could scarcely believe it, but here she was. There had always been an image, a dim, fading image deep within his mind that sometimes surfaced upon meditation. It was one that had perpetually troubled Master Munraito, and it automatically triggered a truly hellish experience. Whenever the memory was triggered, Master Munraito was able to make a Quantum Jump straight into what could only be described as Hell itself. Upon arrival, he would become cloaked in total darkness and choked by simmering heat, seared by unholy flames and tormented by the moans and shouts of people being tortured. He was often able to walk around in the searing blackness, which he could only describe as warping to the core of an active volcano. Standing in the darkness, this woman beckoned him into the eternal fires of damnation. He was always able to resist the vision, and in many ways, it had tempered him to become the strong, stalwart servant of the Light that he had grown into...still...he could scarcely believe that she stood before him, here, on this night, out of the blackness of space.

"Yes...my dear Haruna...It has been so long. I have not spoken to you since our time in primary school together. What has the Universe taught you in your travels?" Munraito asked, already having an idea of what the answer would be.

"Oh, so much, Master Munraito, I would love to tell you about the Republic and the things I have seen since I left this planet for the New Berlin Space Colony more than 14 years ago. I'd be happy to join you at the Festival tonight," Haruna said, joyfully.

Suddenly, Master Munraito, the youngest Grand Master of the Lightbringer Order in history, felt very, very torn. Here he was on top of his world one minute, and in the very next moment, was confronted with a dilemma that he never thought he would have to encounter. A little girl from his long-distant childhood was now a beautiful young woman of immense power and prestige, and he, Hikari Munraito, the man his peers called 'The Light and the Savior,' was faced with his greatest temptation ever. He tried to block the feelings that wracked his body with jabbing pins and needles, but it still felt as if someone had just fed him hemlock poison. The way her hand fit so neatly into his, it...it was almost like fate. Furthermore, he had very erotic visions of this woman in the depths of Hell itself, for he knew that such a romance could be the utter ruin of his life and happiness...yet he could scarcely resist it...he believed that he could overcome any challenge that came his way. Visions were one thing. Reality was completely different. The repressed memories of his childhood flooded back like an endless torrent of summer days - hot, sultry nights and days growing up in Muranahe, the main city on Oumi.

In every one of those memories, Haruna was there, by his side, exploring the world and experiencing the follies of childhood and young adulthood. Now, after nearly 15 years, they were standing together again, on one of the most magical nights of the year, Sakura Matsuri. The experience felt just like all those dreamy childhood summers many years before, when they were only children. And at that very moment, with Haruna standing in front of him, Munraito realized that there might be more to life than simply studying and praying in an ancient castle. He felt like a little boy again, like a boy who could truly be himself.

"Come, Haruna, and join the festivities. Bring all of your friends with you. Lord Annunaki is welcome too. This is a happy moment, the happiest moment of my life. Welcome home, sweet Haruna," Munraito said, with a smile on his face.

"Thank you, Munraito," Haruna said, wrapping Master Munraito in her warm embrace.

The music playing on the bandstand switched to a song sung by many young men in love during the spring, "A Valediction of a Golden Heart."

"A golden heart has ceased at last its steady rhythm,

in the sultry twilight of a summer's day...

Afar, waifs and strays of the day flutter, no more lamenting over what was lost...

Afar, waifs and strays of the day flutter, no more lamenting over what was lost...

What to lament for, the night is brilliant...the moons shine like silver beacons in the sky...

a falling star shines for a moment, but then leaves this world anon...

It carries the dreams of all who see it, and dies quietly above a tranquil sea...

It carries the dreams of all who see it, and dies quietly above a tranquil sea...

I stand alone in a summer field...a gust of wind carries my wish away.

For my joyful youth is fleeting, and nothing in the gone do I bewail.

For my joyful youth is fleeting, and nothing in the gone to I bewail...

I feel no pity for the squandered love...the heartbreak, the loneliness, the goodbyes...

For all there is is life, and I am but a man in love...

A fire slowly burns in my heart, bright like the spring flowers in the yard,

and it warms me evermore...

A fire slowly burns in my heart, bright like the spring flowers in the yard,

and it warms me evermore...

Yet the flowers, delicate and beautiful, will not last forever, and neither will you and I...

Someday we shall perish, pure and somber...and shine like the stars in the sky...

So for now, my love, take my heart in your hand,

as the summer wind is rising, and tears fill my eyes...

Then close your eyes, and say with me as follows...

a golden heart beats again once more...

Then close your eyes, and say with me as follows...

a golden heart beats again once more..."

 Koda, Munraito's new apprentice, could scarcely believe what had just transpired. He walked over to his master and stood nearby as the two of them stood silently, embracing each other for dear life. "Master, she's beautiful...how did you meet her?" Koda asked.

Munraito did not respond, for he was too lost in Haruna's embrace.

"Hahaha...Koda, you might want to speak to him later. He's a young man in love," Veteran Miyagi chuckled.

Lord Annunaki stared calmly at Munraito and Haruna and smiled peacefully, his radiating body of light shining brilliantly in the night air. His other followers removed their masks to show their faces; more than 50 men and women, all dressed in the same type of elaborate outfits as Haruna with makeup, masks and jewelry.

"All bask in the glory of the Return of the Light! May He be blessed."

Lord Annunaki's echoing voice boomed across the Ookazi Fields, as his followers applauded.

Haruna finally let go of Munraito, and Munraito was quick to ask questions.

"Haruna, can you introduce me to these people?" Munraito asked, knowing very well who Annunaki was.

"I'm happy you asked. These people are the Baron-Administrators of the New Berlin Space Colony, and Lord Annunaki is the Viceroy of the Naruhol Ihr Imperium. Lord Annunaki is perhaps the greatest being in the Universe. He and his race are beyond human comprehension and use their radiating bodies of Hvareno. They can appear to humans in any number of forms. They can alter our perceptions of reality. They can implant thoughts and illusions into our minds. The can control the weather on planets. They can effortlessly manipulate organic evolution. They can remove our consciousness from our bodies and enter our bodies as energy, granting humans extraordinary powers. They can easily control organic life through these means. They can travel invisibly at the speed of thought across the Universe and through the infinitely-existing different dimensions and the seven levels of consciousness. They have no beginning, they have no end; they are infinite. Millions of years after we die and are forgotten, they will endure. The Naruhol Ihr have been influencing humanity for thousands of years, to the point where they have power over each and every one of our lives. They have masterful illusory capabilities...and their agenda is far beyond that of every human in the

Universe...except for us. The 50 Baron-Administrators here are the only humans in the Republic that know the true agenda of the Naruhol Ihr. Lord Annunaki is Light and Salvation...and he has shown me the Light, just as the Lightbringers have enlightened you," Haruna said, finishing her explanation with a flourish, proud of what she had learned and now felt obligated to share with others.

Munraito looked skeptical.

"Do you know Lord Annunaki's agenda yourself?" Munraito asked, curiously.

"No, Munraito. I do not, but I can assure you there is nothing to be afraid of. I don't know why Veteran Miyagi is so offended by Annunaki's presence," Haruna replied.

"She speaks the truth, Master Munraito. Long has Haruna studied under my tutelage; she has seen many worlds across this vast galaxy, and now she has returned to you. She told me that the day you left her for Heiei Castle was the most difficult day of her young life, because you two were inseparable when you were younger. Childhood is a magical time of discovery, and your lives took you apart far before you were meant to be away from each other. After 14 years of training, I have brought her back to you. She is here for you, Master Munraito. Treasure her and take care of her, just as I did, and she will reward you with happiness and the lifetime of satisfaction that all you organic beings seek," Lord Annunaki said, tapping his scepter of light on the ground.

"Thank you, Lord Annunaki. Bringing Haruna back to me is proof that my faith has been rewarded. I am without words," Munraito replied.

"Such events are more than coincidence, Lord Annunaki. There are powerful forces in this Universe, energies that permeate everything that exists. Haruna radiates this energy as brightly as the brightest star in the night sky, shining with the light of a thousand suns. She has always radiated that light, and now it shines brighter than ever," Munraito said.

"It is my pleasure to see organic life in a state of happiness, after all the suffering my people have caused over the countless eons of our existence...Come, followers of the Light, it is time to rejoice in this world's festival. Tonight, we are the Sun and the Moon, and the end of all time."

Lord Annunaki, his 50 Disciples, Munraito, and his congregation all returned to the Festival grounds, just as the band began playing another tune on the bandstand with the silver moons sparkling in the sky. Munraito sat down under a cherry tree with Haruna, her head resting on his shoulder. He closed his eyes, gently stroking Haruna's deep red hair and entered a deep, meditative state of torpor. Focusing all his energies on a single point in time and space, he reached out to the Universe for guidance. In an instant, he timed his thoughts with the speed of light, and broke through the space-time barrier, entering the quantum plane in a flash of brilliant white light. He sat with Haruna in an empty void, surrounded by a flashing, brilliant aurora as quantum strings danced before him. He was now outside of space and time, and no longer in a physical place.

As he sat with Haruna in the tranquility of "otherspace," he opened the parts of his mind hitherto closed off to the outside world, and began to see worlds unfolding before him. His and Haruna's collective consciousness were leaving their bodies, traveling at the speed of thought through the vacuum of space to various worlds; a beautiful tropical planet here, and a cold, snowy, winter wonderland world there. He could tell that these images were of the worlds that Haruna had visited in her travels with the New Berliners, because he could feel Haruna's unique "handprint," or energy, that she had left on the Universe. More and more planets began to appear as Munraito's consciousness soared through space like an angel on shimmering wings. He stooped, zoomed and wheeled through the cosmos, like a Republic starfighter pilot in the heat

of a dogfight, using the stars and his own intuition to guide his journey

through Haruna's past. Munraito flew past a comet, which dazzled him

with a frigid, icy tail as he flew through it, avoiding the huge chunks of

rock and ice streaming off of its nucleus. As he wheeled through the

heavens, he felt more liberated than he had ever felt in his life. Everything

around him looked brighter, deeper, and altogether more inviting.

Haruna's energy was undeniable. It was beautiful, effortless and flowing,

much like her long red hair or the folds of her dress. It filled every ounce

of his consciousness, allowing Munraito to visit every world she had ever

been to, actively retracing her path through the Universe. In all, Munraito

realized that Haruna had visited more than 25 planets with the New Berlin

Space Colony, from the watery paradise of Lilliana V to the Royal House of

Serenna.

What she uncovered on those far-flung worlds was a mystery, but Lord

Annunaki probably showed her sights beyond her wildest comprehension.

In order to best understand Haruna's worldview, he thought it best to

physically travel to those planets, with her by his side, so she could

personally show him what wonders she had uncovered. And so in an

instant, Munraito was back in "otherspace," and slowly, his consciousness began to return to his body. His eyes opened, and there he was, sitting right beside Haruna, who had fallen asleep on his shoulder under the cherry tree. The Festival was over; he must have been traveling around the Universe for hours. Hundreds of other festival attendees were also asleep under the cherry trees, wearing their warm festival robes. All slept peacefully, except for Lord Annunaki, who had taken the form of a huge, shimmering bird perched high in a camphor tree. He stood like a silent sentinel over Oumi's verdant Ookazi Valley, in the shadow of Heiei Castle, his feathers glimmering in the ethereal red light. Firefly Cicadas called peacefully in the trees, as a warm spring breeze blew through the leaves, upturning their undersides and creating a lovely rustling sound. The ambiance and environment slowly soothed Munraito to sleep. It was only a few hours until morning, judging by the position of the stars, Amaterasu and the 5 moons in the sky. Munraito gently closed his eyes, rested his head against Haruna's upper body, and promptly fell into a deep sleep, a sleep enjoyed only by those who were truly at peace.

Chapter 2: Killer Lady

Munraito awoke, feeling a sweet kiss on his cheek, refreshed and restored from his sleep. He looked up at the position of the sun and saw Haruna looking back at him, smiling; it had to be at least noon by that point. All around him, he heard the sounds of people slowly waking up from the previous night's festivities, some of the purely biological humans still visibly hung over from a night of heavy drinking. Haruna was probably headed inside to speak with the Elders; Munraito remembered Haruna as being a very curious little girl. She was always looking for something to read, and continually stayed busy. Perhaps she had gone to help Elder Master Nomato in preparation for the daily meditation session.

Munraito slowly staggered to his feet and slipped his sandals on, walking carefully to avoid stepping on anyone else still sleeping. His Lightbringer robes were slightly soiled by sleeping on the ground, but they were easily dusted off. As Munraito made his way back towards the castle, his apprentice, Koda, was there to greet him. Eager as always, he waved to him and called for his attention.

"Munraito-sama, come this way! Haruna is in the castle, helping the Elders," Koda said, enthusiastically.

"I thought as much. She was always very curious as a little girl. I have wondered for some time what was going on inside that mind of hers," Munraito added, walking past some endemic Ookazi Roses.

"Well, she's certainly grown into her body, that's for sure. She's one of the most attractive women I have ever met. I guess living on one of the space colonies your whole life will do that for you," Koda said, admiring the new arrivals from the New Berlin space colony.

Munraito knew that during the age of the Republic, life on a space colony was preferable to life on a planet. With the development of hologram-like avatar bodies for Mankind during the 21st century, humanity became a new species altogether; Homo ultimus, the 'Ultimate Man.' Immortal, perfect and eternally youthful, humanity embarked on a quest to walk under the light of other stars, and millions of years later, more than half the known Universe had been mapped and explored. Though purely biological humans still existed, these were few and far between; Veteran Miyagi and Elder Master Iori were the only two that Munraito had ever met. Munraito himself had become an avatar at age 25, as was custom in the Republic. Haruna had become an avatar at that age as well. Still, the space colonies were the home of the privileged, and neither Koda nor Munraito had ever lived away from Oumi.

Koda looked up at the gigantic colony ship high overhead, admiring its sleek contours and gleaming-white chromium hull. The ship slowly rotated in two segments to generate artificial gravity.

"Wow, it must be nice living on one of those things. No angry wildlife, no cosmic radiation storms from Amaterasu and no bad weather...your girlfriend's got it really easy. Why would she come back here? I don't understand," Koda wondered aloud to Munraito.

"Koda, allow me to explain something to you. Our Universe, vast as it is, is home to a tremendous variety of life and worlds of all kinds, from the exotic jungle moon of Lunara to the tranquil Global Lake of Lilliana V to the icy paradise world of Arcana II. This life, from the greatest marine organism to the smallest bacterium, gives off energy, the energy of life itself. This energy acts as an attraction, drawing all other forms of life to it...and sometimes, two beings meet that become inseparable. When two organisms whose atoms were joined together before the Big Bang meet as a result of this universal attraction, they join together, living as one body, one mind, and one soul. We are each a piece of a whole person. There are many worlds, many homelands, many voices, but one mind, one soul and one race. It is even written into the Republic motto. Haruna came back to me because her energy drew her here, it is something that I sensed the moment she placed her hand in mine. The energy that radiates from Haruna is undeniable. I feel that she came home because the Universe beckoned her back to me, " Munraito said.

"Did you just scientifically explain soulmates?" Koda asked, incredulously.

"In a matter of speaking, yes I did," Munraito replied.

Munraito and Koda proceeded into Heiei Castle and walked through the luxuriant, wood-paneled hallways. As the two of them walked into the main atrium, they found Haruna sitting perfectly still with Elder Master Nomato and several other Lightbringers, in deep meditation. Haruna was introducing some new topics into the Lightbringers' thoughts; her immensely powerful avatar mind literally planting thoughts in their minds as they sat in a circle. Munraito could sense their thoughts; Haruna was entertaining the Lightbringers with stories of far-flung worlds, exotic places, extraordinary people and wondrous civilizations. Most of the Lightbringers didn't know what to think about Haruna's sudden arrival and her much greater travel experiences. Some of the Lightbringers were a bit confused as to exactly what Haruna was communicating.

Haruna sensed Munraito entering the room and promptly came out of her trance; along with the other Lightbringers, with whom she continued to discuss her travels verbally.

"Oh, good morning Munraito-kun, I was just having a conversation with the Elders. I hope you don't mind," Haruna said.

"That's no problem at all. Did you sleep well last night?" Munraito asked.

"No, actually, I was awake all night telling the Elders of my life aboard the space colony," Haruna replied.

"Haruna, you know better. Your avatar still needs rest every night. That's not healthy," Munraito said.

"Haruna has seen so much...she is very blessed," Elder Master Nomato said, still amazed at what Haruna had seen.

Munraito and Koda walked past Haruna as six more guests entered the main hall...and when the Lightbringers gazed upon them, they could scarcely believe their eyes. Standing 12 feet tall and wearing exquisitely ornate, regal outfits, six Hyperboreans took their seats at the head of the table. The first woman had long, flowing blonde hair, shimmering green eyes and an elaborate, ornate blue formal dress with many pagan, runic themes adorning it. Her dress was topped by a black cloak and hood adorned with a Ragnarok rune over the whole ensemble. Munraito recognized this woman as Gwenlynn Stormweaver, the Director of the Imperial Society of Human Antiquities, based on the Republic capital world of Stronghold. The second member of the group was also a woman, wearing a long red formal dress adorned with brilliant flower patterns and a hood with blue lining to it. Her hair was long and silky brown, and she had a devilish look to her face. Her eyes were pale blue. This was Mistress Ai Takada, the leader of an esoteric sexual liberation cult based on the icy paradise world of Arcana II. The third woman was immediately identified as Elohim, an extraterrestrial species nearly identical to a Hyperborean human and often lumped into the same category, as much as the Elohim would tell you otherwise. She wore an extremely elaborate, shining-white, gaudy, non-Euclidean outfit that seemed to defy the laws of physics. She possessed shimmering pink eyes and a bald, hairless head characteristic of all Elohim females. This was Sei Ikkiku, the Queen of the Elohim Consortium; a vital ally and founding member of the Republic. The other three were none other than Alik Arditi, Astari Marduk and Sylphain Anteon, the Most High Troika, the three leaders of the Andromedan Empire. This was a mighty Imperial civilization that completely controlled the Andromeda Galaxy and possessed the largest military in the known Universe; their radiant forms filled the entire dining hall with light.

'Greetings, Most Holy Lightbringers. We bring the honor and justice of the Astari Intergalactic Command to your world, on behalf of the Republic and the Andromedan Empire,' Anteon said, his huge, hologram-like body shimmering in the sunlight streaming in through the windows.

"Munraito, these are our partners in our current project. I trust you all know who they are by now," Haruna said, confidently.

"What sort of project would require the assistance of the Troika, the Elohim Queen and the Director of Human Antiquities?!" Munraito gasped.

"Master Lightbringer, Haruna Otohime has been placed in charge of the Universal Life Project, a Republic-led initiative to bring all the advanced civilizations across the Cosmos together in greater goodwill and universal brotherhood," Queen Ikkiku said, softly.

"The project is being facilitated by the Troika and the Republic High Chancellery, with my people being close advisers to both ends of the project. Miss Stormweaver is the archaeological adviser to the Chancellery, and Miss Takada...well, no one really knows why she signed up for this project, but we appreciate her assistance nevertheless," Queen Ikkiku said.

"Hey, don't everyone look at me like I'm the weird one..." Takada said, slowly running her fingers through her hair.

"Takada, what is it that you actually do? You've built quite a fortune for yourself and more people on Arcana II recognize you than the currently-elected Chancellor," Munraito asked.

"Oh, Munraito, dear, you've been trapped in this dank, isolated fortress for far too long. Here, take this."

Takada flipped a small holodisk at Munraito, which he caught in midair.

"That is my tell-all, an interstellar best-seller describing my actions, profession and passions, Confessions of a Renegade Sinflower. I recommend you read it. You never know if you'll find a new temptation..." Takada said, with an evil looking smirk on her face.

"Something tells me she has serious ulterior motives..." Koda whispered to Munraito.

"Tell me something I don't know..." Munraito grumbled.

"I open-mouth kissed a cat once. That's something you don't know," Koda joked.

"Koda, must you always be so strange? I'm not even going to comment on that," Munraito said, slightly disgusted.

"You might actually be her type, Koda. From what I hear, Miss Takada is one of the most well-known deviants in the entire Republic. You should get to know her a little better," Munraito suggested.

"Oh, absolutely not, she and her cult are way out of my league," Koda said, vehemently.

"I don't think you give yourself enough credit," Munraito said.

"Are you kidding me? I'm half their size, they would literally kill me," Koda said to Munraito.

"Well, you do have a point," Munraito realized.

"We will be staying here for a while...we may as well get comfortable," Gwenlynn said twiddling her thumbs as they all became accustomed to their new environment.

"An old Japanese castle, wow, I could get used to this..." Takada said, quietly, licking her lips in anticipation.

"That woman is an absolute lunatic..." Koda whispered to Munraito, reading the contents of Takada's memoir.

"Tell me about it...are you seeing this stuff that she does?" Munraito showed Koda some of the sexual depravities that Takada had inflicted on willing participants.

"That is absolutely insane...some of this stuff is so twisted that it should be criminal. I hope all of this is conducted in the online Universe. Why would she show any interest in a diplomacy mission?" Koda said, audibly, causing Takada to notice that he was talking about her.

"Quiet Koda...I think she heard you..." Munraito cautioned.

It was too late, however. Takada stood up from her chair and walked calmly over to Koda, reached down and literally picked Koda up by the collar of his outfit, holding him at eye level with her.

"You were talking about me, weren't you?" Takada hissed.

"Not...really..." Koda said, gasping for breath as Takada was hanging him from his own shirt collar.

"DON'T LIE TO ME, YOU FILTHY LITTLE SHIT! I'LL LET YOU HANG TO DEATH FROM MY OWN HAND!!"

"Ai Takada, release him this instant!" Munraito demanded.

Takada responded by letting go of Koda, dropping on the ground with a thud, while he gasped for breath, bruised from the fall.

"Tell your friend to mind his mouth. I will not tolerate slanderous remarks, thank you."

Takada returned to her seat and promptly pulled out her datapad, reading through some of the information on it.

The rest of the Lightbringers' gazes were squarely fixed on Takada.

"What are you all gawking at me like that for?! Stop it!" Takada screamed.

Most people who chose the Hyperborean avatar were already much stronger, egocentric, smarter and more ambitious that those who chose the standard avatar body, but Takada's personality was so exaggerated that it bordered on psychosis. The fact that such a woman could build a truly interstellar following despite being such a psychotic, sex-crazed witch was truly mind-blowing for the Lightbringers, who epitomized humbleness and self-sufficiency. She was a toxic individual to have in Heiei Castle and everyone knew it. She had to have a decent streak in her somewhere for the general public to like her so much; surely, she could not be like this all the time.

"Haruna, is Takada always this confrontational?" Munraito asked, quietly.

"No, not really, she's just very insecure and quick to anger. She sees her career, if you can call it that, as a form of religious liberation, the fame she has built is only a by-product of her...'unique' methods of prayer and religious devotion. She hates being famous and only wishes to enjoy her life in peace..." Haruna said, calmly.

"Well, she would do well to contain herself here," Munraito said.

"Ha, good luck with that, Munraito-kun. That woman cannot be tamed," Haruna joked.

As the Lightbringers finished their meditation, Haruna and her six guests began discussing their upcoming mission with the Republic government.

"Emperor Arditi, are your fleets prepared for any eventualities resulting from our mission?" Haruna asked.

"Yes, Haruna, the Astari Galactic Command can mobilize the Armada at a moment's notice. All we need to do is give the order. We are the most powerful society in the known Universe. The Sangresaara Imperium and the Sigtyr Ascendancy wouldn't dare behave in a way that compromises universal harmony and peace," Emperor Arditi said, referring to two civilizations with a history of being hostile towards their neighbors.

"Emperor Arditi, those two civilizations you mentioned, are they dangerous in any way?" Munraito asked, admiring the radiant forms of the assembled dignitaries.

"Not necessarily. The Sangresaara are a synthetic species descended from a reptilian ancestor, they stand an imposing 12 feet tall and have four massive arms, along with two legs with huge hooves. They are a proud warrior race, commanding enormous armadas of warships and completely controlling the Orion Arm of the Milky Way galaxy. Their leader, Warmaster Lumen Ash, is a being of great wisdom, although he is also one of great hostility. The Sangresaara live and die by the blades of their plasma swords, and they have been known to be quite hostile to outsiders.

The Sigtyr are a bizarre humanoid species living on a world of liquid hydrocarbons, orbiting an antimatter star. Their planet is dark, frigid and drenched in seas of liquid methane and ethane. Life on this planet, however, exists in a profusion unlike anywhere else in the known

Universe, with as much biodiversity there as anywhere else in the Universe. The Sigtyr live in colossal cities on the coast of the great methane oceans, thriving in the frigid temperatures. They are all female and have many mammalian and reptilian characteristics; they breathe hydrogen, exhale nitrogen, are not DNA based organisms, communicate through telepathy and bioluminescence and have an extremely strong sense of nationalism to their home planet. Their enormous starships can carry more than five million of them at once, and cross the cosmos with ease. They have been known to be quite hostile to outsiders and have even resorted to acts of violence against others, making them a concern for our mission," Emperor Arditi explained, having learned most of the spoken human languages in preparation for his interaction with the Republic.

"Interesting, the Orion Arm is one of the areas of space nearest to the Republic center, which implies that the Sangresaara often come very close to Republic space. I wouldn't doubt that they account for the majority of extraterrestrial encounters amongst human travelers," Munraito responded.

"Indeed they are very close, and their encounters with humanity are not always friendly, because they never expect to see humans in deep space.

They have created various servant races through genetic engineering, and even though these beings are far more often encountered than the Sangresaara themselves; occasionally a Republic trade vessel will be approached by a Sangresaara warship, which is never a pleasant experience," Emperor Arditi explained.

"This is our aim, Munraito. We seek to make the Universe a more unified place, one where interstellar and intergalactic communication between civilizations is free and simple. We aim to create a place where economies can grow, citizens can prosper, and all life can enjoy bounty, prosperity and peace," Sei Ikkiku added.

"It is the sovereign wish of all Elohim people that the glory and peace of Belisaria shine upon all life in the Cosmos. For untold millennia has our race been the peace shield of the Milky Way Galaxy, what our diplomats failed to solve, our War Wyverns more than made up for. The White Tower shines eternally, and as long as our race defends the Crown, the light of justice shall always prevail," Sei explained, folding her hands in a very unnatural way, impossible for a human.

"Haruna is the steward of our project...she has been appointed by the Republic to lead the diplomatic missions to other star systems," Sei said.

"Oh, and by the way, Munraito-kun, there was something I've been meaning to ask you. I haven't been on Oumi in years, and I'd like to see the old capital, Muranahe, again. Would you mind showing me around after everyone is finished acclimating?" Haruna asked, politely.

Immediately, Takada's head perked up at this request.

"Oh my God, dear, is it a date? How sweet, just in case you need any advice, Munraito, I'm here for you as well..." Takada said, a very devilish tone in her voice.

"No thank you...I'm sure I can manage on my own," Munraito responded, not wanting anything to do with Takada or any of her antics.

"Haruna, I'd be happy to show you around," Munraito said, pleasantly.

"Thank you so much!" Haruna said, happily.

At that moment, Haruna turned to Munraito and raised her hand, pulling a small object from her pocket telekinetically and placing it between her fingers.

"Munraito, this is my personal datapad, I never leave my apartment without it. I'm programming our date into the system set to begin three hours from now. I suggest you take this time to get ready, as I will be getting ready as well. Farewell, until later," Haruna smiled, kissing

Munraito on the cheek, sending the other Lightbringers on their way and

entering a command into her datapad. She then walked calmly out of the

room, towards the guest rooms in Heiei Castle.

"Looks like you've got a date, Munraito-san," Koda said.

"It would seem so," Munraito replied.

Koda was still visibly shaken from his confrontation with Takada, who had

since left the table to explore the rest of the castle. The rest of the

Lightbringers went about their daily duties, studies and conversations, as

Munraito and Koda walked calmly away.

"Koda, does any of this surprise you in the least bit?" Munraito asked,

thinking about everything that had happened over the past 12 hours.

"What do you mean, 'surprise?'" Koda asked.

"The fact that Haruna came back to Oumi even after the events of

fourteen years ago is nothing short of miraculous. She told me before she

left that she never wanted to see this planet ever again. However, here

she is, with us once again," Munraito said.

"What do you mean? What are you talking about?" Koda asked, curious about Haruna's apparently troubled past.

"Fourteen years ago, Haruna and I were classmates at Muranahe Primary School, when Haruna found her parents dead in her house one day after school. Both of them had been killed by a single blaster bolt to the back of the head, and there was no sign of a struggle. Haruna was devastated, and the police never caught the perpetrators. Whoever killed her parents did a truly professional job of it. I have tried using my Hyperspace Meditation to find the perpetrators by reaching across space-time, but apparently they even prepared for that eventuality, because whenever I arrive at the scene of the crime, I am immediately thrust into a bizarre psychedelic universe full of fanciful, ridiculous scenes meant to cover up what really happened. It is a projection by the perpetrator, because this, in his mind, is what really happened. I don't even think the killer knew what he was doing. Psychosis is a very powerful shield against mind probing. It is something you will learn in time, Koda," Munraito lectured to his Apprentice.

"That doesn't make sense. How could the killer not know what he's doing and be so precise about it, without leaving a shred of evidence?"

"That is what still eludes me. The case went cold years ago. I've been trying to solve it ever since, but the fog of time is growing too dense. Soon, it will be impossible to return to the scene of the crime through Hyperspace Meditation, because other events in the time stream since the crime occurred will have clouded the truth too much. The exact event will be lost in the quantum clutter. I fear the case will never be solved," Munraito said, with a heavy sigh.

"Some things just cannot be known, Munraito-san. We can reach across the cosmos to see things beyond most people's comprehension, but we cannot alter the past or know everything. Sometimes, we need to learn to accept things we cannot know or change," Koda reminded him.

"Perhaps, sometimes your wisdom exceeds even mine, Koda," Munraito said, smiling.

The two of them continued down the Patron's Corridor; a section of the castle built with traditional Japanese architecture, letting the brilliant red light from Amaterasu into the building. Oumi's habitable zone was large, but beyond that, complex life was very scarce. Along the Patron's Corridor, lines of crimson-red Ookazi Roses, with their black stems and blood-red flowers, sat in elegant vases. However, as beautiful as

Amaterasu was, the star could be very violent. All red-dwarf stars were prone to massive solar flares, which would blast the entire day side of the planet with deadly storms of cosmic radiation. Most life native to Oumi had evolved with adaptations to survive the occasional solar flare; however, the species that humans had brought with them to Oumi possessed no such adaptations, and massive wildfires amongst introduced plant species were very common. Building construction on Oumi needed to be heat and radiation resistant. Heiei Castle was built from the same ultra-strong composite materials as every other building on Oumi. Among the occasional earthquakes, volcanic activity, solar storms, massive hurricanes, hostile wildlife, and the constant winds from the massive temperature difference between the day and night sides of the planet, Oumi was not the easiest place where humans could live. However, the technology that Mankind had brought with it allowed people to eke out a living on a hostile yet beautiful foreign world.

Munraito and Koda arrived in the castle's enormous library, containing holographic records of most of humanity's knowledge, contained within vast Matryoshka brains and immediately accessible to the Lightbringers in their efforts to understand the Universe through their pursuit of Pantheon Doctrine. Munraito walked over to one of the AI interfaces and asked the friendly hologram that appeared in front of him for the Otohime murder case records.

"Still trying to solve that case, Munraito-san?" the person generated by the AI program said, curiously.

"I have a renewed interest in it...Haruna Otohime is back on Oumi and in the castle. I just spoke with her and I'm going to show her around Muranahe in a few hours. I'm just getting some work in before then," Munraito responded.

"Very well then, the records are being downloaded to your neural interface. Place your hand on the contact panel, please," the AI personification said as Munraito placed his hand on the computer panel, and immediately downloaded the full case file into his mind.

"Thank you very much," Munraito said, sitting down and mentally reviewing the case file, using his immensely powerful synthetic brain to do so. He perused through the various police files, scanning through them and picking out bits and pieces of data relevant to his theory about how the murderer managed to accomplish his goal without leaving any evidence. Just then, Munraito noticed something in one of the many images of the crime scene displayed in the case file. At first he thought he was imagining it, but then he looked at it again and saw the same thing. He didn't understand how the police could miss it, with their sophisticated AI systems scanning every piece of evidence leading up to the crime thousands of times. Perhaps this was just one of the many flaws of having AI in control of almost everything in society. AI, as sophisticated as it was, simply couldn't rationalize complex things such as a police investigation. Police had become so reliant on artificial intelligence that an obvious clue had been completely overlooked.

In one of the still shots from the Otohime family's home security system, one picture showed a dark shadow moving away from the camera, apparently holding something in its left hand. Perhaps the AI scanners had missed this shadow, determining that it may have just been a trick of the lighting or simply irrelevant to the investigation...however, it took a human eye to see the significance of this bit of evidence. The shadow was very tall and had a definite shape, although the details were not noticeable from the camera shot. However, it was definitely something of note. The odds of police actually catching this killer 14 years after the murder had happened were very slim, however. Whoever had done this could actually be anywhere in the Cosmos at this point, and Republic Security Forces on Oumi could only do so much. Perhaps just the

Defenders could solve this crime at this point. In the age of the Republic, large-scale militaries were a thing of the past. Instead, the Republic had invested heavily in 'Defenders,' squads of highly-trained Marines and vast armies of self-replicating AI units; the Defenders were elite super-soldiers wielding vast, seemingly supernatural powers to defend humanity from existential threats. Many different types of Defenders existed, but all were extremely potent warriors with a single mission: Defend the Republic from all potential enemies, foreign and domestic.

At that moment, Munraito formulated a plan of action for what he had found. He would bring the new evidence to the attention of the Security Forces in Muranahe, and leave it to them to sort out the truth from the video files. Then, he would focus on some much-needed personal time to reconnect with Haruna in Muranahe itself.

Munraito quickly closed the case file and stood up from his chair, walking rapidly towards the library's exit.

"Munraito-san, where are you going?" Koda asked, curiously.

"I must meet with the Republic Security Forces in Muranahe. I believe I have found evidence relevant to the Otohime murder case, information related to the being that killed Haruna's parents. Check up on Haruna while I'm gone. Tell her I'll be back in time for our date in Muranahe."

"Yes, Munraito-san, I'll get right on that," Koda said, walking away.

Munraito walked back down the Patron's Corridor back towards the rear doors to Heiei Castle, near where the transports were kept. Munraito could not stop thinking about what he had just found. Had he really done it? Had he really just found the first solid lead in the case, the first hint at a possible suspect? Perhaps, but no one could say for sure until the police looked at the footage for themselves. As Munraito walked towards the castle doors, he encountered Takada again, this time loitering around in the courtyard and enjoying the sunshine, presumably waiting for some action or the thrill of a new temptation.

"Where are you headed to in such a hurry?" Takada asked, curiously.

"It does not concern you, go about your business," Munraito said, deeply disturbed by Takada's behavior earlier.

"Ok...whatever," Takada grumbled, sitting on a bench enjoying the morning light.

Munraito left the courtyard and walked over toward the garage, where several mechanics were repairing a few of the superconductor vehicles the Lightbringers used to travel to Muranahe along the Inari Highway. This superconducting highway ran through the Panarin Mountains, offering a breathtaking view of the huge volcanic caldera of which the mountains formed the outer rim. Oumi was a much older planet than Earth, and most of its volcanoes were extinct or had such long repose times than they had not erupted for as long as humans had lived there. However, the bubbling hot springs, mud pots and fumaroles were proof that some volcanoes on Oumi were still active. The caldera that had formed the Panarin Mountains was created by an explosive eruption that dwarfed even the largest explosive eruptions in Earth's history. Thankfully, there were no human colonists present for that cataclysm; however, in the Fourteenth Age, human beings had long mastered the weather and earthquakes and volcanoes could be controlled.

Munraito approached the three mechanics and requested a vehicle for his errand.

"Sure thing, Master Lightbringer, the cars are right over there."

The mechanic pointed at three sleek, streamlined, wheel-less vehicles hovering over the garage floor on magnetic superconductors. The cars were self-driving and piloted by sophisticated AI programs, and could travel at nearly 400 miles per hour with almost no fuel. All Munraito had to do was speak the address he desired and let the vehicle carry him there automatically. Munraito walked over to the nearest car and waited for the doors to open automatically. Sitting in the driver's seat, Munraito spoke the address of Muranahe Police Headquarters into the car's AI system, and immediately, the doors shut. The car powered on, slowly hovered out of the garage and zoomed away from the Lightbringer Temple down the Inari Highway, towards the forbidding snow-capped volcanic mountains. As the car reached its top speed, Munraito felt the G-forces from traveling so fast. Despite these cars' impeccable safety records, Munraito always felt nervous whenever he had to drive anywhere. Maybe it was just paranoia, or maybe he thought that going 400 miles per hour on any road just wasn't safe, no matter what Rothus Engineering and other car manufacturers would try to make him believe. There were few cars on the Inari Highway that day, but that was not unusual. Oumi was rather sparsely populated due to its location, far from any major hubs of civilization and the fact that the planet was so hostile to human life.

As Munraito admired the scenery, suddenly, he saw a dark shadow pass over the car. Looking out through the windshield, he saw the sinister form of a Velvet Impaler shadowing his car. To his amazement, the Impaler was keeping pace with the car, and he was driving at more than 300 miles per hour! Munraito could hear the creature's loud sonar pings bouncing off the body of the car. Cars were not a typical target of Velvet Impaler attacks, but these creatures were huge, powerful, and among the top predators on Oumi. Perhaps this one was just very hungry, and there was nothing that Munraito could do to avoid it at this point. Munraito just had to hope that this giant creature would lose interest. Munraito looked out the window and shuddered. The huge, batlike creature was flying directly alongside the car, and Munraito was staring directly at its bulbous head. Its massive, lance-like mouthparts extended more than six feet beyond its spiderlike head; an Impaler's lance was harder than titanium and hollow, containing a drill-like tongue that injected an extraordinarily powerful venom, liquefying the prey's interior in seconds. Just the impact of an Impaler striking its prey at full speed was instantly lethal, and most creatures never even knew what hit them.

These statistics were a sobering thought for Munraito as his car zoomed through the mountains with the Impaler following close behind. Despite their brute strength, Velvet Impalers were actually quite intelligent and would investigate foreign objects in their environment, often by swooping in very low and pegging the object with waves of sonar. A simple inquiry was apparently what this Impaler was doing to Munraito's car, and it realized that the car was not a prey item. Still, having one of the top predators on Oumi shadowing one's car was a very unnerving experience.

Eventually, as the car passed over the caldera rim, the Impaler lost interest and pulled away into the thin mountain air. Munraito breathed a sigh of relief as the car passed through the Geldern Tunnel, a huge tunnel that made its way through Geldern Peak, the tallest mountain in the Panarin range. This mountain was far more than a mere geological formation. The mountain had been hollowed out by excavators and now contained a small town, called Asagi City. As Munraito's car entered the tunnel, it zoomed past various exits leading deep into the mountain. These were marked with street signs indicating Asagi City's main hubs: the Shopping District, the Business District and various other areas built directly into the mountain itself. The city was a true marvel of engineering and a testament to the technological achievements attained by both humans and transhumans as they spread across the stars. Munraito looked at the car's speedometer, which indicated that the car had reached its top speed of 400 miles per hour, zooming along on a magnetic cushion created by superconducting materials. At this speed, he would arrive in Muranahe within ten minutes. In the span of 5 seconds, Munraito had zoomed through Geldern Tunnel and had emerged on the other side of the Panarin Mountains, inside a vast caldera basin, at the center of which sat Muranahe City, surrounded by miles and miles of suburbs. All around the caldera rim, huge mountains rose up together like a gigantic amphitheater. In the skies above Muranahe, Munraito could see various starships coming and going, including the massive New Berlin Space Colony, from which hundreds of smaller ships were descending into Muranahe itself.

"It appears the New Berliners are enjoying themselves in Muranahe..." Munraito thought to himself.

The car slowed down automatically as it began entering the suburbs surrounding Muranahe City. High mountain peaks and natural scenery gave way to towns and conurbations, all constructed with self-assembling nanomaterials and reaching hundreds of stories tall. Many other cars clogged the streets as Munraito approached the city center. People, driving cars or riding bicycles were everywhere, walking down the street and enjoying the sunny, tropical weather. They enjoyed the constant breezes blowing from the frozen night side of the planet. There was no grass on Oumi, just a low carpet of reddish-brown, leafy plants that bloomed with many species of crimson-red wildflowers, and these plants made up the majority of plant life on most of the homes' lawns. The entire city was bathed in an eerie, perpetual red twilight from Amaterasu, giving Muranahe a unique personality found nowhere else in the Republic, much like the floating cities and multicolored suns of Lilliana V or the icy beauty of Arcana II.

As Munraito's car drove through the suburban streets, the buildings gradually began to grow larger as he approached the main city center, and residential apartment blocks gradually gave way to corporate skyscrapers and office buildings. Looming high above the city was the corporate spire of Rothus Engineering's Oumi branch. Rothus was the primary vehicle manufacturer in the Republic, producing most of the vehicles used by civilians, as well as many different types of starships used by the Defenders. The largest ships in the Republic were produced by Kraid Drive Yards, based around the industrial world of Kraid in the Cygnus Constellation. Rothus had produced the car that Munraito was currently driving, and as it moved through the city streets, a small alarm beeped on the car's computer console, indicating that it was approaching its destination.

As the car drove towards the Security Headquarters, it passed by a group of Defenders standing on the sidewalk, immediately identifiable by their unique armor and decorations. Each Defender possessed a specialized set of armor, as there were hundreds of different varieties, some quite standard, others rather exotic. The weapons used by these super-soldiers were just as diverse and varied. The different abilities wielded by their synthetic bodies were also immensely varied. Each Defender was an army unto himself, an elite unit, free of all weakness. This platoon of Defenders had apparently been flying aboard the New Berlin Space Colony, and they were simply taking time off from their duties to enjoy the city on Oumi.

Munraito's car turned a corner and pulled directly into the Muranahe Security Headquarters, in the shadow of Rothus Engineering's building complex. Perhaps placing the police headquarters immediately adjacent to the wealthiest company on Oumi gave the ultra-paranoid corporate bigwigs a sense of greater security. As Munraito's car parked in the visitor's lot, the seatbelt unfastened itself and Munraito stepped out of the car, walking swiftly towards the sliding door entrance to the police station. Walking through the door, he approached the reception counter and was immediately greeted by an AI program acting as the receptionist.

"Can I help you?" the AI personality said, with a cooing, almost soothing voice.

"I would like to speak with the Chief of Police. I have new evidence in the Otohime murder case," Munraito said.

"The Chief is not here right now, but you can leave what you've found with me. I will present it to him when he gets back. Can I have your name please?" the simulated personality asked.

"Master Sukui no Munraito Hikari, of the Lightbringer Order."

Suddenly, the AI program's facial expression changed.

"Master Lightbringer...we were beginning to think you would never figure this out. After all these years...what could the other AI programs have missed? Place your hand on the contact panel to download the information you have uncovered into my database. I will have the Chief look at it personally when he gets back," the simulated receptionist said.

Munraito placed his hand on the contact panel and downloaded the case files into the AI's computer database.

"Thank you very much. The data has been received. Have a wonderful day, and the Chief will be in touch with you as soon as possible," the AI personality reassured as Munraito walked back out the door towards his car. Munraito spoke the coordinates for the Lightbringer Temple into the car's computer system, which promptly gave the estimated travel time back to the Temple...he would be back just as Haruna was getting ready. As the car pulled away from the police station, Munraito passed by the group of Defenders again, each one clad in his own unique set of armor, mostly with adorning surcoats or cloaks. They always wore their visors, so no one could ever see their faces. Munraito watched the Defenders as the car slowly drove past them, and noticed that an ethereal energy field surrounded the Defenders, as if their bodies were radiating energy themselves. This was the innate ability that all Defenders possessed...the ability to channel pure energy into the most powerful weapons in the known Universe. Defenders were not just supremely powerful warriors, but they were cunning diplomats as well, often defusing conflicts before they could even begin. It was largely because of the Defenders that the Naruhol Ihr had been defeated more than 80 years before...it was a profound era of peace. Munraito was glad to see the Defenders doing their job, protecting the citizenry and standing on guard for peace.

Despite the Republic's general peace and prosperity, human beings had not changed a bit since antiquity. Crime was still commonplace, and with a completely immortal population, prison terms were no longer effective. What was 30 years in prison to someone who was never going to die? Police had long ago needed to find ways to prevent crime from happening in the first place; however, the near-accurate forms of corrective action, such as mental reprogramming to delete the urge to commit crimes from the offender's brain, was the closest the authorities could come to complete prevention in a democratic government. The technology to eradicate all crime existed, but implementing it for that purpose was a major violation of the Republic Constitution.

Munraito thought about all of this as he drove out of the main city center, and asked himself whether the Republic Constitution was always in the common citizenry's best interests. If the Republic had decided to use the appropriate technology to prevent all crime, Haruna's parents would still be alive today, and she would have never had to endure the suffering that she had experienced. Was it really 'immoral' to police a potentially violent individual's thoughts if it could save lives? In the interest of protecting those he cared about, he disregarded the Republic Constitution in this respect. His sense of justice was too profound. This lack of competence on behalf of the Republic government in protecting its own citizens sickened Munraito. Why did an innocent girl like Haruna have to suffer at the hands of truly rotten criminals because those elected to lead humanity were too concerned with 'moral questions?' The only 'immorality' in that question was the government not taking every step necessary to ensure the safety of every man, woman and child...and as a member of the Lightbringer Order, Munraito was one of the few people in the Republic with the power to change anything.

Munraito thought deeply about this as his car zoomed out of Muranahe, towards the Panarin Mountains once more. While sitting in the car, Munraito entered a deep trance, one characteristic of a Lightbringer's Hyperspace Meditation. As his consciousness drifted across space-time, Munraito could see Haruna going about her daily activities at the Lightbringer Temple, preparing for her day in Muranahe with Munraito. Haruna was very tidy and organized, actually making an itinerary for the day out in the city, writing her plans down in her data assistant. This was the first time Haruna had been in Muranahe in more than 14 years, and she wanted to keep track of everything that happened.

Munraito chuckled to himself when he saw how precise Haruna was being.

"What kind of person makes an itinerary for a date?" Munraito wondered to himself, deep in meditation. As the car zoomed through the Geldern Tunnel, Munraito's consciousness began to wander elsewhere; back to the wondrous worlds that he had visited the night before at the festival, the ones from Haruna's memories. He recognized a few of them, namely the tranquil Global Lake of Lilliana V, the icy skyline on Nox Aeterna on Arcana II, and the exotic jungles of Lunara, a habitable moon of the gas giant Wellingtonia, orbiting a binary star system in the Cygnus Constellation. Several, however, he did not recognize, indicating that they were not worlds under Republic control. Haruna was on an intergalactic diplomacy mission, involving many different advanced civilizations, so some of the foreign planets and moons may very well have been under the control of another civilization. Munraito couldn't wait to ask Haruna about her travels aboard the New Berlin Space Colony, it was a world far removed from the peace and prosperity of Oumi.

As Munraito's car passed through the Panarin Mountains on the return trip, he scanned the skies nervously for any signs of the Velvet Impalers; thankfully, there were none. The car passed over the high mountain passes and offered a breathtaking view of the Ookazi Fields far below, with the Heiei Castle complex rising like a beacon out of the sea of red and brown flowers and plants. To the southwest lay the borderlands of the Jukai, or 'Sea of Trees,' the largest tropical forest on Oumi, growing as a result of the constant moisture coming in off the Umi-no-Ai, the vast, tropical ocean that made life on Oumi possible at all. The creatures that inhabited the oceans were just as diverse as the ones that inhabited the land, if not more so, with gigantic, gliding Festoon Rays breaching out of the water and gliding over the ocean surface. These massive creatures filtered prey by skimming the water's surface with huge, beak-like snouts, which usually consisted of thousands of species of crustacean-like creatures called Sylphswimmers. These creatures were even more diverse than life in Earth's oceans were; as the Sun had continued to age, conditions on Earth had been slowly getting hotter and hotter, despite the massive Dyson sphere that had been constructed around the entire Solar System. Much of Earth's massive supercontinent, Pangaea Ultima, was covered by deserts in the North, though the South was much more verdant thanks to a large inland sea in the center of the continent. Most of the human civilization on Earth during the Fourteenth Age was in the South of this continent, the North contained many massive cities as well, though they were all clustered around underground aquifers. Munraito looked out across the vast panorama of Oumi, and took a deep breath.

This was the only home he had ever known, and the return of Haruna, with all the stories she carried with her, tempted Munraito with far more than what the Order of Lightbringers could offer him. He had learned all he could from his studies and his meditation...he now wanted to go out and see the Universe for himself.

As Munraito's car pulled up to Heiei Castle's grounds, the car drove past a group of Lightbringers talking to Ai Takada again. They looked very entertained by Takada's conversation, gesturing and laughing at Takada's stories. Munraito stopped the car and rolled down the windows, curious to see what was going on.

"Oh, hello Munraito, dear, your friends and I were just having a little conversation, I hope you don't mind," Takada said, with her usual attitude.

"About what, dare may I ask?" Munraito said, still leery of Takada after her behavior earlier.

"Master Munraito, calm down. She's really not that bad when you get to know her. She's actually quite interesting to talk to," one of the other Lightbringers said. Munraito closed his eyes and sighed. He rolled up the windows and continued towards the garage, where the vehicle mechanics were busy playing a game on their break.

"Welcome back, Master Munraito. We really enjoyed your speech last night at the Festival. I wonder why the Naruhol Ihr showed up," one of the mechanics looked up, and said to Munraito.

Munraito nodded in acknowledgment and thought about the same thing...the fact that the Naruhol Ihr would come to Oumi, so far from any centers of civilization was very odd. As Munraito walked back through the courtyard and into the castle once again, he encountered the radiant form of Viceroy Annunaki hovering down the hallway. He was being followed by several Lightbringers conversing with him.

"Oh, hello there Master Munraito. I trust you are enjoying the lovely weather," Viceroy Annunaki said.

"Indeed, Viceroy. Is there any reason why you and the other Naruhol Ihr leaders are here on Oumi?" Munraito asked.

"Master Lightbringer, they are here to further the cause of Miss Otohime's efforts. Our civilizations will benefit immensely from our greater cooperation," Viceroy Annunaki said, very calmly.

"Speaking of which, where is she...she said she'd be ready by now," Munraito said, looking at his pocket chronometer.

"I don't know where she went...perhaps you should go looking for her," Viceroy Annunaki said.

Munraito walked away from Viceroy Annunaki and went to look for Haruna, who was nowhere to be found. Munraito walked back down the Patron's Corridor towards the library, where he saw the Troika of Andromedan leaders perusing the archives with the assistance of Gwenlynn Stormweaver. She was studying the ancient architecture of the prehistoric Zanthril civilization, which had built monuments on Earth's Moon, Mars and various other places in humanity's ancestral Solar System. The Zanthril civilization still existed, with several outposts in Republic space in the constellation Lyra, but the colonies in the Solar System were abandoned many thousands of years before the rise of humanity as a major force in the Universe. Gwenlynn appeared to be very busy analyzing the data, so Munraito politely declined to interrupt her. Munraito continued past the library and towards the Grand Staircase, leading up to the second floor and the Lightbringers' living quarters.

"Haruna, I'm back!" Munraito yelled up the stairs, in an effort to find Haruna.

"Damn it, where did she go?" Munraito grumbled to himself.

"Oh! Munraito-kun! Hi!" Haruna yelled from upstairs, seemingly struggling with something.

"Good afternoon, Haruna-chan. Can I help you with anything?" Munraito walked up the stairs and found Haruna trying to decide what to wear for her day out in Muranahe, she had put on a very nice outfit, but the choice had come down to either a red synthetic nano-cashmere cardigan over her shirt, or a black one.

"Munraito-kun, can you help me decide which one to wear? I can't decide whether to wear the red one to match my hair, or the black one to match my pants..." Haruna asked, her voice trailing off in an uncharacteristic display of self-doubt.

"Does it really matter, Haruna?" Munraito sighed, realizing that Haruna's dilemma was a trivial one at best.

"Munraito-kun, I don't think you understand the importance of me looking my best at all times. I am employed by the Republic Department of Internal Affairs. Everything I do, everywhere I go, I am under the microscope. I represent the interests of the Republic to all who meet me, and in any sort of political position, first impressions are everything. I must always project the image of success and that of an upstanding citizen, so, knowing that, which do you think looks better on me, the black one, or the red one?" Haruna explained, very frankly.

"Well, that depends. Which one do you like better?" Munraito asked.

Haruna paused at this question, unsure of how to respond.

"I don't know which one I like better, I need you to tell me," Haruna said, with a very serious look on her face.

"I think the red one looks better on you," Munraito said, conceding to what he thought was just a silly request.

"Thank you," Haruna said, kindly.

Haruna placed the red nano-cashmere on over her shirt and walked out of the bedroom with Munraito in tow, walking back down the spiral staircase and towards the Patron's Corridor.

"This place is truly beautiful, wow, you're so lucky to be able to live here," Haruna said, marveling at the splendor of Heiei Castle.

"Thank you. This has always been the home of the Lightbringer Order; we have lived here for as long as there has been an Order on Oumi, though our headquarters is at the Temple of the Sun in New Tokyo, on Earth. Earth in this day and age has become so altered from its natural state that the planet itself is essentially an artificial structure by this point, and is gradually being moved to a new orbit as the Sun continues to grow hotter and brighter. However, Earth is still a world of ancient beauty, quite unlike anything else in the known Universe," Munraito explained, walking past the library, where some of Haruna's guests were still studying.

"Wow...so there are even more places like this, where your Order does everything in its power to advance the cause of humanity. That is a truly amazing thing," Haruna said, walking with Munraito towards the exit to the courtyard. Munraito and Haruna stepped out into the sun, where they saw Takada again, only this time she was sitting in the sun and talking to some of the mechanics.

"She does nothing except run her mouth..." Munraito groaned, walking right past her without her even noticing.

"Yeah, Takada's a real socialite and a dedicated romantic...you know what she's famous for, right?" Haruna said, smiling.

"Yes, I do...I read that book she wrote, at least some of it. Not my thing. I think her behavior borders on criminal," Munraito grumbled.

"Chill out, seriously. Every one of the people she's done that to have volunteered themselves and paid her huge sums of money for it. It all takes place in the online Universe as well. She makes a great living for herself; the only downside is that she has a bit of a temper issue, which I'm sure your apprentice Koda can attest to," Haruna said.

"I don't care what she is or how she makes her living, I don't like her, nor will I tolerate that behavior in Heiei Castle. This is a place of respect, and I expect all guests to uphold that standard," Munraito said, walking into the garage and approaching one of the cars parked inside.

"Ok then...fair enough," Haruna said, stepping into the car with Munraito in tow. Even in situations where she was not in charge, such as when Munraito was driving, Haruna took the lead. Munraito took his seat behind the controls and entered Muranahe City Center into the car's AI systems. Immediately, the doors closed and the car pulled out of the garage, headed down the Inari Highway for the second time that day. It was at this point that Munraito turned to Haruna and asked her the question he had been waiting to ask:

"Haruna, where have you been all this time?"

3. Breakthrough

"Well, Munraito, where do I begin? The last time I saw you, I was

preparing to board the shuttle craft to the New Berlin Space Colony to live

with my relatives, shortly after my parents were murdered. I settled in

nicely with my aunt and uncle on the Valhalla Apartment Block aboard the

New Berlin Colony, which is one of the most prestigious space colonies in

the Republic. Everyone living there is of either European or Japanese

descent, as the colony was inspired by the 19th-century völkisch

movement. This mindset resulted in the glorification of European and

South Asian heritage. In the spirit of the movement, the colony prides

itself on being a naturally grown, organic society in Earthly harmony, and

the colony has an emphasis on its own version of populism, in terms of being in harmony with nature and having a romanticized heritage. This perspective is maintained while attempting to reject the slow-paced Republic bureaucracy and rampant technological 'over-civilization.' I was presented with all the luxuries of being a New Berlin resident, including membership in prestigious youth organizations, many of which have produced individuals that have gone on to lead the Republic. I was also granted admission to some of the finest universities in the Republic. During my travels across the Republic with the New Berliners, I went to a private academy, was a leader in the New Berlin Youth League and graduated with high honors from Sol Invictus University. As you know, Sol Invictus is one of the most prestigious Universities in the Republic. I eventually plan to run for the office of Republic Secretary of State," Haruna explained.

"We must have become so wrapped up in our own lives that we simply drifted apart over the years...but the winds of the Universe have brought us back together. What about the office of the Chancellery? Why not go all the way with that background?" Munraito suggested.

"Oh no, flattering me is nice but...with my political views I could never be elected," Haruna said, embarrassed.

"Why not? With the right campaign strategy, I think you could accomplish anything," Munraito asserted.

"Well, my stance on mind-reading technology to prevent crime is not exactly popular and my foreign policy stance towards such belligerent civilizations such as the Sangresaara and Sigtyr won't make me many friends in conservative circles...but I suppose my beliefs wouldn't be that unpopular," Haruna explained as the car began climbing the Panarin Mountains.

"What exactly is your stance on the mind-reading technology, Haruna?" Munraito asked, curiously.

"Well, I think it's wrong, contrary to what the rest of the general public thinks. If we allow the government to read the minds of anyone it considers to be a potential threat, we will effectively create a very slippery slope in which the government could conceivably grow into a totalitarian police state, where people aren't even allowed to think freely, let alone speak their minds or let their voices be heard. I believe it is detrimental to democracy," Haruna said.

"An interesting stance coming from someone whose parents could have been saved by the implementation of this technology," Munraito said, somberly.

Haruna froze at that statement.

"Well, I have come to believe that without my parents' death, I would have never been able to live the life that I have, and I probably would not be in the position that I am today," Haruna said, with a smile on her face.

"So you recognize the positives in every situation, I see. Perhaps you and the current Chancellor have more in common than you realize. He is more of an idealist than a realist. His policymaking, however, has had a noticeable effect on the economic development of the Outer Rim, beyond the reach of the Grand Alliance, which includes the Astari and Elohim," Munraito said, referring to the current High Chancellor, Phoenix Oberholtzer.

"That is an interesting statement. So you believe that Chancellor Oberholtzer has good intentions, but does not always seem to have the realities of our lives in mind. Keep in mind that any and all human beings in government are mere figureheads; it is really immensely powerful AI brains and computers that govern our society. The vast majority of military force within the Republic consists of AI units; the Defenders and Marines are just the human arm of the military," Haruna reminded Munraito.

"Yes, you do make a good point. Human beings scarcely have to do anything these days," Munraito responded.

"Thank you," Haruna said.

"I prefer it that way, anyway. Robots and computers are the only truly efficient way to govern a society that spans over millions of star systems," Munraito responded.

"I would have to agree with you there," Haruna said.

"The task of governance would be impossible for a human being in our scenario," Haruna responded.

"Either way, I praise you for overcoming your parents' death and making such a successful life for yourself," Munraito said.

"Thank you so much...that means a lot to me," Haruna replied.

The car was passing over the high mountain passes again towards the Geldern Tunnel, with Haruna gazing in awe of the volcanic mountain ranges that she hadn't seen in 14 years.

"I've almost forgotten how incredible these mountains are...to think that these were formed by one of the largest volcanic eruptions known to science is a very humbling experience. Oumi is a much older planet than Earth, and its volcanoes are far less active than the ones on Earth. When they erupt, however, they erupt with a far greater ferocity than any volcano on Earth, ever," Haruna said, recalling the nature of Oumi's volcanism versus that of Earth's. The eruption that formed the caldera in which the city of Muranahe sat released an estimated 15,000 cubic kilometers of tephra, most of which raged across the land as pyroclastic ignimbrite flows, as determined by Republic geologists. These eruptions dwarfed anything seen on Earth in its entire history; humanity had lived through many super-eruptions at this point, and had developed technology to prevent them from happening in the first place by the Fourteenth Age. A repeat of these caldera-forming eruptions on Oumi would almost certainly constitute an extinction-level event for that planet. As the car zoomed into the Geldern Tunnel, it accelerated to its top speed as it moved through the mountains.

"Haruna, do you ever get nervous when these cars hit their top speed?" Munraito asked.

"No, not at all, I love the feeling of zooming at top speed down the highway, or sailing through space on a starship. I just love the feeling of going fast. I used to dream about being a pilot or a starship captain when I was younger. It's funny how life turns out- you have your heart set on being one thing, but then as your grow up, you realize that you want to be something else...and when you finally reach that point in life, you never want it to end," Haruna said as the car zoomed past Asagi City in the heart of Geldern Mountain.

"I suppose. As a Lightbringer I was taught differently. The desire of all Mankind is to learn and grow into a higher spiritual awareness. Much as the Elohim and Astari do, our species seeks to achieve its ultimate goal: absolute omnipotence and supreme power over Nature. Our Order seeks to achieve that goal through the Pantheon Doctrine and our Hyperspace Meditation...we channel the Universal Energy, much like the Defenders do, for this energy is what would have been thought of as God in an earlier time. For us, life is a constant balancing act, between light and darkness, justice and injustice, truth and lies, knowledge and ignorance, hate and love, and all other human emotions. I, above all else, seek to better understand the Universe in which I live and work to make it a better place for all by any means necessary. To elaborate on your earlier point about mind-reading technology, I fully support its introduction. The only thing 'immoral' about that is the government not taking every step necessary to protect its citizens," Munraito stated.

"Well, that philosophy does have its merits, I suppose. It is a very noble aim to dedicate your life to the betterment of Mankind. However, I would advise you to tread cautiously in this territory. Some of the worst atrocities in human history have occurred under the guise of 'the betterment of Mankind,'" Haruna cautioned as their car came zooming out of Geldern Tunnel, into the vast panorama of the caldera basin and Muranahe City far below.

"Well, there it is, Muranahe City," Munraito said.

"There's the New Berlin Space Colony, my home for the past 14 years," Haruna said, pointing at the massive starship hovering over the city, on the banks of a huge lake in the center of the caldera. The colony sat in geo-synch orbit with smaller ships coming and going from its massive hangars, ferrying people to and from Oumi's surface. Munraito looked up at the massive colony and wondered just what it was like aboard one of the most prestigious places to live in the entire Republic. It was a truly different world aboard one of the colonies, a world of rarified luxury and unprecedented wealth and privilege. Haruna was no longer the little girl from Oumi that Munraito had once known, but now a woman of immense social standing and prestige. He wondered if Haruna still cared about him or Oumi, or if she was only passing through on her way to achieving her own dreams. Either way, it was very reassuring to Munraito to have Haruna back on Oumi...it was as if a long-lost part of him had returned. All he wanted from her was companionship and compassion...he wanted to feel something that he had never felt before from anyone, not the Lightbringers, not his mentors, nobody. As the car began its descent from the mountain passes into Muranahe City, Haruna was overwhelmed by a wave of nostalgia.

"This is the street my friends and I used to play on..." Haruna said of one suburban street surrounding Muranahe City. Munraito looked out the window at the nondescript suburban street, lined with rows of middle-class housing units and fresh lawns of red and orange flowers and other native plants. Some children played on the sidewalks outside the mid-sized homes, enjoying their childhood, blissfully unaware of all the concerns of adult life that Munraito and Haruna dealt with on a daily basis.

"Where exactly did you live? I know we went to the same primary school," Munraito asked.

"I lived on Usagi Street, in one of the housing developments with my family," Haruna said, warmly reminiscing on her childhood.

"Usagi...that's up near the Imperial Heights area. Haruna, that's a really nice neighborhood, it must have been nice growing up in a neighborhood like that," Munraito said.

"My father was a Senator in the Republic capitol on Stronghold, and my mother was a lawyer, practicing in Muranahe, but she also had law offices on Lilliana V and Stronghold as well, two of the most respected worlds in the Republic. The police believe that my parents were assassinated by a lone-wolf gunman acting alone...I just think it's very odd that even after 14 years, the police and the Defenders, for that matter, would have almost zero leads in the case. I have long believed that my parents' murder was part of a much larger series of events; if it was just a rogue assassin acting alone, the police would have caught the killer a very long time ago and I would have since moved on from this event...however, the lack of closure has been very difficult for me to accept going forward. I have been forced to accept that this case will likely never be solved," Haruna said, solemnly.

"Well, Haruna, I have not given up on that pursuit. For the past 14 years, I have been studying the case inside and out, analyzing every possible aspect of the incident and tracking down every lead involving the murder of your parents...and just today, I found something in the Archives. I believe it is a key piece of evidence involving the murder of your parents. Earlier I came to Muranahe and dropped it off at the police station. Don't ever give up. There is always hope," Munraito said, reassuringly.

"You did that for me?" Haruna asked, incredulously.

"Yes. I did not forget about you," Munraito said.

Just then, the car stopped suddenly, the AI systems detecting a road closure ahead.

"This is odd...I was just here an hour ago on an errand...this road was open."

At that moment, Haruna received a call on her neural implant.

"Yes...what?! Ok, understood," Haruna said, incredulously.

"I don't believe it. There was a terrorist attack against the Oumi Security Forces...it just happened not even 20 minutes ago...I don't understand. This doesn't happen on Oumi. We're too out of the way, too peaceful, why would terrorists attack here?!" Haruna said, panicking.

"Don't panic, Haruna. Why would they attack the police station?" Munraito exclaimed as the car rerouted around the road closure and proceeded into the city center.

The centermost part of the city was thick with police officers and heavily armored and armed Defenders, all redirecting traffic and keeping people away from the site of the attack, which was apparently confined to the area around the police station. A large column of smoke was billowing out of the side of the building. It appeared from first examination that a single explosive device had been detonated inside the police station where Munraito just was less than two hours before, and various groups of police officers and Defenders were examining the blast zone. The Defenders' tiny, hovering android assistants, called Waifs, were examining and scanning the blast area. Their weapons- grenades and psychic abilities- were held at the ready, just in case of a second attack.

"There sure are a lot of Defenders around here, Haruna...I don't know if I've ever seen so many in one area."

"Well, I certainly feel a lot safer with them around. They are humanity's best defenders and have a truly legendary history in service of the Republic. The defeat of the Naruhol Ihr is just the most recent exploit that they have achieved for us," Haruna said as the car pulled into a parking garage on the other side of town, outside of the police barricades. Haruna and Munraito stepped out of the car and into the garage, surrounded by the sounds and sights of Muranahe. Everywhere, police and Defenders patrolled the streets, with Republic armored vehicles and various other combat assets in position, prepared for the worst.

"Wow...the Republic is just on full alert right now...it's going to be difficult to have a normal day out at this rate," Munraito said as both of them walked past two Defenders in full armor standing by the parking garage. As Munraito and Haruna stepped out onto the city streets, a police armored vehicle hovered past them, with a SWAT officer on the gun turret.

"This is crazy...I mean, it was just the police station, wasn't it? Why are they rolling out all of their assets as if they are anticipating an all-out invasion?" Haruna wondered.

"Perhaps they know something we don't," Munraito said, ominously.

As Munraito and Haruna proceeded down the city streets, they passed by multiple clearly-concerned passersby, many of which had bewildered looks on their faces. Perhaps the extreme reaction to the bombing was a result of the extremely low crime rate on Oumi. The city of Muranahe hadn't seen so much as one violent crime in the past 5 years, let alone a terrorist bombing...and this one was with absolutely no warning, no prior threats, and no indication that anyone had anything against the Muranahe Police Department. Yet, the police had determined that the explosion was not accidental. For the people of Muranahe, this was an extraordinarily disturbing turn of events, and the fact that it seemed to coincide with the arrival of the New Berlin Space Colony began to make many residents of Oumi suspicious of the off-worlders. They had not forgotten what had happened the last time the New Berlin Space Colony visited Oumi. Haruna's parents, the powerful Otohime family, had been murdered within days of the colony arriving on Oumi. People on Oumi were generally very close-knit and large numbers of visitors from elsewhere in the Republic were rare, so naturally people began to develop all sorts of wild conspiracy theories every time something as monumental as a colony ship appeared in the skies over Oumi. Most of these theories were utter nonsense, with no basis in reality. However, people's paranoia whenever something went wrong was very real, and it was palpable that day in Muranahe, with everyone seeking some sort of additional safety. The threat was, in all likelihood, far more imagined than real. Still, the amount of police and military presence out in force was disturbing. Perhaps the Defenders had only been deployed as a means to combat panic, as crime on Oumi was so rare. Still, Munraito couldn't shake the various brooding thoughts from the back of his mind.

Munraito and Haruna walked into a boutique, which was still bustling with its usual camaraderie of guests and customers, despite the commotion outside. People were concerned, but they trusted that the worst of the commotion was over and that everything was under control. As Munraito and Haruna stepped up to the counter, they were greeted by an AI program acting as the cashier, who promptly appeared as a hologram and greeted them. The AI automations employed by most retail outlets across the Republic could do their respective jobs far better than a human being ever could, and most AI programs were simply part of the building itself, with every object in that building capable of interacting with customers and patrons. Every building on every planet, space colony and settlement in the Republic made use of this technology, a true wonder of the modern age. Haruna and Munraito sat down at one of the boutique's outdoor benches and watched as the Republic armored vehicles and Defenders walked past, checking every inch of the city for the perpetrator of the attack on the police station.

"Wow...this is really wild...it'll only be a matter of time before they catch the person who did this..." Haruna said, commenting on the sheer numbers of police and Defenders scouring the area. As Haruna and Munraito began talking, Haruna took out her datapad and tapped the screen with a stylus. She then placed the assistant back in her shirt pocket.

"Haruna, what was that about?" Munraito said, curious as to why Haruna took her assistant out instead of talking to him.

"It was my itinerary for the day. I just checked off going to a store and enjoying the sunshine," Haruna laughed.

"Who makes an itinerary for a date?" Munraito asked, jokingly.

"I like to be very organized," Haruna said.

"My datapad is my life these days," Haruna sighed.

"Isn't it for most of us? I was always taught that technology was a distraction, which kept us from the things that really mattered," Munraito said, watching as the Defenders marched past.

"What you say is true, I guess. However, without this technology, we would still be cavemen living on Earth, and, I know that's not what you would prefer," Haruna said.

"I can't say that I don't agree with you. However, Haruna, don't you miss the good old days, where we used to go outside and just explore the world? We didn't care about things like technology, deadlines and schedules. We were young and full of life...and now look at us...when did we become so boring?" Munraito asked.

Haruna smiled and looked at Munraito.

"Munraito, you live a truly blessed life. You live in a castle, surrounded by beautiful scenery. You are surrounded by hundreds of people that love and care about you. Everyone respects you wherever you go, and I still believe you are going to change our existence so radically that this world will be unrecognizable by the time you're through with it...Sadly, the same is not true for me. My parents are dead; I'm an adult. I have a career now, and I have my own life and responsibilities. You never had that innocence ripped from you. It is something you can never truly understand. I have no one," Haruna said.

"No, Haruna. You have me," Munraito said, warmly.

"You mean more to me than anything in this Universe; I always considered you my girlfriend growing up, even when we were too young to truly understand the complex emotion we call love. Love is the strongest force in the Universe, Haruna. It transcends time and space, reaches across generations, and always brings each and every one of us back home. You came back here for a reason, Haruna, even if you do not believe so. Something inside of you drew you here...I can sense it...you are still haunted by the demons from your past...do not worry. As long as I am here, nothing will harm you," Munraito said.

"Thank you..." Haruna said, quietly, her voice becoming more child-like, as she wistfully recalled recent events.

"I feel the same way. Something about Oumi, something about you...that's what brought me back here. It all started a few months ago when I had a dream...no, more of a premonition, of me returning to Oumi. I conferred with Viceroy Annunaki aboard the New Berlin Space Colony, and he told me to come back...and sure enough, you were the first person I met here. It was almost like it was meant to be, like something was pulling me back here. Is that love? I wouldn't know...however, the one thing I do know is that I feel like I truly belong with you...and nothing can take that away from me," Haruna said.

"Haruna, what you are experiencing is the law of attraction. Energy seeks energy...and when two energies bound by time, body and space meet...we call it love. However, it is just another force in our Universe, and the strongest one that exists. It transcends time, space, gravity, dark energy, the nuclear forces, and everything else. It knows no boundaries, and crosses entire Universes. All intelligent life feels this force, and all life radiates this energy. Entire civilizations have been built using this power as an energy source; take for example the Astari and the Elohim...these are the energies of the Cosmos itself, emanating from the Universal Energy. It is what we would call God in an earlier time. The Astari and Elohim's vehicles and technology radiate it and shine with the brightness of a thousand stars because of the power they possess. All life in the Universe is subject to the same laws of attraction...and we are no different," Munraito said to Haruna as he noticed a police officer walking towards the store. The officer looked odd, like he hadn't slept for days.

"Wow. That's extremely profound. Such things are normally believed to be pure luck...however, you claim to know otherwise. There's no such thing as luck. Everything happens for a purpose, but that purpose is nothing special...it is just the natural flow of energy through the Universe..." Haruna said.

"Precisely, everything is connected, Haruna-chan," Munraito replied.

Munraito and Haruna shared another warm embrace with a parting look into each other's eyes, both of them overjoyed that they had finally found each other again. In an earlier age, it would have been seen as divine intervention. However, in the age of the Republic, it was simply a law of the Universe. As both Haruna and Munraito prepared to leave, they were approached by the odd-looking police officer, who had another officer with him now. Munraito looked at the two officers and noticed something very unusual about them. Their eyes were an unnatural color, and their skin seemed extraordinarily pale. They looked sick, even diseased.

"Are you Hikari Munraito, of the Lightbringer Order?" the police officers asked, with an extremely disturbing look on their face.

Munraito made a very skeptical face and identified himself. "You need to come with us to the station. This matter requires immediate attention.

You aren't under arrest or suspected of anything. We just need to speak with you."

Munraito turned to Haruna and nodded to her.

"I'll be back," Munraito said.

"Wait, can I come with him?" Haruna asked.

"You may," the police responded.

Haruna and Munraito followed the two police officers out of the boutique and back towards the Republic armored vehicle, towards three Defenders and several armored police officers. They assisted Haruna and Munraito as they stepped into the armored personnel carrier, which promptly headed off in the direction of one of the auxiliary police stations around the city. As Munraito and Haruna sat in the back of the carrier, Haruna couldn't believe the extreme set of circumstances they were suddenly thrown into.

"Munraito, what happened? What did you do?" Haruna said, concerned.

"I have no idea. The police just want to speak with me for some reason. As a Lightbringer, I hold a very high-ranking position in society. Perhaps they think I can help them with the investigation," Munraito said.

The armored vehicle hovered through the city streets and eventually arrived at the 13th Street Auxiliary Police Station, which was heavily guarded by various armored police forces and Defenders. As the Defenders opened the rear hatch to the APC, Munraito and Haruna stepped out of the vehicle and were escorted into the police station, where they were met by the battalion chief, clutching a pulse rifle and flanked by two Defenders, both carrying sniper weapons. The Chief looked at Munraito very coldly as he entered the police station, and even though the officers at the cafe had told him that he was not under arrest, the police chief was looking at him like a common criminal. He also had the same sickly appearance; in addition, his eyes appeared glazed over.

"Miss Otohime...I did not expect to see you here again," the police chief said, almost mockingly.

Haruna seemed very unnerved by the police chief's attitude towards her and Munraito. Even the two Defenders seemed to think that something was amiss, as they were communicating telepathically to each other from behind their helmets.

"Come into the back room. We need to have a word with you," the Chief said, very coldly.

"Haruna, you stay right there," the police chief instructed to a very uneasy Haruna, who promptly sought security with the two Defenders, who seemed just as concerned with the police chief's behavior as Haruna was. The Defenders reassured Haruna that nothing was going to happen as long as they were present, which gave Haruna some comfort.

As the police chief led Munraito into the back room, Munraito thought to himself about the implications of this sudden turn of events. The police chief seemed to be on edge, but this was likely a result of stress and dealing with the attacks. Surely, there was really nothing wrong. He was a Lightbringer, a Grand Master of the Order, what could he possibly have done to anger the police? The Chief sat Munraito down in one of the interview rooms used to interrogate suspects, where the Chief pulled out a small data file and placed it on the table in front of Munraito.

"Ok, 'Master Lightbringer,' where did you get this picture?" the police chief sneered, revealing the image that Munraito had found in the Otohime case file and had turned into the police just hours before.

Sensing that something was wrong, Munraito kept his steely-eyed cool and responded calmly.

"I found it in the Otohime case file."

"Where did you get that case file?" the Chief barked.

"It was in the Archives of the Lightbringer library. I have been researching the case for many years, as Haruna is a childhood friend of mine," Munraito responded.

"A childhood friend of yours...is that right? So, let me get this straight, you've been conducting your own investigation into the Otohime murders for the past fourteen years out of charity for your childhood friend, and you turn in evidence that you think was conveniently overlooked...Hah, I thought you Lightbringers were supposed to be smart," the police chief chuckled.

"Chief, what are you talking about?!" Munraito snapped.

"You don't know the half of it, do you? This little bit of evidence you found was something that must have been missed fourteen years ago...something that wasn't destroyed when the order was given...it is of no concern at this point. This is just a minor inconvenience for us, and will not impede our overall goal. Unfortunately for you, Master Lightbringer, I'm afraid I cannot let you leave this station. You and Haruna both must be dealt with. The Departed God's will be done...and now, I'm going to finish what was started fourteen years ago!"

Just then, the doors to the interview room flew off their hinges, as the police chief was immobilized by a blast of plasma energy. One of the Defenders, hovering through the air and shrouded in a static storm of energy, had immobilized the police chief just in time. He drew his huge sniper rifle and placed it against the police chief's head.

"Chief Aleistair Watts, you are under arrest for the murder of Seta and Reina Otohime, among many, many other charges. Master Munraito, congratulations. You just uncovered the biggest case of police corruption in the history of the Republic," the well-armed Defender said to a stunned Munraito.

"Where is Haruna?" Munraito yelled.

"She's in the armored vehicle, and you might want to take cover, Master Munraito."

"No. Take me to her now," Munraito ordered, just as the building's wall blew down in a massive explosion.

The Defender cloaked himself in plasma energy again, hovering through the air. Two other Defenders joined him, also pulsing with radiant energy and drawing their weapons. As soon as they did so, a group of armored SWAT police burst in, firing their plasma rifles on full automatic at the

Defenders, who promptly unleashed withering waves of energy attacks and rifle fire. The Defenders were dealing plasma, fire, electrical and telekinetic damage to the SWAT police, who quickly crumpled from the assault. Just then, one of the Defenders' fiery assaults completely annihilated the police station's other wall, blasting debris out in all directions and scattering passersby screaming as plasma fire rocked the crowded city street corner. All over the city, Defenders were making arrests of corrupt police officers, all with the same sickly looks on their faces, but this was the only corrupt precinct that wasn't going down without a fight. As Munraito kept his distance from the fighting, he thought about the implications of this revelation. If the police had killed Haruna's parents, then the police were probably responsible for the recent terrorist bombing...but why would the police bomb their own headquarters? It just didn't add up. Munraito had more pressing matters to contend with at this very moment, however, like not being shot by a corrupt police officer during the firefight.

The Defenders continued their battle with the police forces, who just seemed to keep coming; even for police corruption, the fact that they would resist arrest so viciously was highly unusual. The police clearly did not want anyone to figure out what they were up to. These police officers were effectively committing suicide by engaging in a direct firefight with three Defenders. They would rather die than be found out in a court of law. Munraito watched as officer after officer fell to the Defenders' attacks, and civilians continued to scatter left and right. The police were putting up a truly ridiculous resistance to the Defenders, and the battle was now beginning to spread beyond 13th Street as yet more police officers, some in armored vehicles firing their plasma turrets, began appearing on the scene, ordering the Defenders to disperse. The police claimed that the Defenders were in violation of Republic law by resisting them. Even at this stage, the police refused to admit any wrongdoing, and instead were blaming the Defenders for this rapidly-unfolding war in the streets. The Defenders began attacking the armored vehicles, frying them like eggs on the pavement and killing hundreds of police officers. Neither side showed any sign of backing down. It looked as if the Defenders were going to have to kill every single police officer in the city of Muranahe, which was something that would surely go down in history as one of the most significant events ever to happen in the history of the Republic.

"This entire damn city's corrupt!" one of the Defenders yelled, throwing an incendiary grenade at an armored vehicle. The blast completely engulfed the vehicle and damaged many of the nearby buildings, scattering more people into cover. The Defenders looked around at the growing devastation, and realized the civilian body count was beginning to climb. They thought to themselves about just how many people had to die in this utterly pointless battle. The resulting mayhem was rapidly turning into one of the greatest tragedies in recent memory for the Republic, and perpetrated by the police, no less.

The Defenders looked around at the devastation and saw heartbreaking scenes all around them. On one street corner, a child was crying over his dead mother's body. On another lay a charred remnant of a human body hit by a treacherous grenade. Burning storefronts filled with incinerated merchandise lined the normally spotless streets, and mangled body parts were scattered all over the ground like children's toys. The Defenders were utterly speechless as they fired their weapons. The only question they could ask themselves was as to how this utter devastation could have happened. What entity in the Republic, what temptation, what motive could possibly corrupt an entire planet's police forces into murdering a Senator and his family and essentially running a completely corrupt enterprise for fourteen years? Equally baffling was the fact that when they were finally caught, rather than go quietly, they started an urban war with the Defenders that killed hundreds, if not thousands of civilians. Chief Watts mentioned something about a 'Departed God.' Whatever the reason for these terrible actions, the motive must have run very, very deep. However, the Defenders couldn't worry about that now. They could only worry about protecting civilians and minimizing further casualties.

Back in the ruins of the police station, Munraito took matters into his own hands. Seeing a weapon lying on the ground, dropped by one of the police officers, he picked it up and prepared to join the battle. Emotions ran hot through his veins. He simply could not believe it. This kind of brutality happening on Oumi made absolutely no sense. What would possess the police to commit such heinous crimes? This chain of events went against everything he had ever believed in. If the police couldn't be trusted, then who could? If this police force was so corrupt, then what about other police forces across the Republic? Munraito was faced with the ugly possibility that this recent turn of events could only be the tip of the iceberg, and that this plot was simultaneously unfolding elsewhere in the Republic. However, he and Haruna were faced with the more immediate task of survival. Haruna was not safe in the armored vehicle, as Munraito had seen multiple armored vehicles go up in flames during the course of the battle. He had to do something to get Haruna out of harm's way.

Munraito felt a sickening worry overtake him. He had just been reunited with Haruna after 14 years. He was not going to lose her again.

Courageously, Munraito stood up and strode through the ruins of the police station as explosions and plasma fire roared all around him. He stepped over broken piles of burning rubble and dead bodies lying on the ground, purposefully making his way towards the armored vehicle where Haruna sat. He had to find Haruna, lest the corrupt police officers find her first. He saw the vehicle parked on the side streets, away from the main area of combat between the Defenders and the police forces, so her current location kept her relatively safe from attack. Munraito quickly ran out of the building through the massive hole in the wall and ran towards the armored vehicle holding the gun he had found on the ground. He opened the back hatch to the armored personnel carrier, his weapon drawn. Inside the passenger compartment, he found a terrified Haruna, at a complete loss for words at the carnage that had unfolded.

"Haruna...I am so sorry," Munraito said.

"How is any of this your fault? At least I now know the truth about what happened to my parents. It's just a shame that so many more people had to die," Haruna continued solemnly, a tone of terror in her voice.

Munraito jumped into the back of the armored vehicle and shut the door. Conveniently, they found two pulse rifles in the personnel compartment, which they took just in case they needed them.

"Are you any good with a rifle, Haruna?" Munraito asked, getting a feel for his weapon.

"No, I can't say I am," Haruna replied, nervously.

"If any of those cops try to get in here, just point and shoot," Munraito directed.

Haruna raised the gun as she became accustomed to it.

"Just hold onto that weapon, and we'll stay right here," Munraito reassured, placing his hand on Haruna's knee.

Haruna looked up at Munraito and took a deep breath. "Ok..." she said, with a deep exhale, conceding to the fact that there was nothing she could do about the situation.

"Haruna, it probably won't be safe for either of us here after all this is over. Whatever motive these police officers had in resorting to this level of violence probably has connections elsewhere on Oumi, and they will probably be looking for us. They're out to finish the job they started 14 years ago by killing your parents, and they probably will not stop until you are dead. That's why you need to leave Oumi, and I want to come with you to protect you. The New Berlin Space Colony should be safe from corruption," Munraito advised Haruna, with a concerned look on his face.

"There are some things that I'd like to investigate on my own. The police chief made a reference to something called the 'Departed God.' If that has anything to do with your parents' murder, I'm going to get to the bottom of it. Haruna, you had me worried sick in there. I just found you again after fourteen years. I will not lose you again," Munraito declared ominously.

"I would support you on that...if we don't get killed here, of course," Haruna said, with a worried look on her face.

"That's not going to happen," Munraito responded, still concerned by the sound of explosions and plasma fire outside. Just then, both Haruna and Munraito felt the APC shudder. Both of them drew their guns, expecting the doors to swing open at any second. Sure enough, they did, but thankfully, two Defenders greeted the barrels of their rifles.

"Hold your fire, you two. We have the situation under control; the remaining police forces have scattered and are being apprehended by

Defender forces across the city. You both can come out now," the hovering Defender said, shouldering his huge sniper rifle behind his long robe. As Munraito and Haruna emerged from the APC, they stared at the devastation around them. For three city blocks there was nothing but mangled buildings, dead bodies, burning wreckage and twisted metal from the urban battle that had erupted around the 13th Street Police Station, as well as several other stations throughout the city. Dazed, bloodied civilians began crawling out of shelters, confused, scared and traumatized by what had just happened. Most of them still had no idea as to what had just occurred. Most believed it was a second terrorist attack and were wondering where the police had all gone. However, when the survivors saw the Defenders rounding up all the surviving police officers, people began to panic.

"Everyone remain calm!" one of the Defenders called out.

"Citizens of Muranahe, your police forces have been deceiving you for the past 14 years! Fourteen years ago, your Chief of Police, Aleistair Watts, became corrupt and dragged the entire city police force into a scheme with him," the Defender proclaimed.

"Plotting in secret, they had Senator Otohime and his wife assassinated for their efforts to prevent police corruption. Upon receiving word that Haruna Otohime, their daughter, had returned to Oumi, they struck again, by destroying their own police headquarters in an effort to create a distraction while they attempted to finish the job they started 14 years before...by killing Haruna. We found out about the plot only minutes before Haruna and her companion were to be killed. A firefight ensued, and now the situation is under control. Medical teams will be arriving shortly to tend to the wounded. Please remain where you are!" the Defender called out, amplifying his voice through his helmet. At that point, the confused people slowly began to come to their senses and realized the magnitude of what the Defenders had just done. Before they could say anything, however, medical teams began arriving on the scene. These medics brought much-needed medical care to the wounded and began the soul-destroying task of collecting the dead, the dying and surveying the damage. This was not just a riot. This was the aftermath of urban warfare. As Munraito and Haruna were led through the fields of rubble, they were approached by several civilians, who asked Munraito for help. As a Lightbringer, he was one of the most respected people on

Oumi. The Defenders, however, deemed that it was unsafe for Munraito and Haruna to remain in Muranahe for any length of time.

"Defender, can you arrange us a transport back to Heiei Castle? We must return and warn the others of the situation," Munraito asked, never wavering from his cool-headed demeanor.

"Yes, Master Lightbringer. We are in the process of doing just that. There's no point in you being here any longer. We'll handle the situation here," the Defender said, clutching his rifle.

Munraito and Haruna stood with the Defenders as ambulances tended to the wounded. GalaxyNet news reporters were on scene covering the unfolding crisis as the Defenders tried to direct medical staff to those most in need of attention. Munraito looked over at Haruna and sighed.

"Sorry I had to ruin our day in town..." Munraito said, with a guilty tone to his voice.

"What makes you think this is any of your fault?" Haruna asked.

"If I hadn't turned those photos into the police station, this would have never happened," Munraito said.

"Munraito, that's ridiculous. These police officers were criminals. They would have tried to kill me either way. If it weren't for that photo in the archives, the Defenders would have never discovered the plot. True, the battle that ensued did cost lives, but you certainly saved my life. For that, I am very grateful to have you around again," Haruna said.

Munraito took a deep breath.

"I guess you're right. Haruna, you are the most important thing in the world to me, more so than life itself. This is just a test of our resolve and our bond. I will do anything to keep you safe and happy, Haruna-chan. You have my word on that," Munraito declared.

Just then, a low hum was heard coming in from the north. Munraito and Haruna looked up and saw a Republic dropship coming in over the Panarin Mountains in the distance.

"That's your ride, you two," The Defender said, pointing at the dropship.

Munraito and Haruna waited patiently for the Republic dropship to land in the ruined city block.

As Munraito watched the dropship coming in, he felt a deep rage boiling inside of him, like a smoldering flame being stoked by the tragedy all around him. He saw crying mothers waiting to hear the fate of their children, walking aimlessly in the town square. In addition, men and women were nursing hideous wounds and plasma burns, their lives shattered by a senseless episode of violence that, in Munraito's eyes, should have never been allowed to happen.

The dropship hummed in for a landing in the city square, with several Defenders already sitting inside the passenger compartment. Munraito and Haruna stepped into the passenger cabin and took their seats, pressing buttons to secure themselves.

"Next stop, Heiei Castle. We're headed back. Just in case they start shooting at us again, keep your heads down," the Defenders said, shouldering their weapons. As the dropship lifted off the ground and into the clear sky, Munraito turned to Haruna.

"Haruna, why did this have to happen?"

"It didn't have to...it just happened." Haruna said as the dropship door shut.

"Why does crime have to happen at all in this day and age? We have the technology to prevent it once and for all, but our politicians would rather kick the can on the issue, because they are too concerned about 'moral implications' and 'constitutionality.' The only 'immoral' thing happening here is that people are dying and suffering at the hands of these horrid, rotten people and our political system, justice system and politicians have failed the people of the Republic. Something else must be done to prevent further tragedies like this, because every crime committed is negligence on the part of the Republic's government. There is no excuse for crime in the Fourteenth Age. We must initiate societal reform on a grand scale, one that would utterly revolutionize our society and pull it out of this Dark Age of crime, corruption and malice," Munraito said.

"Munraito, do you hear yourself right now?" Haruna said, incredulously. "What you speak of is a violation of constitutional rights in the extreme. We cannot make exceptions to democracy, no matter how horrible a tragedy occurs," Haruna reminded, very concerned about Munraito's comments.

"Haruna, you are merely repeating the political doctrines espoused by the Republic government, the same ineffectual dialogue that has permeated the issue of crime ever since the mind-reading technology was developed. We cannot afford to have anyone suffer like this ever again. Something needs to be done. Someone has to take the initiative and put a stop to this barbarism," Munraito said, very strongly. "Democracy has become counterproductive to the needs of the people and public safety. Sometimes, more aggressive action is needed on behalf of the ruling powers that be," Munraito added.

"That sounds like a dictatorship to me. Munraito, you have to understand, as pressing as the issue is, the rule of law must be upheld. The government cannot make rash decisions, for risk of making the situation even worse. As powerful as the Lightbringer Order is, it is not above the rule of law. It cannot pass judgment upon those it sees as evil," Haruna responded.

Munraito said nothing and just stared out the hatch windows at the majestic Panarin Mountains far below. To him, Haruna's words were meaningless. Justice needed to be served, the righteous needed to be protected, and the unrighteous dealt with accordingly. It could be delayed no longer. The Republic had failed its own people, which made the Republic government just as guilty as the criminals they had done nothing about.

The dropship flew high over the mountains, towards Heiei Castle as Amaterasu began to dip towards the horizon once again. The day had been something of a revelation to Munraito and many others across the

Republic watching the evening GalaxyNet news channels...something

needed to be done about the criminals still running riot across the

Republic. Perhaps the Constitution had become its own worst enemy.

Haruna would never admit it, but even she had to believe that something

had to be done. Even the police couldn't be trusted anymore. There was a

certain urgency for action now that the tragedy in Muranahe had

occurred, and this would doubtlessly spark another round of vicious

bickering between the Senators and Congress about implementing the

mind-reading technology to prevent all crime from ever happening in the

first place...Munraito had absolutely no faith in the system, as he knew

that the debate would go nowhere...and he wasn't willing to wait any

longer. The moment the dropship returned to Heiei Castle, he would

begin his plan of action, to do what no others could, to take action when

the government would not.

As Munraito felt the dropship begin to descend, he prepared himself for

what he was about to do. It was something that no Lightbringer had ever

attempted to do in the history of the Order, an action that would put

everything he held dear in danger. His dedication to protecting the people

of the Republic, Haruna and advancing the cause of humanity took

paramount over all else, however. To him, the risks were worth the reward. Munraito looked over at Haruna as the dropship prepared to land at Heiei Castle. This reaction, above all, was for her, so that no one would ever have to suffer through the horrors of human evil ever again. As the dropship landed, Munraito stepped out of the passenger compartment and walked calmly through the courtyard and into the luxuriant halls of Heiei Castle. Haruna followed close behind as they walked into the main hall, where they found the rest of the Lightbringers, the Troika, Sei Ikkiku, Gwenlynn and Takada being briefed on the situation in Muranahe.

"Welcome back, Master Munraito. We are so glad you and Haruna are safe," Elder Master Iori said.

"It's good to be back, Master Iori," Munraito said.

"These miscreants will continue to pursue you to the ends of the Universe if something is not done immediately to stop them," Arditi said to Haruna, his radiant form hovering above the floor.

"The Astari Galactic Command will do all it can to secure a future for Miss Otohime, in the face of this scenario," Anteon added.

"That's very reassuring, but I believe the problem needs to be solved by a solution much closer to home," Haruna said. "I want to know who's trying to kill me. Munraito thinks that the police being corrupt wasn't the half of what happened today, and that this plot runs much, much deeper," Haruna explained, giving a rationale for her point of view.

"If what you say is true, the Defenders must be alerted to a potential Republic-wide plot to induce disorder and unrest. I believe anarchist or communist groups are to blame, in this case. It's time for those beliefs to die a slow, painful death," Gwenlynn said, in her Scandinavian accent.

Haruna didn't know what to say.

"This is all good discussion, but us sitting here is not solving anything. There are terrorists and criminals on the loose, and us sitting at a table discussing a plan of action is not going to solve the problem. Haruna, I sincerely enjoyed spending time with you today, regardless of the outcome of the day's events. However, at this point, I feel it is best if I excuse myself from the table and meditate on this matter in private," Munraito said, standing up from his chair. He walked away from the table and down the Patron's Corridor, towards the huge staircase that led to the Order's living quarters. Walking up the stairs, Munraito had full knowledge and understanding of what he was about to do. However, as a Lightbringer, he believed that it was his sovereign duty to do whatever was necessary to protect Haruna and all citizens of the Republic, regardless of what the Republic citizens believed in. Haruna was the one living thing he truly cared about most of all at this point, and he would do whatever it took to keep her safe.

Munraito reached the top of the staircase and walked into his bedroom, near the Pontiff's Balcony where he had just given the invocation the night before. Sitting down on the cushion in the center of the room, Munraito immediately entered a deep trance, his mind reaching across space and time. Munraito's consciousness permeated every crease in the fabric of space-time, searching for the answers to what had happened in Muranahe that day. As he sat in deep Hyperspace Meditation, his consciousness flowed like a raging river across the Cosmos, penetrating the hearts and minds of thousands of living creatures, and searching for any ounce of responsibility for the day's actions. It did not take Munraito long to find a lead in the case. After his consciousness invaded the minds of the corrupt survivors of the battle earlier that day, he discovered a name and a face to go along with the operations on Oumi: Asaga Kanagashima III. Could he have been the 'Departed God?' Perhaps, however, Asaga's location in space-time was not clear, as he had taken measures against Lightbringer mind penetration...he was clearly a suspect in this case, but Munraito couldn't prove anything at this point. However, one thing was clear. Those in Defender custody were guilty of hideous

crimes against Haruna's family. All twenty-five of them were equally

guilty. There was only one just thing to do at this point. Munraito focused

a huge pulse of quantum energy at the twenty-five corrupt officers sitting

in holding cells. This energy immediately struck them at once,

overwhelming their bodies' neural circuitry and killing them all

instantaneously. Munraito saw them die in their cells, the only just

outcome for what they had done to Haruna and so many others who had

spoken out against them or had tried to reveal the truth of what was

going on for fourteen lengthy years. At long last, justice was finally

served...and Munraito was the only one who could pass judgment upon

these unrighteous fiends. After the brief time spent in meditation,

Munraito returned to the physical world, immensely satisfied at what he

had done. This was to be a complete secret, and not a soul could ever

know what he was doing, for knowledge of the great cleansing that

Munraito had planned would cause utter chaos. This was nobody's

business but his. Munraito was doing this for Haruna, for the Republic and

for the good of all Mankind and every being in the galaxy, human or

otherwise. For Honor, for Pantheon and for Humanity...this was the

Lightbringer way. Munraito stood up from his cushion in the center of the room and walked towards the door, fully aware of the potential consequences of what he had just done. Munraito walked down the hallway towards the grand staircase and walked back down the stairs towards the library, headed for one of the AI terminals. Munraito walked calmly into the library and approached a terminal, entered a few commands, and proceeded to manually enter a message into the terminal to be broadcast from every computer in the Oumi Sector. This message was to be received by the entire Republic, which controlled most of the Milky Way Galaxy and many points beyond. Oumi, a colony seldom mentioned anywhere in the Republic, was about to take center stage amongst the races of the Milky Way and Andromeda Galaxies. The message simply read:

"THE HAMMER HAS FALLEN. THE MAN AGAINST TIME IS HERE."

Munraito calmly sent the message out across the entire GalaxyNet, where it would soon be seen by billions of Republic inhabitants, both human and non-human. Munraito thought about how the various races that constituted the Republic would react to the message. The more militaristic races, such as the Sangresaara and Sigtyr who occasionally had disagreements with the Republic governance would likely applaud the arrival of a man willing to take matters into his own hands, as the

Sangresaara and Sigtyr emphasized self-sufficiency and self-reliance above all else. However, more pragmatic and peaceful races, such as the Elohim, would be very skeptical of this message. The Chancellery and the Republic Department of State were seeking to bring the races of the Republic closer together with Haruna's mission, but the Senators were doubtful of this mission's probability of success. The arrival of a "Man against Time" would surely create divisions within the Republic at a time when such divisions were not desirable. However, Munraito had his own agenda, one that would not cease until his goal was achieved.

Munraito turned away from the computer terminal and walked back out of the library, back towards the main gathering hall, where the rest of the Lightbringers were having their evening meditation sessions. Haruna's guests had joined them as well. Takada was sitting in Munraito's usual seat, but at this point, he knew she was just doing this to goad him. Munraito simply ignored Takada, not giving her the acknowledgment she so desperately craved.

"Well folks, it's been a whirlwind of a day, and I'm glad we're all in one piece after the catastrophe in Muranahe," Munraito said, somberly.

"Whoever is ultimately responsible for the crimes committed today deserves nothing less than death," Gwenlynn said, with her usual aggressive overtone. She held the position of Chief of Human Antiquities, but there were many rumors about her floating around in the Republic government, some of which suggested that she held some decidedly un-democratic belief systems and that she believed human rights were conditional, not universal. Of course, she always denied these rumors. Statements like that did little to dissuade people from believing them, however.

"Indeed, Gwenlynn, justice must be served in this case. I am normally against all forms of capital punishment, but in this case I believe it to be appropriate for the circumstances," Sei Ikkiku added.

"I think we should just fry every single one of them. These criminals absolutely need to be stopped. Isn't that right, Munraito?" Takada said, jokingly.

Munraito turned to Takada and smiled coyly. There was no way she could have known what he was doing, could she?

"My people have just contacted me...they tell me that a great disturbance in the quantum strings is coming..." Anteon said.

"We cannot leave any stone unturned or any potential world of criminality innocent. We must find the perpetrator of this crime," Arditi said.

"As such, the Astari Imperium will not allow for any more horrors to befall our civilizations. We will go to war if necessary," Marduk responded, his head twisting around in a very bizarre manner.

Munraito sat down at the table and fixed his gaze squarely on the Troika. So this is how it began...a rising conflict within the Republic, and some of the most high-profile individuals in existence were in fact assisting him. He was now opposing one of the most dangerous forces in the known Universe, with nothing but his wits and his intelligence. The 'Departed God,' whatever that was, was powerful enough to corrupt the entire Muranahe police force. Such a force could easily destroy him and everything he cared about with a minimum of effort. Munraito needed to leave Oumi and go somewhere where the Departed God wouldn't as easily find him...and fast.

Munraito kept his usual cool head as he sat in silence, thinking about the day's events, under the watchful gaze of the Troika. Haruna was not present at the table, for she had retreated to her guest room, presumably to come to terms with what had just happened in Muranahe. Seeing all that suffering and pain was a very difficult thing to bear. Munraito was concerned about her, worried that whatever had corrupted those police officers would eventually come for her. Munraito had intended to ask Haruna if she wanted to join him at the table that evening, but he respectfully gave Haruna some space; her well-being, above all, was his greatest motivation.

"Takada, where did you say you were from?"

"I live primarily on Arcana II, but I also have homes on Lilliana V, Kraid, Orphea and Lunara. Why do you ask?" Takada responded.

"I was just wondering if you'd be willing to let me into your world for once," Munraito said.

"I like the sound of that...When we leave this planet, join us on the New Berlin Space Colony, I'll show you everything," Takada said.

"Ok then," Munraito responded.

Munraito stood up from his chair and walked back towards the library, where he was known to spend long hours deep in thought. As he did so, however, Sei Ikkiku stood up and slowly walked over to him, her ethereal, shining garments flowing behind her like a river of crystal glass.

"Master Lightbringer...There is something about you that...seems very familiar to me," Sei said, with genuine curiosity in her voice.

"I can't say I've ever met you in person before today," Munraito responded.

"Perhaps the years have clouded my memory, as I am preparing to celebrate my eighty-fourth millennium of life," Sei said.

"Your body has not failed you at all," Munraito said.

"I am a synthetic just as you are. I've just been around for much longer than you have. My race is among the most ancient in the Universe, along with the Astari. However, as young as you are, I do believe you are meant for great things," Sei continued.

Munraito was growing suspicious of Sei's comments. Could she possibly be reading his mind? Could she already know what he had done to those criminals?

"What kinds of things am I meant for, Sei?" Munraito asked, a look of suspicion on his face.

"You've asked me this question before...and my response is the same...if you had to do it again, why wouldn't you?" Sei casually walked past Munraito and out into the hallway.

"She knows..." Munraito thought to himself. He walked briskly out of the dining room and towards the Great Library again, his mind racing a million miles per second. Apparently, Sei could read minds, but the Astari couldn't. However, Sei did not seem to be against what Munraito was doing. She almost seemed like she wanted to help, which was something Munraito could use to his advantage. Munraito thought about this possibility, how the resources of the Elohim Consortium could assist his coming crusade...but that was something for another time. For the moment, Munraito only wanted to get lost in a book after a long and very eventful day. His concern for Haruna was never-ending, but even he needed a break from the stress of daily life. Munraito took his usual walk down the Patron's Corridor towards the Great Library, stepped up to the AI hologram assistant and requested a book to read. Downloading the content of the book into his neural interface, he sat down and began to read, thinking about his actions...and Sei's offer of assistance. Something was coming, something far greater than anything that had ever happened before, and this was only the beginning.

4. Vacate

The next morning, Munraito was awake very early as usual, standing on the Pontiff's Balcony, absorbing the radiant warmth of Amaterasu. He had not forgotten about Sei's subtle hints the night before, and was promptly dressed to see her that morning. Munraito walked out of his bedroom and down the grand staircase, leading down to the Patron's Hallway. To his surprise, he saw his apprentice, Koda, waiting for him.

"Munraito, did you hear? All the suspects from yesterday's massacre were found dead in their cells this morning."

"What? What happened?" Munraito responded, making a very convincing lie.

"The Defenders don't know. Every single one of them was found dead," Koda said.

"Do they think it was suicide?" Munraito asked.

"That's what they ruled it as...must be tough to deal with, going to a prison where half the inmates were put there by you, although there was no clear evidence of suicide. They don't know how they did it," Koda said, quizzically.

"Interesting, the Defenders may be a bit presumptuous in their assessment of the situation," Munraito said to Koda.

"You honestly think someone else killed them?" Koda asked, incredulously.

"We cannot assume anything at this point, but I don't think these men died at their own hand," Munraito said.

Just then, Haruna came around the corner dressed in a red Japanese summer kimono and gave Munraito a warm hug.

"Good morning, Haruna-chan. What do you want to do today?" Munraito asked, very sweetly.

"After what happened yesterday, I think we need a do-over. We never got to see most of Muranahe or spend much time with each other. It's a shame that so many people don't know how to act civilized," Haruna said.

"You are absolutely right. Come with me, we'll go out into the courtyard together this morning," Munraito replied optimistically.

"Ok," Haruna agreed, taking Munraito's hand as they both walked towards the exit to the courtyard.

"I'm glad to see him happy," Elder Master Iori said.

"He always works so hard for what he believes in. I think Haruna coming back is the best thing that could have ever happened to him," the Elder Master responded, with Sei Ikkiku and the Troika watching as Munraito and Haruna stepped out into the sunlight, like two strange shadows in the morning light.

As Munraito and Haruna stepped out into the morning light, they saw Takada sitting on a bench underneath a huge cedar tree. She was wearing a different, more revealing outfit than the one she was wearing yesterday; it looked very exotic, to say the least.

"You like my outfit, Munraito?" Takada teased. "It's my Draconis Marunae Tropica style, I designed it myself. I wear it mostly when I'm in a more playful mood," Takada said, clearly coming on to Munraito.

"Hey, back off, weirdo. Are you serious? He's with me," Haruna called out loudly, not appreciative of Takada's jokes.

"Come on, Munraito-kun. We don't need to be bothered by people like her. That woman does not know boundaries. Not at all," Haruna grumbled.

"I noticed she has a tattoo on the back of her neck...what is that for?" Munraito inquired.

"It's a Kanji character symbolizing love, lust and life, three things that she's very well known for," Haruna said. "I'm surprised you noticed that underneath her brown hair," Haruna added.

Munraito and Haruna continued past Takada and towards a wooden bridge over a koi pond.

"So, I hear that the perpetrators of the attack yesterday died suddenly in Defender custody," Munraito said to Haruna.

"What, how?" Haruna asked, confused.

"The Defenders in charge don't know how. They decided that the perpetrators killed themselves," Munraito said.

"Well, that would make sense. It must be a difficult prospect going to a prison where half the inmates were put there by you," Haruna said.

Just then, Takada came walking over to them, her Hyperborean avatar body towering over the two of them.

"What are you two talking about?" Takada inquired, being her typical nosy, immature self.

"Do you ever leave us alone?" Munraito asked, standing at eye level with Takada's belly.

"I'm just curious as to what you're discussing. I hear that those rotten criminals were found dead this morning, and those poor Defenders don't know what happened to them," Takada said, in her usual mocking, almost sarcastic tone.

"Yes, you heard correctly. However, our conversation does not concern you at this point. Haruna is right. You need to learn boundaries, honestly. You just seem to do whatever you damn well please, and that's not going to work for me," Munraito said, emphatically, showing his growing impatience.

"Fine then, I was just about to offer you my expert opinions and assistance with this case, but with your lousy attitude, I guess I won't," Takada said, turning and walking haughtily away.

Munraito watched her as she walked back across the bridge towards the castle courtyard again.

"You really don't like her, do you?" Haruna said to Munraito, glaring at Takada as she walked calmly away.

"I'm sorry, she made a terrible first impression on me and she has done nothing since then to rectify that," Munraito said, rather sternly.

"You should give her a second chance, Munraito-kun. She may yet surprise you," Haruna said.

Haruna and Munraito continued down the path through the grove of trees, their beautiful red flowers and black leaves rustling in the constant breezes that blew across the planet's surface. As Haruna and Munraito walked through the woods on the castle grounds, they listened to the sounds and scenery of Oumi's deep dry forest, which could be one of the most dangerous places on the planet for a human being. There were many predators in these woods capable of killing someone, and they were not afraid of coming close to human habitation. Suddenly, Munraito heard a faint rustling noise coming from a thicket about 25 feet away from where he was standing.

"Haruna...don't move," Munraito said, realizing what could be behind those bushes.

No sooner had he said that that a massive, black, flightless bird-like creature stepped out from behind the bushes, staring at Munraito and Haruna with its massive yellow eyes. It was covered in shaggy black, hairlike feathers with a handsome white ruff around its neck, along with a murderously sharp, shredding bill that could make quick work of any prey item. Its three massive toes were adorned with sickle-like slashing claws, and the creature's stumpy wings possessed ripping claws as well. Munraito knew immediately what he was looking at. This was an adult male Shinigami Bird, endemic to Oumi and one of the major reasons why the dry forest was such a dangerous place during the summer months. The large males would patrol vast territories, and were fiercely protective of their space.

"Don't move a muscle..." Munraito said. The huge bird stared at Munraito and Haruna intently for a few seconds, and then let out an ear-piercing squawk, its massive yellow eyes practically bugging out of its head as it did so. The huge bird lunged at Munraito, its massive, axe-like beak aimed directly at his head. In an instant, however, there was tremendous flash of white light, a crash like an explosion, and a very dead Shinigami Bird, with a massive, cauterized wound slitting its gullet open.

"What the..." Munraito said, turning around to face a 12-foot tall being in an immensely sophisticated suit of armor, holding a searing hot blade in its hands. The armor this being was wearing was far, far more sophisticated than anything the human race possessed at that time. At that moment, the being came to rest on the ground, and its armor retracted back into its common outfit on its own, much like a second set of organs or skin. To Munraito's shock, the being that had killed the Shinigami Bird was Sei Ikkiku, having heard the bird's angry screams from inside the castle.

"Wow...you certainly have a convenient way of showing up," Munraito said, still in shock about what he had just seen.

"The Elohim race will not tolerate harm to you by any living creature. Trust me, we have an entire star cluster of warriors prepared to fight at a moment's notice. Our technology is among the most advanced in the Universe, and our sole goal is to achieve a higher spiritual presence. There are many that wish to imitate us; however, none have succeeded. Come inside, Munraito. I would like to speak with you in private."

Munraito and Haruna followed Sei back through the woodland path towards the castle again, this time Sei leading the way, just in case of further attacks by hostile wildlife. Needless to say, Munraito and Haruna felt more secure with Sei leading their way. Haruna, Munraito and Sei walked back through the courtyard, where they found Takada sitting in the courtyard, as if she was waiting for them.

"What happened?" Takada said, with concern in her voice.

"Nothing serious, Munraito and Haruna just encountered a very hostile form of life in the woods behind the castle."

"What was it?" Takada asked, in the most inquisitive voice Munraito had heard from her in a while.

"A Shinigami Bird, the males can be very territorial," Munraito said, annoyed at Takada's incessant nosiness.

"Interesting...you know, not much separates us from animals." Takada said, rather coyly.

"What do you mean?" Haruna asked.

Munraito flinched, not wanting to engage Takada's now-grating personality.

"Well, did you read the third chapter of my book?" Takada asked.

"A while ago, though I did not fully understand what you meant in those stories," Haruna said.

"Well, the example I gave from my own life was the fantasy I have about the Prophet Mohammed and his wives. In the dreams I have, I travel back in time using Republic warp technology and entering the Prophet's home in the dead of night. As I enter, I sneak into the chambers of his wives, dressed in my finest Draconis Marunae Tropica styles, holding a knife in my hand. I lean down to each woman as she sleeps and put the blade to her throat, slitting them cleanly and licking the blood from the knife edge. Once they lay dead, I creep into the Prophet's chamber and awaken him with a whisper in his ear. Within a few seconds, he is under my spell, and all night long I violate him in every possible way, cleansing the filth of Islam from his body and changing the history of the world for the better. The point I try to make here is that humans have the same animal instincts as any other species."

"In contrast, over time, our society and culture has dulled these instincts to the point where we think of ourselves as superior to all other forms of life. My stories and actions prove that we are not. Any species that has the arrogance to call itself anything more than an animal is rather ridiculous to me. Human beings eventually reached a point where religion died a peaceful death, and now, we can all have a joyous laugh about how human beings were ever ignorant enough to believe such high-and-mighty nonsense," Takada explained.

Munraito rolled his eyes at Takada's explanation, still finding Takada's memoirs to be insensitive, if only to those that came before her.

"Haruna, that woman is a complete trainwreck...the only reason she's famous is because she wrote a book about her tawdry version of crazy and now everyone is obsessed with her," Munraito whispered, leaving Takada behind.

"Please, Munraito-kun, would it kill you to be a little nicer to her? Your opinion of her life does not matter. You have no right to police people's lives, Munraito. She is a celebrity for the book she wrote about her deviant behavior, although she would rather not be. She also had a difficult upbringing. She grew up in the Holy City, one of the less affluent parts of Nox Aeterna, the main mega-city on Arcana II," Haruna said.

"Excuse me, Haruna. I am a Grand Master of the Lightbringer Order. I have spent my entire life trying to improve the lives of Republic citizens through our work here on Oumi and our representation of the Oumi Sector in the Senate, so if I can't say that that woman needs help, who can?" Munraito stated.

Haruna rolled her eyes.

"Munraito, sometimes your arrogance is palpable. Takada's really not such a bad person once you get to know her. Please, just give her a chance," Haruna asked.

Munraito said nothing.

Haruna, Munraito, Takada and Sei walked back into Heiei Castle and through the Patron's Hallway, where Sei took Munraito to the Grand Staircase.

"I'm sorry you two, I must meet with Munraito in private," Sei said.

"Alright then, talk to you later, Munraito-kun," Haruna said, kissing him goodbye and walking back towards the library with Takada right behind her.

"Very well then, now that we are alone, I trust we'll be free of the opinions of the unenlightened," Sei said to Munraito. Munraito and Sei climbed the stairs and walked toward one of the guest rooms where Sei was staying.

"What you witnessed in the woods today was just a minor demonstration of what my race is capable of. The Elohim are one of the oldest races in the known Universe, having built a vast Empire in the Seven Sisters Cluster...and we know a great many things that could assist you in your endeavors as a Lightbringer."

"Like what?" Munraito asked, with astonishment.

"Don't you think it's a bit odd that those criminals died in their cells today and a message has been found, referencing the arrival of a 'Man against Time?'" Munraito froze...perhaps Sei did know what really happened.

"I think the police are being a bit presumptuous in their ruling of the deaths as suicide. They don't know what we know. I called you in here to express my concerns that we are dealing with a murderer, one who murders in the name of justice...just as the ancient prophecies of my race have foretold." Sei said to Munraito.

Munraito thought for a second, and then smiled...he knew that she understood his true intentions.

"Sei, that's ridiculous. How could anyone have murdered those criminals in their jail cells? They were under 24-hour surveillance; I don't understand how anyone could have killed them," Munraito said, incredulously.

"There are many ways to kill someone, Munraito. Trust me as an elder. I have seen more pain and suffering in my own life than you could ever know...and I have seen much stranger deaths in my time than you have. This mention of a 'Man against Time' is all the proof that I need," Sei said, a decisive tone in her voice.

"What, exactly, does that imply?" Munraito asked.

"I do not think you are ready to know the true implications of what could be about to transpire. That is why I recommend you leave Oumi with us, aboard the New Berlin Space Colony. You will learn much more there than you could here...with us, you will learn to use your true power...the power to save Haruna and everything you hold dear."

"Sei, this is the only home I have ever known. What makes you think I'll even be able to acclimate to such a different environment?"

"Your species is not meant to spend eternity on a planet's surface," Sei responded. "You know as well as I do that space travel is essential to our survival. I feel it is no longer safe for you to remain here with the other Lightbringers," Sei said, concerned. "You will be much safer with us aboard the colony," Sei continued with her vague attempt at an explanation.

"I don't understand. What could be so dangerous as to make it imperative that I leave?" Munraito queried.

"Just follow my lead, Munraito. You'll see the value in what I say soon," Sei said, standing up from her chair.

Munraito stood up as well and walked out of the room, with a very stoic look on his face. It was quite clear that Sei knew that he was in fact the Man against Time. Her grave concern over the events in Muranahe was disturbing, however. Sei was going to be a formidable ally, and so long as she did not speak of Munraito's true intentions, everything would be fine. Perhaps traveling aboard the space colony would give Munraito an advantage over his enemies...and allow him to be with Haruna. Munraito slowly walked back towards his room, making sure Sei was not following him. He entered his bedroom and sat down on his meditation cushion in the center of the room and took a deep breath. In an instant, Munraito's consciousness streamed out of every pore in his body, permeating every thread of space-time, traveling at the speed of thought to the farthest reaches of the Universe. In his mind's eye he saw them, hundreds of convicted criminals sitting in prisons across the Republic...going about their daily activities as they served their sentences, going through the re-programming process that would remove the urge to commit further crimes from their brains...however, Munraito knew that this policy accomplished nothing. The only true deterrent for crime was the fear of God Himself. Munraito focused his energies onto cell after cell of criminals in the prisons, detonating a quantum blast within their consciousness, killing them instantaneously. Man after man, woman after woman fell to Munraito's judgment, all in the name of protecting the ones he loved. Haruna had suffered enough at the hands of criminals. It was time to set the record straight.

Munraito carved a path through the cells of the unsuspecting criminals with complete silence and complete anonymity. Hyperspace Meditation was completely untraceable and was almost impossible to defend against.

These wrongdoers had no idea what hit them. Just then, however, Munraito heard a knock at his door. Munraito slowly exited his Hyperspace trance, stood up and opened the door to find Haruna standing in front of him.

"Oh, hello there Haruna-chan," Munraito said.

"Hi Munraito...I just wanted to tell you something. Sei was talking about you coming onto the space colony with me...she seems really concerned about what happened yesterday. I just wanted to tell you that you are welcome to travel with me. I'd be happy to have you on board," Haruna said, cheerfully.

"Thank you. Sei has been acting a bit jittery since yesterday. I guess the attacks rattled all of us," Munraito continued.

"Munraito, Sei is very, very old. Once you reach her age, you start worrying about everything. She's more than 90,000 years old. Don't be put off by it. She's just concerned about you and your well-being. Besides, I heard that Belisaria is very beautiful," Haruna said of the Elohim home world.

"What's it like there?" Munraito asked, inquisitively.

"I've never been there, but Belisaria is supposedly one of the most astounding worlds in the Universe. It is a gigantic ringworld, covered in an entire city and held around its star by centrifugal force. The entire Seven Sisters Cluster in our galaxy is inhabited by the Elohim, with enormous ring-worlds constructed around many of the brilliant white stars within the Cluster itself. These worlds are truly enormous, held in place by a centrifugal force. They are home to untold trillions of Elohim, as well as truly gigantic 'shield worlds,' massive artificial planets that serve a purpose to protect the entire star cluster from harm. They are the epitome of a Type-III civilization, a civilization that has explored its entire galaxy and consumes more than 1036 watts of energy per standard year. Having colonized the Local Group with trillions of self-replicating nanomachines, their Empire has expanded outward from the Cluster at the speed of light, colonizing every planet and moon in the galaxy, constructing factories on each world they encounter. There the machines lie dormant, patiently waiting for any intelligent life to find them. This is how the human race first made contact with them, by finding their factories on the Moon and on Mars. They are among the most ancient of races, and have dedicated their existence to achieving a higher level of spiritual presence. They seek to transcend the very Universe itself," Haruna explained.

"Wow..." Munraito said, realizing just how powerful Sei truly was.

"Sei is one of the most ancient of her race; for ninety millennia, she has presided over the Elohim Consortium and has witnessed the rise and fall of hundreds of civilizations across the galaxy. She has lived many, many lifetimes before this, creating new bodies for herself as her synthetic forms have slowly degraded over time. That being said, she is much, much older than 90,000 years old. The rise of the Republic and the consequential ascension of humanity were perhaps the greatest achievements of our species. From our own interstellar travels, we have seen the ruins of many societies that did not make it," Haruna said.

"We have encountered many worlds whose atmospheres are heavily irradiated, and many others whose climate has become too hot to support life. These barren, dead planets are all that remains of societies that failed to make that quantum leap from a regional civilization to a planetary one. Take, for example, the tragedy of Lushar and Cressil, mentioned in the Elohim Archives on Erzat, one of the Elohim Ringworlds. Lushar and Cressil were two brothers of the feline Ashtar race living on the planet of Avyon. Rivals who pushed each other like only brothers could, Lushar and Cressil began a competition with each other to see who could become the more powerful of the two, as they were from a very privileged family. The competition was friendly at first, but as the two brothers became more powerful, they became the bitterest of rivals and eventually enemies, until eventually they had divided the entire planet in half between themselves. Inevitably, a colossal war broke out in which Lushar and Cressil sought to annihilate each other. Eventually, the war became so intense that Queen Sei of the Elohim was forced to intervene, but it was too late. The brothers had already unveiled their superweapons and had used them, which destroyed the entire species and rendered Avyon completely uninhabitable. Now, nothing more than bacteria survives on the ravaged surface of that broken world, a stark reminder of the perils that all civilizations face on the road to immortality," Haruna explained.

"Humanity faced many perils on its route to the stars as well. The greatest challenge humanity ever faced was during the 21st century, with rising global temperatures, overpopulation and natural resources being strained to their limit on Earth. Just when it appeared that all life on Earth was doomed, a group of technology companies unveiled synthetic human bodies. These bodies allowed humanity to solve these problems and eventually reach the stars. Not all civilizations make that transition: as a matter of fact, archaeological records suggest that most of them don't and are thus wiped out long before they reach Type-I status. Only an extremely small percentage of civilizations survive long enough to reach a Type-II or Type-III level, which explains why the mathematics of the Universe suggest that there should be thousands of Type-III societies, but in reality there are only a few. The Elohim Ascendancy, the Naruhol Ihr race and the Astari Empire are the only three that we know of, besides humanity," Munraito responded.

"Well, in that case, that may be for the best, because Type-III societies are so powerful that they can control the fate of their respective galaxies, and if there were hundreds of such societies in a single galaxy, there would be quite a power struggle between civilizations," Haruna responded.

"Where did Sei go, anyway?" Munraito asked.

"Oh, she went back outside to talk to Takada for a bit. I think she and Takada have become very good friends in their travels together," Haruna responded

"What about Gwenlynn? She's not very talkative," Munraito asked.

"No, she's really not. She has always craved solitude and has a severe case of nyctophilia. She's drawn to dark, strange, otherworldly places and would really like nothing more than to spend her eternity drifting through space alone. She is an absolutely brilliant archaeologist and scientist, however, and gets along better with most nonhuman races than humans. Just a few weeks ago we were on Chalheim, a Sangresaara stronghold world to meet with Warmaster Lumen Ash. He is the leader of the Sangresaara Imperium, a society that completely controls the Orion Arm of the Milky Way Galaxy. Ash is not one you would want to take lightly. He stands more than 12 feet tall, inhabiting a synthetic, reptilian body wearing an elaborate, ornate suit of shielded armor that vaguely resembles that of a medieval shogun from Japan. The Defenders have fought multiple skirmishes with the Sangresaara and their seven subservient races which form their Empire, including one mission that took them into the heart of Shinaeal, the Sangresaara capital world. Gwenlynn, even face to face with a very suspicious Warmaster, did not flinch. She spoke clearly, aggressively and definitively, and eventually convinced the Sangresaara to sign the Treaty of Chalheim, which stated that the Sangresaara would cease all raids into Republic space, in exchange for granting the Sangresaara control of three contested worlds, all three of them uninhabited. This conflict resolution was all thanks to Gwenlynn's diplomacy. She is a tremendous help to us on our mission. She gets along better with aliens than she does with people," Haruna explained.

"Haruna, there is something I've been meaning to tell you. All this talk about diplomacy, a higher calling and the future of the Republic got me to thinking, ever since the tragedy in Muranahe yesterday, I have discovered the Republic's critical flaw. The Naruhol Ihr are correct. Humanity has become immortal, but it lacks something it has always possessed: those capable of doing great things, those individuals that become more than they ever thought possible. They discover extraordinary things. They compete and win every battle they fight, in ways that no one thought possible. There are those that are satisfied with everyday life and routine, and those with the audacity to break it and take humanity forward. So ask yourself, Haruna. Will you merely step forward? Or will you take a quantum leap?" Munraito queried Haruna as he walked calmly past her to find Sei again.

Haruna looked at Munraito curiously as he walked by her and back down the Grand Staircase. She didn't know what to think about Munraito's statement, other than the fact that it seemed rather out of place. She had to admire Munraito's will and determination, however. Munraito walked back down the Grand Staircase towards the library, where he saw Sei and Gwenlynn poring over computer data in the library's archives.

"I don't know, Queen Ikkiku, the idea of a Man against Time enforcing moral justice seems like exactly what the Republic and humanity needs. I believe the Naruhol Ihr are correct in their assessment of the human race, that humanity now lacks what allowed it to reach its pinnacle in the first place: the force of human will. The Naruhol Ihr's war against the Republic was a test of our will, and were it not for the Defenders, none of us would be here today. I think this Man against Time has taken it upon himself to restore humanity's greatness," Gwenlynn said to Sei, as they looked over the various GalaxyNet chatter about the so-called 'Man against Time' and his alleged purges of criminals.

It was not even clear that the deaths of the criminals on Oumi and now in various prisons across the Republic were attributable to the Man against Time, or even if the Man against Time was a real person. A significant portion of the population had drawn a connection between the deaths of the criminals and the Man against Time rumors, however.

"Regardless of the Man against Time's intent, we must be sure that this is the real one this time. My civilization has seen many individuals claim to be the Man against Time, only to be revealed as impostors later on. This is a glorious day for the Universe indeed," Sei told Gwenlynn, feeding into her ambitious personality.

"For one so old, you possess an enormous amount of youthful idealism. The world needs more people who are willing to do what others won't," Gwenlynn said, decisively.

Sei closed her eyes and sighed. Her 90,000 years of wisdom had seen nearly every possible political scenario unfold. She had seen plenty of so-called 'revolutionaries' lead innumerable societies astray, and far more often than not, the outcomes of such revolutions were less than ideal. Gwenlynn was far too young to realize the potential consequences of what was to come, which was the real danger in this case. If the Man against Time could gain enough support from the young masses of Republic citizens, it would be very difficult for anyone to stop him if the public opinion swung were to swing largely in his favor. The issue of crime and the fact that many people believed that not enough was being done to stop it would make the Man Against Time popular among many citizens of the Republic, and this issue weighed on Sei greatly. Gwenlynn, however, did not seem too concerned. She thought the ideals espoused by the Man against Time were just what the galaxy needed. Sei was not so sure. Long had the legends of her people spoke of a great warrior rising to save the Cosmos from destruction. However, now that the warrior appeared to be manifesting himself, Sei didn't know what to think.

Munraito approached Sei as she was looking over some data in the Archives.

"Sei, I was just wondering when we would be leaving, and where our next destination would be," Munraito pondered.

"Our next destination is Shinaeal, the Sangresaara capital world, to tie up some loose ends with Warmaster Lumen Ash. He has requested our presence for an unspecified reason, and rest assured, we do not want to keep him waiting for long," Sei said.

"Wow...I've only heard stories about the Sangresaara...they are a very proud race with a valiant history," Munraito replied.

"All the stories you heard are true. The Sangresaara are every bit as imposing and powerful as the stories suggest. They and their 7 subservient races form a vast Empire that controls the entire Orion Arm of the Milky Way Galaxy, but it maintain a bilateral relationship with the

Republic; however, their military is much, much larger than the Republic's and they are known to be hostile to Republic vessels entering their territory. This has been a point of contention between the Republic and the Sangresaara for years, and just a few weeks ago, we struck a deal with Warmaster Lumen Ash to cease all raids into Republic territory. The fact that Ash has summoned us to his capital world on such short notice is very unusual. I hope nothing has happened," Sei said, worried.

"All right then, I will prepare myself for that in the meantime," Munraito said.

Munraito sat down in the library next to Gwenlynn and asked her what she was reading.

"I'm studying the works of Julius Evola and various other futurist philosphers. These works, while generally considered to be from a bygone age, are relevant again after the war with the Naruhol Ihr. Their philosophy is much like that of Evola's and various other human right-wing thinkers. The Defenders are our last link to a glorious past, Munraito. I think this Man against Time is doing the Republic a great favor," Gwenlynn said, reading the book 'Metaphysics of War' through her synthetic neural interface.

"Munraito, I believe the Defenders are the continuation of Evola's visions. Operating in fireteams of 4 and possessing physically-augmented, synthetic super-bodies, their armor, weapons and combat abilities are truly unmatched. The only reason the Republic won the war with the Naruhol Ihr was due to the abilities, armor and weapons of the Defender teams, not the Republic Marines, not the self-replicating AI, not the Navy and not the scientists who helped reverse-engineer the Naruhol Ihr's technology. Defenders know that they could die any day, and know very well that they probably will someday. However, they do their jobs knowing that this is what they were born to do, and that is what they will always do. They do not regret not having a childhood. They do not regret being trained from a very early age. They feel that they were born to fight and defend humanity from any and all threats. You saw them in action in Muranahe, and if the Man against Time could garner their support, he would be unstoppable," Gwenlynn said.

Munraito smiled...he now knew what he needed to do. The Defenders were part of the Republic military, and to garner their support, Munraito would need to reach a position where he was trusted by the Defenders to protect the Republic. As a Lightbringer, he was already in a very strong position to do so.

"A very interesting observation, Gwenlynn, you seem to understand how this man thinks," Munraito remarked.

"Munraito...the career I have with the Department of Human Antiquities is only my public face. I have a second career, a second life that makes me a good bit of money. I am a traveling philosopher of sorts, one that uses music as a medium of speaking to the masses. I create under the persona of Moonrise, a woman who speaks to the masses of unenlightened commonfolk through atmospheric, symphonic black metal," Gwenlynn elaborated.

Munraito looked at Gwenlynn curiously.

"Interesting, so in a way, you see your music as espousing your own personal values; like a teacher to a pupil," Munraito replied.

"What do you think of this 'Man against Time?'" Munraito asked.

"He is...a very complicated man, I would have to say. He's fighting for justice, but at the same time he is conflicted as to where he stands in society. He would be a very interesting character study, to be sure," Gwenlynn replied.

"Indeed he would, Gwenlynn..." Munraito responded. At that moment, he devised a plan of action. He would assist the Defenders in their investigation of the tragedy in Muranahe and advise them once they discovered the Man against Time...all the while working closer to his own goal of creating a safe world for people like Haruna.

"Now, if you'll excuse me, I must be going. I have other matters to attend to," Munraito said, standing up and walking out of the library, back down the Patron's Corridor. He was headed for the garage once again, this time to head back into Muranahe to assist the Defenders with their investigation into the police uprising there the day before. As Munraito walked through Heiei Castle, he passed Takada and some of the other Lightbringers, as well as Viceroy Annunaki of the Naruhol Ihr.

"Where are you headed, Master Munraito?" Viceroy Annunaki asked.

"To Muranahe, I have business there that I must attend to. I believe the Defenders could use my help in their investigation of the police riots that happened there yesterday," Munraito replied.

"That sounds like a decent thing to do. They could use a Lightbringer's assistance," Viceroy Annunaki said, turning and slowly hovering away. Munraito left the Viceroy and Takada behind and walked through the sliding doors into the courtyard, where he immediately noticed that the humidity had risen, and dark clouds were building over the Ookazi Fields.

"It looks like a storm is coming in..." Munraito thought to himself as he walked towards the garage. Suddenly, Munraito heard someone calling out for him as he was getting into a car to leave.

"Wait!"

Munraito looked behind him to see Haruna running out after him.

"Viceroy Annunaki said you were going into Muranahe to help the Defenders...Elder Master Iori wanted to see you about something first," Haruna said breathlessly, words tumbling out of her mouth like the rapids in the Geldern River.

Munraito stepped out of the car and approached Haruna.

"All right then, take me to him," Munraito directed.

Haruna led Munraito back into the castle and back down the Patron's Hallway, past the library and past the Grand Staircase, towards the Inner Sanctum, where the Lightbringers practiced their Hyperspace Meditation in group worship sessions. As Munraito and Haruna entered the utter silence of the Sanctum, Munraito saw Elder Master Iori sitting alone in the center of the room, with two burning candles on either side of him.

"Welcome, Master Munraito. Come sit in front of me," Elder Master Iori said, instructing Munraito to take a seat on the floor cushion. Munraito sat down opposite Elder Master Iori as the old man reached for something in his robes.

"Master Munraito, I am one of the last purely biological humans on Oumi, and one of the few left in the Republic. As such, my life span is finite. For more than 150 years I have lived on this world, and not once have I seen someone exemplify the Lightbringer philosophy as you do. Now as you undertake your mission in Muranahe, Munraito, I would like to bestow a great honor upon you. This is something that I wanted you to have when the time was right," Elder Master Iori said, presenting Munraito with a small, golden-orange talisman on a lanyard.

"Master Iori...this is the Talisman of Uehara, the treasure of the Lightbringer Order...are you sure you want me to have this?" Munraito asked, incredulously.

"Absolutely, with that talisman and your mastery of Hyperspace Meditation, you will do the wonders of the gods themselves. This I am fully confident of," Master Iori said, sure of Munraito's abilities. Munraito proudly placed the Talisman around his neck, and watched as it began to glow radiantly as it reacted to Munraito's power and prestige.

"The Talisman has accepted you well, Master Munraito. Take it with you into Muranahe. I believe with it you will be of great assistance to the Defenders in their efforts to discover the truth behind the police corruption," Master Iori said.

"Indeed I will be, Master Iori. With this Talisman, my powers exceed even that of the Defenders. I will carry this mantle with great honor and distinction," Munraito said, standing up from his seat and walking towards the door with Haruna in tow. Munraito walked out of the Inner Sanctum with a newfound sense of power and pride. The other Lightbringers saw the Talisman around Munraito's neck and bowed in respect as he walked past. Koda, his apprentice, walked up to him and congratulated him on his immense accomplishment.

"Koda, prepare for departure. You are coming into Muranahe with me to investigate this matter further. The Defenders will need our help," Munraito instructed.

"Yes sir!" Koda said, with an official tone in his voice.

Koda and Munraito walked back down the Patron's Hallway and towards the garage again, with Haruna looking on, worried. She had no knowledge of what Munraito and Koda would find in Muranahe, but the presence of the Defenders made Haruna feel a little more secure. If the Defenders could defeat the Naruhol Ihr, then they could certainly handle an army of corrupt police officers.

As Munraito and Koda walked out into the courtyard, the skies darkened considerably, and there was a heavy smell of ozone in the air.

"Smells like a typical summer storm," Koda said.

"I agree. It should give the thirsty plants in the woodlands some much-needed rainfall, this area of Oumi is far below average for rain this year. A solar flare could spark an enormous firestorm," Munraito said, getting into a car in the garage.

As Munraito and Koda strapped themselves into the car, Munraito programmed Muranahe City Center into the car's computer systems. They were headed directly for ground zero, the site of the police uprising just the day before. The Defenders and the Republic Marine Corps had taken temporary control of the city until the root of the corruption in the city's police force could be found, so there would be plenty of military personnel around once Koda and Munraito arrived. Perhaps they had made some progress in the investigation.

As the car pulled out of the garage and began its journey down the Inari Highway, Koda turned to Munraito and asked him the same question that was on everyone else's mind.

"Munraito-san, what do you think of this 'Man against Time?' I mean, one could argue that what he's doing is good for society in the long run, but still, the Elohim and the Astari seem to be very concerned about these events. The Naruhol Ihr don't seem to be too worried, however. I think the Naruhol Ihr like the idea of vigilante justice, as their society values heroism and warrior pride more than anything else. The whole reason they attacked us in the first place was as a test of our resolve, and thanks to the Defenders, we won," Koda said, in an attempt to answer his own question.

"I believe that the Man against Time has good intentions. He strikes me as someone who has a very strong sense of justice and a very strong moral compass. He is someone who believes that society does not always have people's best interest, and that sometimes, the people need a hero to believe in. He and the Naruhol Ihr would get along very well. I would not be surprised if the Man against Time is of the Naruhol Ihr race," Munraito said.

"You really think so? The Naruhol Ihr terminated hostilities with humanity more than 80 years ago. Why would they start this kind of violence now?" Koda asked.

"The Naruhol Ihr probably do not see these actions as hostility, instead they see them as doing the human race a favor," Munraito said.

"Well, if that is the case, then the results of this foray remain to be seen," Koda said.

As the car zoomed down the highway into the Panarin Mountains, Koda looked around at the breathtaking vistas all around him.

"It's amazing, this landscape. To think that this entire mountain range was formed with one act of geological violence...it proves that what destroys can also create monuments that last forever," Koda said, looking at the high mountain peaks.

"What you say is true, Koda. Everything exists in a cyclical balance. What destroys also creates, and what creates also destroys. It is one of the four Pantheon Pillars, the Philosophy of Self-Containment. Represented by the serpent consuming its own tail, this philosophy states that all things in the Universe are self-contained; they create, destroy, live and die in equal measure. Every being leaves a footprint on the Universe, and all of these footprints serve to drive the ultimate engine of universal creation and destruction forward. This energy that permeates every corner of the infinite Universes is the power that all living beings possess, but only a few are able to harness. The Elohim, Astari and Naruhol Ihr have long since mastered the use of this energy, the energy of the Universe itself. Our species is just beginning to learn how to use it, however, and as Lightbringers we have long since been able to harness it through our Hyperspace Meditation. The rest of humanity is just beginning to elevate itself to our level of consciousness," Munraito pontificated.

"Well, I have been practicing myself. I think I'm close to understanding how to break the space-time barrier open," Koda said.

"Good. Keep up your hard work. Only through repetition will you be able to master these skills," Munraito encouraged.

As the car prepared to enter the Geldern Tunnel, the storm that Munraito had sensed arrived. The heavens opened up and a torrential downpour began, forcing Munraito to activate the car's inclement weather features to ensure that they arrived at their destination safely.

"Wow, it's really coming down out there..." Koda said, listening as rain drilled the car's windshield.

"It's just a summer storm, Koda. There's nothing unusual about it." Munraito said as the rain poured down.

"We've been in the worst drought in years...we haven't had this much rain in months...and it's the dry season. This weather is bizarre for this time of year," Koda said.

"Come to think of it, the humidity did rise noticeably in just the past half-hour...This could be Sei Ikkiku."

"What, you think that old crone can control the weather?!" Koda yelled, incredulously.

"You would do well to respect her, Koda. She is the leader of a Type-III civilization, one of the most ancient societies in the known Universe. Her civilization has technologies and weapons that we cannot even conceive of; have you ever seen an Elohim starship? They are enormous, masterful works of art and engineering. Sei's mind is so powerful that she can alter the very fabric of the Universe with her own thoughts. Changing the weather for someone like her is as easy as changing an old-fashioned light bulb," Munraito explained.

"I don't understand, though. Why would she create this storm?" Koda asked.

"Who knows? Perhaps she senses something we don't. Perhaps this storm is a projection of her own concerns for us," Munraito said.

"Can she perform Hyperspace Meditation, too?" Koda asked.

"Yes, and far, far more efficiently than you or I can. With her mental abilities, she can alter the fate of the Universe itself. There are some in the Republic who believe that encounters with the Elohim civilization are responsible for most of the human religions that originated in antiquity. The Republic has tried to make sense of Elohim technology for years, and we are only now just beginning to understand the true nature of their technological wonders. Most of the other advanced civilizations try to emulate the Elohim in some way, though not one of them has been able to do a very good job of it," Munraito explained.

"Well, the Republic Navy has had some success at reverse-engineering Elohim technology. The Republic warships' shields and warp drives are much more efficient now after the adaptation of the Elohim technologies to our ships. However, the majority of our upgrades came from the Naruhol Ihr during our war with them. Without the Defenders and our scientists cracking their technology, we would not have won the war," Koda replied as the rain came down even harder.

The car received a brief respite from the driving rain as it entered Geldern Tunnel, giving the windshield wipers a break from the driving storm. As the car accelerated to its top speed, it zoomed past the exits for Asagi City, built deep in the heart of Geldern Mountain.

"I wonder what it's like, living inside a mountain," Koda thought out loud.

"It must feel very secure with a constant temperature. Living in the heart of a mountain definitely has its benefits," Munraito said.

As the car zoomed out the other side of the tunnel, it entered the roaring storm once again, and at that point, Munraito began to realize just how enormous this storm was. From horizon to horizon, the storm stretched with its dark, dense clouds, and lightning flashed across the sky in all directions. Wind buffeted the car as it cut through the storm, the lights of Muranahe shining in the distance. By this point, Munraito and Koda were keenly aware that something was amiss; in the middle of the dry season, a storm like this was completely unheard of. The idea that this storm was being caused by someone using Hyperspace Meditation was becoming more and more likely by the second. The closer Munraito and Koda came to Muranahe, the stronger the storm seemed to become.

As the car neared the outer suburbs of Muranahe proper, harsh gusts of wind began slamming the car, as if to impede Munraito and Koda's progress. At that point, Munraito knew that if this storm had been caused by Hyperspace Meditation, Sei Ikkiku was not likely to have been the culprit. This led Munraito to the ugly possibility that the corrupt police officers were just the tip of the iceberg as to what was really going on in Muranahe...however, he had the Talisman of Uehara now. With the help of the Defender fireteams, whatever was causing this storm wouldn't last long.

As the car reached its destination, Munraito came upon four Olympian-class Defenders standing in the road. The Defenders were divided into three categories depending on their augmentations, abilities and armor classes: the Olympians, the Sorcerers and the Stalkers. Within these three categories, there were numerous subcategories and specialty classes that allowed the Defenders to take on almost every mission imaginable.

The four Olympian Defenders stood around the car like Greek war gods in their armor, holding their weapons at the ready and prepared to use their superhuman abilities at a moment's notice. Each soldier's armor was unique, customized to fit his or her unique personality and mission profile.

"Master Lightbringer, I am Airsaidh Starhunter of Defender Fireteam Isis. We were made aware of your arrival by the Elohim Queen. You'd best get out of that car and come with us, as we're dealing with a bit of a situation here," Defender Starhunter instructed as Munraito and Koda's car pulled under a shelter from the torrential rainfall. Munraito and Koda stepped out of the car and joined Fireteam Isis, who were clad in their individualized armor. Their entire bodies were shielded and armored from the raging storm outside.

"So, Defender Starhunter, what's the situation here in Muranahe right now?" Munraito asked.

"We and several other Defender Fireteams have remained in Muranahe for the past 36 hours, and in that time we've found quite a bit more about the police corruption. Searching through the police archives, Fireteam Odin discovered evidence of a much larger conspiracy originating elsewhere, but the exact location had been intentionally deleted from the Archives, so that no one could find it. However, someone is not happy that we've uncovered this information and is presently creating an enormous atmospheric disturbance above Muranahe as a result. However, the Archives did state the location of several data files in Muranahe that could lead to more information. Our job is to find them and recover them," Defender Starhunter said.

"I'll be happy to assist you in any way I can," Munraito said.

Defender Starhunter tossed Munraito and Koda a pair of exotic-looking pulse rifles.

"You might want to take those with you then. Let's move out. Just try to keep up with us," Defender Starhunter said.

"Wow...this is Elohim technology!" Koda said, marveling at the gun in his hands.

"Easy there, Koda. That's extremely powerful. Just try to keep up with Fireteam Isis," Munraito instructed.

Munraito and Koda followed Fireteam Isis through the blinding rain, struggling to keep up with the squad's extremely fast pace, thanks to the augmentations to their synthetic, superhuman bodies. Defender Starhunter led the way, his unique helmet distinguishing him from the rest of his squad mates; all four of them were armed with different weapons, each one suited to their preferred style of combat. Each member of the fireteam specialized in a different tactic; one was the heavy weapons specialist, the other a long-range marksman, one a tech specialist and the other an assault specialist. Together, Fireteam Isis was nearly invincible, and they feared absolutely nothing.

Munraito and Koda followed Fireteam Isis up to what looked like an abandoned building. Standing by the door, Defender Starhunter activated a small computer function built into his armor.

"Activating the ORACLE, let's see if anyone's been through here."

Immediately, the computer scanned the entire building, both the interior and the exterior, revealing the building's specifications and layout on the squad's Heads Up Displays.

"Bingo. Prepare to breach entry," Defender Starhunter ordered.

"Watanabe, Sale, you go in first. Hutch and I will take the rear. Master Lightbringers, you come in once the all-clear is given," Defender Starhunter instructed.

"On my mark...3...2...1...BREACH!"

Defender Starhunter yelled as Defenders Watanabe and Sale blew the door clean off its hinges, bursting into the room and fanning out, making sure that the room was clear of potential hostiles.

"All clear, come on in, boys," Sale yelled.

Starhunter and Hutch cautiously entered the building, followed by Munraito and Koda, soaked from the rain.

"That's strange...this building seems empty," Koda said.

"Not quite," Starhunter said, pointing across the room.

"Watanabe, Sale, place a breaching charge on that floor panel shown on your heads-up display," Starhunter ordered.

"Yes sir, I'm dying to blow something up," Sale said.

"Just get us down there without killing us, OK Sale?" Watanabe said, sarcastically.

Sale placed three small charges on the area of floor that appeared to have a slight indentation, stepped away, and then pulled a small remote detonator.

"I'm going loud!" Sale yelled, just as the three charges detonated, creating a cloud of pulverized cement and floor tiles. Sure enough, the hole in the floor revealed a flight of stairs leading down into the ground. Clearly, this was something the builders of this warehouse wanted to keep hidden from view.

"Sale, you take point. Watanabe and Hutch, you cover Sale. The Lightbringers and I will bring up the rear. I don't like the look of this, stay close and stay frosty." Starhunter ordered.

"Why do I always have to go in first?" Sale joked.

"Cut the chatter and just get in there, will you?" Watanabe yelled.

"Master Lightbringers, stay close to us. This place has been sealed for years. We have no idea what's down there," Starhunter warned.

Sale descended the staircase first, followed by Watanabe and Hutch, and finally Starhunter and the Lightbringers. As they entered the dark passageway, Munraito began generating a light from the Talisman of Uehara, creating a radiant glow around him and Fireteam Isis as they descended deeper into what appeared to be a vast network of underground tunnels.

"These tunnels are what's left of an incomplete subway line...no one's been down here in years...and this place seriously gives me the creeps," Sale said, looking around at the ghostly ruins of what would have been a subway station. The vast ruins had a very spooky, almost haunted feel to them. It was enough to make anyone nervous.

"Watch your motion trackers, everyone. Be prepared for hard contact," Watanabe said.

"I honestly don't know if anything could even be down here...this place looks completely abandoned...hold on...I've got a reading. Something's moving down on the train tracks. It's emitting very strong energy signatures...probably something mechanical." Hutch warned. Hutch and Watanabe walked cautiously over to the source of the movement. Suddenly, two orbs of plasma shot up from the corroding train tracks, tracing rapidly through the air like ball lightning, making a loud static discharge as they did so.

"Watch out!" Starhunter yelled as the orbs whizzed by him. The two orbs landed on the ground directly behind Fireteam Isis, and instantly exploded into a flurry of digital pixellations, which promptly assembled themselves into three insect-like creatures, glowing orange and covered in a silver chromium finish. At that moment, the three strange entities let out a blood-curdling screech, and began firing bolts of orange plasma energy at Fireteam Isis.

"Hostiles found!" Munraito yelled as Fireteam Isis took defensive positions behind support pilings and other pieces of cover. Munraito and Koda did the same.

"Weapons free! Take offensive formation!" Starhunter yelled as Fireteam Isis returned fire with their white-hot plasma weapons. Koda and Munraito both fired their Elohim Plasma Casters at the strange hostiles, who moved remarkably quickly and could teleport by digitizing their bodies at will. It was difficult just tracking these things, let alone shooting them. However, these enemies' tactics were not foolproof. Watanabe caught one of them between two support pilings, and promptly blasted it with her pulse rifle, causing it to explode into a bizarre puddle of golden-orange jelly, which quickly evaporated.

"These things are some sort of defense-AI, origin unknown!" Watanabe yelled.

"Wait for them to stop moving!" Watanabe suggested, firing her weapon in short, controlled bursts.

Sale caught one of the AI-based soldiers dead in his sights and annihilated it, and Starhunter did the same moments later against the final defense-AI.

"All hostiles eliminated. Great job, squad," Starhunter said.

"Woo-hoo! Eat plasma, you stupid machines!" Sale cheered.

"Back to the scrap heap, gearheads..." Hutch grumbled.

Fireteam Isis stepped out from behind their cover and looked at the jellylike remains of the three hostile AI soldiers scattered about the old subway station.

"What the hell were those things?" Sale asked.

"Some sort of defense AI programs. They definitely weren't Elohim," Watanabe said.

"Then where the hell did they come from?" Starhunter asked.

"I'm activating the ORACLE and performing a scan of the area. We'll find the source of these bolt bags soon enough," Hutch said, scanning the entire network of subterranean tunnels beneath the vast city with the ORACLE computer systems integrated into his armor.

"I've got a reading...it's further down the tunnel, away from the station. We need to move," Hutch said.

"Hutch, Watanabe, offensive positions. Lightbringers, you follow us. Keep your weapons ready," Starhunter said.

Hutch and Watanabe jumped down onto the old maglev tracks with Sale and Starhunter following close behind. The sound of a fully-armored, fully-augmented Defender hitting the ground after jumping was extremely loud, to say the least. Defenders weighed more than half a ton in their armor, and only they could wear it. Any ordinary soldier would die immediately if they tried to move while wearing the armor system, which was custom made to channel the Defenders' tremendous telekinetic abilities. The armor also protected the Defenders from the fall from the platform. Munraito and Koda had no such protection and instead climbed down a service ladder onto the maglev tracks, long abandoned and never used. Munraito and Koda quickly caught up with Fireteam Isis, who were now advancing into total darkness. Munraito's Talisman of Uehara began glowing again to generate light; Fireteam Isis needed no such light sources, as they had powerful infrared scanners in their helmets, allowing them to see flawlessly in the darkness.

"This place is unbearably creepy..." Koda said.

"Calm down, Koda. There's nothing down here except for those AI personalities," Munraito said.

"Keep your wits about you and your weapons ready," Watanabe reminded everyone.

Just then, three more plasma orbs appeared in the tunnel, and just like before, the orbs materialized into hostile AI programs. These ones were different, however. Unlike the smaller hostiles that had attacked them in the station, these enemy AI beings stood upright and possessed the same orange glow, with the same insect-like appearance. These warriors carried a sort of weapon that did not look like any weapon used by any known faction.

"There are more unknown hostiles ahead!" Watanabe said, firing her weapon at the closest enemy. Unlike the previous encounter in the train station, these enemies did not make any effort to evade.

"Trespassers sighted! You will submit!" One of the hostiles proclaimed, firing its weapon at Starhunter, whose shields promptly repelled the blast from the enemy's weapon.

"They're using some sort of close-range weapon! Keep your distance!" Sale said, backpedaling and firing his weapon at the enemy that had just fired at Starhunter. Thankfully, these enemy AI beings were not very resilient. The targets quickly vaporized after being hit with a sustained burst of plasma fire, being reduced to a cloud of golden-orange embers. Suddenly, the last remaining enemy came charging at Munraito, who promptly opened fire with his Plasma Caster, obliterating the hostile contact and rendering it harmless.

"Well done, Munraito. You scored your first kill," Watanabe said, jokingly.

"What are these things, Watanabe?" Munraito inquired, a slight tone of panic in his voice.

"Hell if I know, but we need to find out fast. This is getting serious. There is a large hostile presence in these subway tunnels. I think the crooked cops were just the tip of the iceberg with what's really been going on here. Let's keep moving," Watanabe suggested, holding her weapon in its ready position. Munraito followed Fireteam Isis down the corridor, sticking close behind the four Defenders, heading towards the source of the reading that they had detected. Suddenly, three more plasma orbs appeared, materializing into yet more hostile AI programs.

"Take them out!" Starhunter yelled. An immediate firefight broke out, in which the four Defenders quickly destroyed the three hostiles in their path.

"Hey Hutch, how many kills do you have today, psycho?" Sale joked.

"More than you, wise guy," Hutch responded.

"Could you keep the comm channels clear unless you have something useful to say?" Watanabe responded.

"When I said I was going to help with the investigation, this is not what I had in mind..." Munraito grumbled to Koda.

The AI programs just kept coming, with more and more of them materializing as Fireteam Isis advanced down the tunnels.

"Take offensive positions! Search and destroy!" Starhunter said, ordering his squad to actively hunt and destroy any hostiles they found. Munraito marveled at the speed and efficiency of the Defenders, carving a path through the hostile contacts as if they were cutting grass. They hadn't even had to use their super abilities yet, as using said abilities on such weak enemies would be considered overkill. Defenders believed in a strict code of conduct, even on the battlefield. Use of excessive force was considered brutish and unrefined. As Fireteam Isis rounded a bend in the tunnel, suddenly a voice chimed in over their communications suites.

"This is Fireteam Odin, reporting topside. The atmospheric disturbance above Muranahe is increasing. Isis, what the hell are you doing down there?!" The other Defender exclaimed, his voice cracking over the communications channel.

"We're working on that, Alnair. Just be prepared to engage any hostiles that emerge into the city itself," Starhunter replied.

"We're having a situation down here!" Sale yelled, firing at more AI units.

"Die, you metalhead pieces of trash!!" Hutch grumbled, destroying three AI units with a telekinetic push.

"Roger that, Fireteam Odin out," Alnair replied, a tone of dry humor in his voice.

"I've got a much stronger reading up ahead. We're approaching a power source of some sort," Sale observed, checking his ORACLE system.

"All right squad, let's move!" Starhunter ordered, running forward with superhuman speed. Munraito and Koda struggled to keep up. There was clearly a sense of urgency with Fireteam Isis, as they were using their armor's thruster packs to dash forward even faster than they could run. The situation in Muranahe was worsening by the second, and Fireteam Isis didn't have much time to find out what was causing the huge storms over the city.

As Fireteam Isis zeroed in on the power source deep under the city, Munraito and Koda thought only about the people of Muranahe and everything the city represented. The cherry blossoms in the spring, the summer festivals, and the warm, dry tropical winters, all of that was in mortal danger from some unknown threat. The corrupt police officers and the Otohime Murders were just the tip of the iceberg. Something was here, deep under the city, hiding in an abandoned subway station. Something that needed to be stopped before it could take any more lives than had already been lost.

Munraito let the energy of the Talisman of Uehara flow through him, engaging in Hyperspace Meditation as he ran. In an instant, he felt the Talisman transform him, becoming a radiant body of energy, easily able to stand toe-to-toe with the Defenders. Koda watched in awe as his master channeled his inner energy, becoming one with the Cosmos and charging forward, hovering above the ground. Munraito zoomed past Fireteam Isis, encouraging them onward.

"Wow...I don't think any of us expected that..." Watanabe said of Munraito's abilities.

"All right squad, form up and follow Munraito. He knows what he's doing," Starhunter ordered.

Fireteam Isis geared up and followed Munraito at full speed down the tunnel. The tunnel seemed to go on forever, an endless winding corridor of decrepit railway infrastructure, the ruin of a failed attempt at transit expansion.

"We're coming up on the power source I detected earlier. Be prepared for hard contact," Sale cautioned.

"Now I'm really going to rack up the kills..." Hutch gloated.

"Just don't get so busy counting that you forget to cover me!" Watanabe reminded, a bit annoyed at Hutch and Sale's constant banter.

Just then, an entire swarm of plasma orbs appeared and promptly materialized into hostile AI personalities, which immediately began targeting Fireteam Isis. Munraito charged forward, his Talisman of Uehara shining radiantly as he unleashed an enormous burst of white-hot plasma from his shining, radiant form. Lighting up the entire tunnel and vaporizing the AI constructs instantaneously, Munraito cleared the path of all hostiles before the Defenders could even react.

"Hostiles eliminated," Munraito announced.

"That was impressive..." Watanabe remarked.

Munraito then realized what he was standing in front of. Fireteam Isis had come upon an enormous power generator, one that looked truly ancient, as if it hadn't been disturbed in thousands of years. Yet the machine was running, generating the AI constructs that had been attacking Fireteam Isis throughout their mission in the tunnels. Munraito slowly approached the machine, only to be greeted by a huge plasma orb rising out of it, which promptly transformed into another AI personality. This one, however, was larger and far more imposing than the others.

"I am the Guardian Eternal, Keeper of the Architects and their secrets. You have made it this far, trespasser, but I assure you, you will go no farther!" The AI personality boomed in its metallic, robotic voice.

"Take him out!" Starhunter yelled as Fireteam Isis raised their weapons to fire.

"Stop, we mean you no harm. We do not wish to steal from you. Tell us what this is, and then we will leave you alone," Munraito said, standing between Fireteam Isis and the Guardian.

"I am a proud warrior of the Architects, the keepers of this realm and the builders of all Creation. For many millennia have I guarded this horde, and only now am I being disturbed. Unless you are the Inheritor, you have no business being here. Others have already stolen from me, and my warriors have been searching this world for those responsible before it is too late," the AI personality said, speaking through its extraordinarily advanced suit of armor. The armor the AI personality wore looked very similar to the armor Sei Ikkiku had worn when she killed the Shinigami Bird in the garden at Heiei Castle. Could this warrior be Elohim?

"Who are the Architects?" Munraito asked.

"The Architects are that they are..." The Guardian responded.

"The builders of this place knew that one day the Inheritor would reclaim their sacred knowledge and technology; however, two decades ago, intruders broke into this sacred ground. I drove them out. The news of what was found here spread through the most unsavory circles of your species, however, until an organization of criminals returned to this place and stole the sacred blueprints to our technology. Since then, I have searched far and wide across this world and others for the stolen blueprints. I have had little success, however. I fear by this point it may already be too late," The Guardian explained, somberly.

"You hear that? Somebody's been here before. This is what the corrupt cops were trying to protect. They were working for a criminal organization who's been harvesting exotic technology from these ancient caches," Watanabe realized.

"Apparently, the reason this subway tunnel was abandoned was because the drillers broke into this cache of technology and were driven out by the Guardian. That tipped off the criminal organization, which promptly swooped in and claimed the technology for themselves. Ever since then, the Guardian has been trying to find who stole from him, but to no avail. This means we have to find them ourselves," Munraito deduced.

"Guardian, we would be happy to assist you in locating whoever stole from you," Munraito told the Guardian.

"Very well then...allow me to gather myself for action," the Guardian replied, vanishing back into the machine from whence he came.

Just then, the entire area began to shake violently. Pieces of rock and tunnel began falling from the ceiling.

"Keep your heads down and run!!" Starhunter barked as the shaking grew incredibly violent. Fireteam Isis and the Lightbringers dashed through the crumbling tunnel at breakneck speed, dodging falling boulders and rocks the size of small cars as they fell from the ceiling. Whatever the Guardian was doing, he was going to take a considerable chunk of Muranahe with him if he wasn't careful.

"We're approaching the exit, don't let up!" Starhunter screamed over the roar of the crumbling tunnel. Jumping back up onto the station platform, Fireteam Isis and the Lightbringers dodged crumbling support beams and falling rocks as they made a mad dash up the stairs to the surface. Rushing out of the abandoned staircase into the warehouse, the building rapidly crumbled from the enormous ground quakes.

Munraito and the Fireteam then emerged from the destroyed building to a jaw-dropping sight. The storm over Muranahe had reached its climax, and when Fireteam Isis looked towards the center of the city, they were utterly stunned by what they saw. A huge portion of the city itself had caved into a massive hole in the ground, and rising out of that hole was a gigantic machine, slowly assembling itself into a 7-story high monstrosity, pulsing with orange and blue light and covered in glowing runes.

"We need to get airborne," Starhunter said, purposefully understating the gravity of the situation.

"No problem," Munraito replied, letting the light from the Talisman of Uehara cloak him in energy. Munraito then levitated off the ground, taking his angelic Incarnate Form as he did so.

"This is Fireteam Odin, reporting in! What the hell is that thing?!" Alnair gasped, clearly winded from running through the city streets.

"It calls itself the Guardian. We encountered it in the tunnels underneath the city. This is what the corrupt cops were trying to keep secret! They were stealing technology from this thing and giving it to organized crime!" Starhunter replied, screaming over the roar of the storm's howling winds.

"Well they certainly stirred up a hornet's nest! I've got hostiles everywhere! The city is under attack!" Alnair responded, frantically.

"We'll link up with you in the Center City district. Eliminate any hostiles you encounter by any means necessary! Protect civilian lives at all costs!" Starhunter hollered, moving towards the rapidly assembling Guardian.

Suddenly, the Guardian stopped moving the moment it had finished assembling.

"I am the Guardian Eternal, Keeper of the Architects and Defender of Justice. Take heed, citizens. There is a realm of existence so far beyond your own, you cannot even imagine it. I am a protector of that realm, and this one. The Architects were true masters of their domain, crossing the cosmos and constructing worlds with impunity, power and honor. Every sentient species in the Universe owes their existence to the Architects. 'God.' 'Oahina.' 'San'ryum' These are just some of the names given to the Architects by various sentient species throughout the Universe, but in the end, what they chose to call us is irrelevant. We simply ARE. We are born of the Universal Energy itself, the purest, most radiant form of consciousness. We the builders of this technology had long since faded into obscurity, but now, the time of our return is imminent. Our numbers will darken the skies of every world, with the coming of the Inheritor...the Man against Time, the Cleanser of Filth, and the Hand of Justice. The Great Purge shall soon begin...and the New Era shall rise," the Guardian announced, with its deep, metallic voice.

Munraito looked up at the Guardian and smiled. He now knew where his destiny lay.

Munraito alighted on the roof of a building near where the Guardian stood, standing in the rain as the wind howled around him. The Guardian was causing the storm to rage, and Munraito stood atop the building, taking it all in. Munraito always knew that he was destined for great things...he just never knew how great.

Just then, however, the Guardian turned and spotted Munraito standing atop the building, still radiating energy from the Talisman of Uehara. The Guardian looked at Munraito with its gigantic, metallic eyes, as if it recognized him from another era or lifetime...and then it began to retreat into its cavern beneath the city. Slowly but surely, the Guardian disassembled into its underground lair, satisfied with its message to the citizens of Muranahe and the rest of humanity.

As the Guardian took its final gaze upon Munraito and the city of Muranahe, Munraito hovered down to the ground with Fireteam Isis and Koda.

"Alright then...you heard the Guardian. An Avatar...a Man against Time is coming. This man will purge all those he sees as unrighteous from the face of the Universe, and usher in a new era of peace and justice using the Architects' technology. This means we are in a race to find this Man against Time, and the organization that stole the Architects' technology. I know for a fact that the Man against Time is responsible for the deaths of the corrupt police officers and the criminals in various prisons across the Republic, and he will likely target the organization who stole the Architects' technology next. This means we have to find them first," Munraito explained.

"Understood, Master Lightbringer, the question is, where do we start?" Starhunter asked as the storm began to ease its grip on the city.

"I shall probe this matter with Hyperspace Meditation later in Heiei Castle; however, I scarcely think Oumi is a safe place for me and Haruna anymore. I plan on temporarily departing Oumi aboard the New Berlin Space Colony once it leaves, and I will pursue this matter further then. Until then, I would recommend that the Defenders and the Republic military remain on high alert to respond to any crises that may arise anywhere in the Milky Way Galaxy. We will get to the bottom of this. For now, Koda and I must return to Heiei. I am fully confident that we will solve this case," Munraito reassured, turning and walking away from Fireteam Isis.

"Master Lightbringer..." Starhunter interrupted.

"It was a pleasure serving with you." Starhunter complemented.

"Thank you very much." Munraito replied, handing over the borrowed weapons and walking towards the Republic Loki-class dropship that had landed nearby. Koda and Munraito stepped into the dropship's passenger compartment with several other Republic Marines. The Defenders would remain in Muranahe to ensure that civilian casualties were minimal.

"Hey, Master Lightbringer...what of this Man against Time, eh?" one of the Marines asked, holding his rifle very tightly.

"What about him? I can't say I know much about him, to be perfectly honest. All I know is that he's the Inheritor of the Architects' technology and that he is trying to purge all the unrighteous from the face of the Universe," Munraito replied as the dropship lifted off the ground, bound for Heiei Castle.

"All I can say right now is that Oumi will never be the same after this," Munraito added.

"Yeah, I would have to agree with you on that one. Not much happens this far from Earth and Stronghold. Oumi is one of the few human colony worlds outside of the Milky Way Galaxy, and you almost never hear about

Oumi on GalaxyNet channels closer to the Core. This is going to change everything," the Marine said, looking out over the Panarin Mountains.

"However, there's nothing the Defenders can't do. They defeated the Naruhol Ihr. If they can do that, they can certainly stop the Man against Time, whoever he is," the Marine continued.

"Who said the Man against Time was an enemy?" Munraito asked.

"We're with the 87th Brigade, stationed aboard the UHR Hannibal, a heavy cruiser in the Republic Navy. The ship is armed with the latest in plasma weaponry and some of the strongest shields ever placed on a spacecraft built by humans. Nothing gets through our fleet in one piece," the Marine continued.

"I like your enthusiasm..." Munraito replied, looking over at Koda.

Munraito and Koda felt the dropship beginning to descend.

"You know, Munraito-san, this is the second time in just as many days that we have completely totaled one of Heiei Castle's vehicles in Muranahe. Perhaps we should find another way of getting into the city next time?" Koda suggested.

"It does not matter. We will both be leaving Oumi very soon, you, me and Haruna. We're going aboard that space colony and leaving with them after this. It is no longer safe for us here on Oumi. I fear that whatever organization stole the Architects' technology will be back to cause more violence and destruction, and when they come back, the Republic will be ready for them," Munraito explained.

The dropship began its descent onto Heiei Castle grounds, where several other Lightbringers, along with a Defender fireteam awaited them. Sei Ikkiku and Gwenlynn Stormweaver were being briefed on the situation in Muranahe and the Guardian's emergence and revelation. As the dropship landed, Munraito and Koda jumped out and ran over to Sei and Gwenlynn.

"Munraito, this is Fireteam Odin, led by a Defender Sorcerer by the name of Alnair. He has told me everything that has transpired in Oumi...and I must say, my worst fears are confirmed. We must move quickly if the Republic is to survive," Gwenlynn explained.

"Munraito, what's going on? I'm scared," Haruna worried, concerned but stalwart in her resolve against the unknown threat.

"I heard there was some sort of attack in Muranahe and that there's this 'Guardian' thing talking about a Great Purge...why? Why only now?" Haruna asked, curiously.

"I don't know..." Munraito lied, calmly and collectively.

"All I know is that we cannot remain here on Oumi for much longer. We're going to have to leave. I will continue to investigate the Man against Time and try to locate those responsible for taking the Architects' technology. We will solve this crisis. It is only a matter of time. Haruna, don't worry. I will make sure you are safe, but you must learn to stand on your own," Munraito encouraged, standing next to Haruna and taking her hand.

"This 'Great Purge' excites me. Come, Munraito. There is much I must share with you." Sei Ikkiku explained.

Munraito and Sei walked back into Heiei Castle.

"This entire saga with the Guardian and the Man against Time has happened before...many millions of years ago. Human history is not what you think it is. For millions of years, humanity, the Elohim and the Astari maintained a vast intergalactic Empire that spanned the entirety of the Milky Way and Andromeda Galaxies. Earth was once a paradise world, covered with advanced cities with its inhabitants using extraordinarily high technology...however, in your species' prehistory, a great plague swept through the Milky Way, decimating the worlds controlled by humans and Elohim, until we were driven back to our respective worlds, Belisaria and Earth. Humans eventually lost touch with who they were, while we maintained our technological prominence. However, the coming of the 'Man against Time,' the Inheritor, will mark the return of our Empire's glory. Human beings are the children of the Architects, and the Man against Time is the Inheritor of the ancient technology...I didn't realize that this was happening until the Guardian was found in Muranahe. The Man against Time will restore our ancient glory, and we will do all we can to support him." Sei explained.

"Sei, what you speak of will be considered treason by the Republic. The Senate will never allow such lawlessness to take over," Munraito replied, stunned by what Sei was telling him.

"This is not a matter of law. It is a matter of human destiny. Knowing this information, I feel it is best for you to spread this as soon as possible. Let the Republic know the truth about human history, and show the Republic what it truly means to be human again," Sei replied.

"Very well then, I shall prepare this in a GalaxyNet broadcast as soon as we board the New Berlin Space Colony," Munraito said as he walked back towards the courtyard again. Sei followed close behind. As the two of them walked out into the late afternoon sun, Munraito turned to Haruna and the others.

"Haruna, Koda, everyone...it is time to leave this world. We must head for the New Berlin Space Colony at once. There is much to accomplish in the coming weeks," Munraito revealed, walking back towards the dropship and Fireteam Odin.

"Munraito is right. We cannot remain on Oumi any longer. The situation that faces us demands that we take action immediately." Sei announced.

"Oh geez, just when I was getting comfortable..." Takada quipped, chiming in.

"I guess it's time to move on..." Gwenlynn added.

The Troika appeared as well, along with Viceroy Annunaki of the Naruhol Ihr.

"We will stand with you in this struggle, Master Munraito," Anteon pledged.

"You are a shining example of human strength. You have the full support of the Naruhol Ihr," Viceroy Annunaki praised.

"This is truly wonderful...I must confer with Master Iori and the other Lightbringers about my leave of absence," Munraito replied, walking back into Heiei Castle for what figured to be the last time for a while, and came upon Master Iori and the other Lightbringers leaving from a daily meditation session.

"Master Iori...the time has come for me to leave this sanctuary. I must leave aboard the New Berlin Space Colony to address the issues currently facing the Republic. The events of the past few days have shown that a crisis is rapidly unfolding, one that cannot be addressed from Heiei Castle. I will be taking Koda with me, as well as Haruna," Munraito declared.

Master Iori looked at Munraito and calmly stated his intentions.

"Master Munraito, you may go. The Universe needs you right now. There is no point in you staying here any longer. Take Koda and Haruna with you, for they will learn much from you on your journey," Master Iori said, his gray beard contrasting against his golden-yellow eyes.

"I shall confer your departure to the people of Oumi once you leave. We wish you the best on your voyage," Iori concluded, turning and walking back into the sanctuary, flanked by his disciples. The other Lightbringers bowed to Munraito in respect, observing the Talisman of Uehara shining around his neck. It was time for Munraito to leave, and start his journey aboard the New Berlin Space Colony. He would fulfill his destiny as the Man against Time, a destiny he knew would eventually come to fruition, regardless of whether the Republic approved of it or not.

Munraito turned and walked back out into the courtyard, back towards the Republic dropship.

"We're getting ready to head back up to the Hannibal; however, we'll be happy to deliver you to the New Berlin Space Colony before we return to our ship," Alnair offered, shouldering his rifle.

"Very well then. We're ready when you are," Munraito replied, directing everyone to board the Loki-class dropship for the trip into orbit. Munraito and his companions stepped into the dropship's passenger compartment as the doors and atmosphere aboard the dropship sealed for the trip into space.

"Get ready everyone, liftoff in 3," Alnair announced as the gunship lifted off the ground and began streaking skyward, towards the infinite abyss of space. Takada looked over at Munraito as the dropship climbed in altitude.

"Munraito, dear, have you ever flown in space before?" Takada asked, still wearing her revealing Draconis Marunae Tropica outfit.

"No, not really, I've only lived on Oumi," Munraito replied.

"Well, then this is going to be a real eye-opener for you," Takada responded as the dropship crossed the atmospheric boundary. Ahead of the dropship, Munraito saw two huge ships, one was an Olympus-class heavy cruiser, and the other an enormous colony ship, three times as large as the heavy cruiser and gleaming silver, instead of the steel-gray reserved for military craft.

"That's the space colony, Munraito-kun. I think you're going to like it there," Haruna indicated as the dropship approached the enormous colony ship's main hangar bay, which was currently playing host to a few smaller ships venturing in and out of the enormous starship.

"This is New Berlin Traffic Control, we have you on our scopes, prepare to enter the hangar bay and dock in slip 113," the traffic controller told the dropship pilots, who slowly maneuvered the dropship through the static shield around the hangar bay entrance and into the colony ship's vast interior. A bright white light shined into the dropship's passenger cabin as the ship descended onto the designated landing pad. As the docking clamps grasped the dropship firmly into place, Haruna breathed a sigh of relief. She was happy to be home again, especially after the wild events of the past two days.

"Well, we're here," Haruna proclaimed.

"I live in Residential Block A-12, which can be reached by the monorail station about three blocks from here. Come. I'll show you where to go," Haruna told Munraito as the dropship doors opened. Munraito, Koda, the Troika, Gwenlynn, Sei, Takada, Haruna and Viceroy Annunaki stepped out of the dropship and into the hustle and bustle of the New Berlin Space Colony. They stood on a catwalk above the main hangar floor, leading straight into one of the main habitation areas aboard the colony. Haruna led the way as the group walked down the gangplank and through a pair of sliding, automatic doors. As they walked through the doors, Munraito found himself in a very different environment from the one he was used to. Lines of high-priced retail outlets advertising their goods stretched from end to end, with hundreds of wealthy residents shopping and carrying around very expensive items in shopping bags marked with high-end labels. Potted plants from all over the Republic lined the avenue, and various flags representing numerous Core Worlds, vital to the Republic's prosperity, hung from storefronts. This was going to take some getting used to, to say the least.

"Munraito, come with me. The monorail is this way," Haruna directed, walking with the others towards the monorail station, which was past several high-end clothing outlets. Takada, being an upper-class socialite, couldn't help but pop her head into the boutique to have a look around. The response from the store owners was immediate, and she was immediately recognized and many other customers came running over to her, plying her with questions about her latest fashion line or her books that she had written about her own life. The store owners immediately tried to make a sale to her, showing her some of the more expensive things on display.

"Haruna, this is going to be a bit of a distraction to our goal, don't you think?" Munraito whispered to Haruna as people continued to ask Takada questions.

"Oh relax, Munraito. She's just in her element right now," Haruna said.

Munraito and the others waited patiently as Takada finished her conversations with her fans and even signed a few autographs before rejoining Munraito and the others.

"Takada, was that delay really necessary?" Munraito grumbled.

"Of course it was, I can't just ignore them, can I? Then what would they think of me?" Takada responded.

"It looks like I'm going to have to get used to this..." Munraito mumbled, experiencing a bit of culture shock from going from Heiei Castle to the New Berlin Space Colony, one of the wealthiest addresses in the Republic. Munraito looked around at all the bright lights, the screens and electronic billboards, all the people walking to and from the hundreds of shops and buildings along the avenue. It was an entire city contained aboard a starship, built to be a permanent home for millions of the Republic's wealthiest and most prestigious citizens. To Munraito, it was completely foreign. Muranahe did have its upscale parts; however, they were nothing compared to what he saw on New Berlin.

"Taking it all in, Munraito?" Haruna asked, smiling.

"You'll all be staying in my apartment. It has ample space for everyone," Haruna added.

"This is my world. I have lived here for the past 14 years, and trust me, it does take some getting used to. Your life will be a lot better here than it was on Oumi. I know mine was," Haruna continued.

"What makes you think that my life will be any better here just because yours was?" Munraito asked.

"This space colony is fantastic...however, you cannot compare your experience to mine," Munraito continued, a tone of admonishment in his voice.

"Are you saying you don't like it here already?" Haruna asked, curiously.

"No, I'm only saying that this is all very new for me, and I just need some time to adjust," Munraito replied.

"I wonder where the Defenders went to," Takada wondered, thinking about the gigantic Olympus-class heavy cruiser in orbit around Oumi.

"Those ships are some of the largest moving objects ever built by human hands. If what Sei Ikkiku said earlier is true; however, humanity is only a shadow of what it once was," Munraito said, quietly.

"Wait, what?" Gwenlynn said, her interest piqued by Munraito's statement.

"What Munraito says is the truth. Darwin and modern archeology don't have the whole story. This was a secret that I planned to reveal to you once the time was right. More than two hundred and fifty million years ago, humanity, the Elohim and the Astari controlled a vast intergalactic Empire which controlled the entire Milky Way and Andromeda Galaxies...but then, disaster struck. A plague, one like no one had ever seen before, decimated the human race, destroying a large part of the Empire in the Milky Way Galaxy. Many survived, however, and settled on planets like Belisaria, my race's homeworld, Earth and Mars. For many thousands of years, humanity and the Elohim existed in harmony as we sought to rebuild what was lost, and Elohim ships made routine visits to Earth throughout human history. Until, however, the Lucifer Experiment began. Some of the people living on Mars rebelled against those on Earth and Belisaria, while cutting themselves off from their Astari brethren in Andromeda. There was, in essence, a war between Earth and Mars following the plague in which everyone on Mars was utterly annihilated and Mars returned to a frozen wasteland from its terraformed state. Earth's population survived, but became so spiritually and consciously degraded by the conflict that the knowledge, wisdom and technology of the glorious past was lost forever, stranding the human race on Earth with no memory of their origin or their past. This is something the Elohim and Astari have been trying to restore for the past fourteen ages of human history, and now, we stand on a threshold. The long-awaited Man against Time, the Inheritor, has finally come, and our job is to find him." Sei explained, leaving out the details that Munraito was in fact the Inheritor.

"Wait, I thought you said the coming of the Man against Time was not necessarily in the Republic's best interest..." Haruna interjected.

"I was not aware that the true Man against Time had returned, as there have been impostors in the past. But the Guardians speak the truth. He is here, somewhere in this galaxy, and our task is to find him before less savory individuals do. Whoever stole the ancient human Architect technology must also be aware that he is here. And, Haruna, the Republic government does not matter in this scenario. There's nothing it can do to prevent these events from happening," Sei elaborated, with a tone of equal concern and anticipation.

"Oh, I doubt that they'll be able to find him. These people are little more than common criminals. Finding the Man against Time will be well beyond their capabilities," Munraito gloated, rather confidently.

"I think the greatest question now is who stole the technology from the Guardian on Oumi?" Gwenlynn asked.

"That is impossible to say at this point, because the only people that knew the answer to that question have been killed by the Man against Time. However, rest assured, it is only a matter of time before they die as well," Sei sighed.

"I fear we will find out soon enough, however," Sei warned as Munraito and the others continued down the avenue towards the monorail station.

After a brief walk down the street, past the rows and rows of shops and restaurants for purely biological beings, Munraito paused briefly as Haruna and the others continued. He was clearly disturbed by something.

"Haruna...something is coming," Munraito warned, sensing a great disturbance in the quantum strings through his Hyperspace Meditation. Suddenly, the entire space colony shook, causing the lights to flicker and people to lose their footing. Several of the Republic Marines stationed on the colony for security started yelling and drew their weapons. Munraito ran to one of the huge bay windows along the street and quickly saw the source of the sudden blast. Crawling out of the Quantum Space tunnel was a flotilla of starships, but starships unlike anything Munraito had ever seen before. Two were large, alien-looking silver ships that looked a bit like giant squids, pulsing with the same orange glow that the AI constructs on Oumi did, and the third was a truly gargantuan point cruiser. This ship was absolutely massive, looking for all intents and purposes like a spacegoing Eiffel Tower on its side with the tip pointed in the direction of travel, just more than 15 kilometers long.

"That's Architect technology, the thieves are here! Everyone take cover now!" Sei Ikkiku said, alarmed.

Munraito watched as the heavy cruiser Hannibal moved to engage the enemy ships as people aboard the space colony began to panic. A space battle was about to unfold over Oumi, and the New Berlin Space Colony was caught right in the middle of it. Munraito overheard several of the Republic Marines communicating with the New Berlin Colony's bridge, recommending an immediate jump to Quantum Space to escape the marauding enemy fleet. Munraito couldn't believe it. His home planet was under attack, and there was absolutely nothing he could do about it.

"We can't just leave!" Munraito protested.

"We have no choice. The Defenders can probably handle it," Gwenlynn said, calmly, watching as the Republic and enemy ships began firing their weapons at one another, their shields flaring.

"Everyone remain calm. The colony is about to make the jump to Quantum Space," the PA system aboard the colony announced. As the enormous ship's warp drives fired up, Munraito could see the stars start to wink out like tiny night lights as the ship slowly made the transition from real space to Quantum Space, a strange state where space-time became so distorted that distances between star systems were reduced to minute levels. As the colony escaped the marauding danger, the rest of the colony breathed a sigh of relief. All, except for Munraito, Koda and Haruna.

"This is bad...if the Defenders fail, Oumi is defenseless. I fear nothing short of genocide if those miscreants get free reign on Oumi," Haruna worried.

"Haruna, there are multiple teams of Defenders aboard that cruiser, they are more than capable of figuring out a way to destroy four enemy ships. Remember, those ancient ships are man-made just as much as this one is," Munraito reminded.

"So the Republic will know what's going on then, as well," Haruna replied, breathing a sigh of relief.

"Yes, they will. How they will react to the news is anyone's guess," Munraito reassured.

Haruna sighed, surrendering to the fact that there was nothing she could do about the situation at this point. She just had to have faith that the Defenders could make the impossible possible once again.

As the colony continued through Quantum Space, Munraito and the rest of the group approached the monorail station, marked with several signs and directories. However, Munraito, Koda and Haruna could not shake the thought of what they had just witnessed in orbit around Oumi. The thought that their home planet was in danger, and that there was absolutely nothing they could do about it was gut wrenching for them. Oumi meant very little to the residents of the New Berlin Colony, their lives were so radically different than those of the colonists on Oumi that they simply could not understand why anyone would choose to live on a planet like Oumi. The risks to human life were everywhere and even the Sun itself was hostile at times. To the New Berlin colonists, the threat of invasion was just one more reason to not live on a planet, especially one like Oumi. Residents of space colonies often had a sense of entitlement that those living on planets did not have. Because space travel was accessible to everyone, living in space was still considered a privilege, not a right, even though technically it was not against the law for middle-class people to live on a space colony. Usually, however, only the very rich could afford such luxuries. The people on New Berlin simply did not care about the people on Oumi, although the implications of what the appearance of the hostile fleet above Oumi meant for the Republic were disturbing. However, Munraito and his group knew, though they did not know exactly what the criminals would do if they managed to defeat the Defenders and the Republic warship in orbit. It was enough to make anyone nervous.

As Munraito and his group sat down in the monorail station to wait for the next train, he wondered about Oumi, and how the battle there was progressing. They would doubtlessly hear about it on the GalaxyNet news later that evening, for sure. Oumi had been in the news a lot the last few days, far more than usual, thanks to the series of attacks on Muranahe. This had culminated in the space battle raging above the planet. Astoundingly to Haruna, nobody seemed to be batting an eye about what had just happened. Haruna knew just how aloof the residents of New

Berlin could be, but their complete lack of empathy for what was happening on Oumi was shocking, to say the least. Perhaps it was simply from a lack of concern, because they thought the issue on Oumi wouldn't affect them.

"Excuse me, but do any of you have any concerns for what happened on Oumi?" Haruna asked a group of people sitting at the train station, reading the news as it unfolded.

"It is a concern, yes, but it likely will not affect us here," one of the other people said in response to Haruna's question.

"I'm from Oumi, and I'm very concerned," Haruna replied, keeping the conversation going longer than was necessary.

"Oh, wow...so I can see why you'd be concerned. Don't worry, though. The Defenders can probably handle it," The train rider reassured, politely answering Haruna's questions while trying to read the news on his holotablet.

"I certainly hope so," Haruna replied, nervously fidgeting as she looked over at Munraito and Sei, who also seemed concerned. Haruna glanced at the other train rider's news headlines on his tablet and saw that the space battle was still in progress, but that the Defenders had put the hostile fleet on the run. Live updates from the ongoing Oumi crisis were streaming in by the minute through the GalaxyNet's livestreaming channels, allowing news to be crowdsourced and reported on as it happened.

"Wow...this is huge," Munraito remarked.

"This is the most attention Oumi has received in Republic media ever...why only now?" Munraito wondered.

"Well, isn't it obvious?" Haruna asked, flabbergasted.

"No, I mean, why did all of this happen now? Why did these criminals choose only now to act? Could it really be as a response to the Man against Time?" Munraito thought.

"That would seem to be the case," Sei said, awaiting the monorail while trying to avoid the curious gaze of many onlookers. It was unusual to ever see an Elohim outside of their home system, let alone the Queen of the entire race. Munraito and his group were attracting quite a lot of attention, to say the least, and it was beginning to trouble Munraito as he anxiously awaited the arrival of the monorail train. High-speed rail transit was one of the primary means of transportation around the space colony, as it was on many Republic colony worlds. Just then, a few more young women approached Takada and asked her about her outfit, which had captured their attention.

"Oh, this is from my summer collection that I released a few months ago, it should be in the stores down the avenue outside. It's really quite lovely for those warm summer days when you're feeling in an exotic, playful mood." Takada explained.

Munraito rolled his eyes. He thought Takada's career was pointless, despite the amount of money she made from it.

The three young women walked away and sat back down, just as a tone rang through the station: the train had arrived.

"All right, next stop, Residential Block A-12, Starlight Division. That's where my apartment is," Haruna announced, proudly.

"I can't wait to see this," Koda said, standing up to board the train.

The group stepped into the passenger car and sat down in a row of seats near the front of the train, away from the other passengers to avoid drawing attention to themselves. The Troika, Viceroy Annunaki and Sei Ikkiku were leaders of their respective civilizations. Not surprisingly, three small orbs of plasma hovered into the train car, surrounded by small metallic plates swirling around them. In an instant, these orbs materialized into three Elohim guards, with blonde hair and matching beards. They looked more like Vikings in cybernetic armor than extraterrestrials, but these were some of Sei's most dedicated protectors.

"Milady, I trust your trip to the surface of Oumi was productive?" one of the guards asked.

"Yes, indeed, Gronveld, I found these lovely young people there as well," Sei replied, pointing at Munraito and Haruna.

"Interesting...The two of them seem rather well-constructed for humans," Gronveld observed, inspecting Haruna and Munraito.

"Where are we headed?" Gronveld asked.

"We are headed to Haruna's apartment for the moment. She has something she wishes to share with us," Sei informed.

"Your highness, you cannot go there! It's against fleet protocol to enter a civilian's home under any circumstances while on duty!" Gronveld protested.

"Calm yourself, Gronveld. She invited us in," Sei responded.

Gronveld looked at Haruna very curiously, as if he was shocked that Haruna didn't know standard Elohim operating procedures when in a foreign environment. As the maglev train pulled away from the station, it passed over a trestle stretching far above an entire city, all contained within a gigantic artificial habitat in space. Green lichen trees from Earth grew in neat rows along streets bustling with pedestrians. Self-driving cars moved through the streets of New Berlin, and various hovering vehicles flew by. The entire station slowly rotated to generate gravity as it flew through space, meaning that everything was always on a slant within the space colony. Thanks to the microgravity environment outside and centripetal force, however, every direction was up, so nobody fell down as the ship rotated.

"So this is where you lived for the past 14 years. Haruna, this is all extraordinary to me. A colony like this is...just so different than what I am used to. I don't think I could live here, to be honest. I grew up in a place full of wide open spaces, where I hunted the animals living on Oumi for sport. This entire place just seems so foreign to me." Munraito confessed.

"It does take some getting used to. I didn't think I could live here for a while, until people started showing me just what the colony had to offer," Haruna reassured.

Munraito looked over at the Astari Troika, standing up against the windows and admiring the view from the train.

"What are they so intrigued by?" Munraito asked.

"We are the Astari, the makers of all things...under the umbrella of our countless generations, we have watched life take deep root in every corner of the Universe. For untold eons we have watched our seeds blossom into flowers, flowers that have expanded and brightened every corner of the Universe. We are the life-giving Sun that all intelligence is eventually drawn to. Organic civilizations rise, advance, reach the apex of their glory and become immortal, adding to the unspoken beauty of the infinite Universe in which we live. We admire this creation of Mankind just as we would a creation of our own, because, in reality, it IS a creation of our own. We seed all planets with life, and wait for it to reach a level of consciousness to contact us...therefore adding to the Universe's total knowledge. Each and every one of you are our children, and we view all of this as such," Anteon explained.

"Are you serious?" Munraito exclaimed, incredulously.

"Everything he says is true, Munraito. The Astari are one of the most ancient species in the Universe. They have colonies in many galaxies across the Cosmos, but it is here in the Andromeda and Milky Way Galaxies that their presence is felt most strongly. All life in our galaxy is traced back to them, and they take responsibility for all things," Haruna explained to Munraito.

"We are all equally their children, seedlings that have flowered towards the radiant light of their Empire. Everything that has happened on Earth and every other planet in the Milky Way Galaxy has grown and thrived under their careful attendance. I guess you could say this moment was meant to be," Haruna said, sweetly.

"I guess you're right," Munraito sighed.

"Haruna, ever since the Oumi crisis started, all I've been able to think about is keeping you safe from harm. I mean, whoever's been stealing the Architect technology also killed your parents and are probably trying to kill you too. I'm happy that we're off-world for now. We should be much safer here," Munraito admitted, a tone of reassurance in his voice.

"Oh, isn't that sweet," Takada jibed, overhearing Munraito and Haruna's conversation.

"You know, I've had more boyfriends than I can count, and each and every time it never worked out for me. They were all the same type of guy for me, Hyperborean avatar, blonde or brown hair and green or blue eyes, but they were never able to stay with me for more than a couple months at a time. I was too much of a woman for them, apparently. I've been single ever since, and I've been absolutely loving it. And by the way, who is that weirdo at the end of the car creeping on us?" Takada explained, pointing at a man sitting at the end of the car reading a tablet. He was pretending to not show interest in the conversation, but Takada and Haruna could tell he was listening.

"Gee, I wonder why guys couldn't stand you," Munraito groaned.

"Seriously, what does he think he's getting away with, reading that tablet and pretending to not be listening to our conversations? That is so lame," Haruna remarked, made slightly uncomfortable by the man's eavesdropping.

"As a matter of fact, I think I recognize him! I know what you're up to, James Cartwright!" Takada yelled, her face taking on an expression of rage.

"Takada, fancy seeing you here," James groaned.

"Why have you been stalking me these past few weeks? I saw you outside the store where I was trying on swimsuits, for Heaven's sakes! We were never friends in high school, you never had a chance with me, grow the hell up already!" Takada exclaimed, making a scene on the train.

"Excuse me, but I think being a celebrity damaged your brain. I am not 'stalking' you, if that's what you think, and I think you're just paranoid as hell that someone is going to find you and reveal some very unsettling details about you," James replied, very ominously.

"WHAT, what the hell do you know?! Who's helping you! I should get up and crush you like an insect right now!" Takada screamed, startling some of the other passengers aboard the train.

"No need to get hostile, I'm just reading the news. I hear you just came from Oumi," James spoke, perfectly calm and collected.

"See?! You are a stalker! How could you possibly have known we were on Oumi!?" Takada shouted, getting irater by the second.

"Ai, calm down, I don't think this man is a stalker," Munraito said, trying to calm Takada down.

"I do believe he knows more than he is telling us, however," Munraito continued.

"You there, James Cartwright, how did you know we were on Oumi?" Munraito asked, politely.

"I had heard from someone else on the colony. It's kind of difficult to miss the Astari Troika and the Elohim Queen. From what I've seen from the live updates, the space battle's over. The Defenders and the Republic cruiser Hannibal successfully repelled the invaders, destroying three of the four ships. However, the largest one got away, but not before the Defenders pulled some incredible information from it. The ships they were using were man-made, except they were unlike any vehicles used by the Republic. The ships had a combination of ancient Egyptian hieroglyphs, Cuneiform writing and ancient Norse runes written on them, indicating that the ancient Norse, Egyptians, Sumerians and Indo-Aryans were the original builders of this technology, but how?" James wondered.

"Should we tell him?" Haruna asked Munraito.

"No. He's lying. He knows already, he's just not telling us," Munraito whispered to Haruna.

Takada was listening in on Munraito and Haruna's conversation, trying to gauge what James was up to.

"Very well then, have a good day," Munraito concluded.

James promptly stood up and walked out of the train car, back through the sliding door.

"Well Takada, he's not a stalker, but he definitely knows more about us than I'd like, and far more than he was willing to tell us," Munraito assessed.

"Oh, I know how to fix that," Takada replied, with a very evil-looking smirk on her face.

"James and I go all the way back to high school, before I even had the Hyperborean avatar body I have now, and he was a creep even then. Second chances don't matter. People never change. I do not forgive, especially people like him. He had better pray he never sees me again, otherwise I may not be able to restrain myself," Takada threatened.

"Ai, I think you have serious anger issues," Munraito said.

"Really, Munraito, I have anger issues? No, I don't have anger issues, you have pacifism issues. Everything in this life is a battle. If you want to win, you must fight. That is something you will never understand as a Lightbringer," Takada lectured, condescendingly.

"Oh, I'm the one with the problem for not getting angry and wanting to fight with everyone? It is my job to assist any citizens of the Republic in any way I can, and just because you have reached celebrity status does not mean you are a perfect, flawless person. Oh, and by the way, you know nothing of what my Order is capable of in battle, literally nothing of what we do. So please, stop talking about something you know nothing about," Munraito responded, quickly correcting Takada's behavior.

"Ok then...I never claimed I was, and I'd really appreciate if you stopped right now, if you know what's good for you," Takada snapped, quickly losing her patience.

"Enough," Haruna dictated, sternly.

"You both have some issues, honestly. Munraito, you can't fix everyone's problems, I'm sorry, but you can't do it. It's just not possible. Ai, Munraito-kun is right. You really need to do something about that anger issue. Now, we're almost at my apartment, and we're going to be getting off the train soon. I expect both of you to get along over the next few days," Haruna said, trying to be the voice of reason between Takada and Munraito.

"I guess you're right...I don't know why I even bother sometimes," Munraito groaned, looking at Takada.

"Hey, why are you looking at me like that, you think I'm the source of the dysfunction!? You really are the most arrogant son of a bitch in the galaxy, do you know that? Just look at you, sitting there ignoring me with that sick smirk on your face, I should rip that right off with my bare hands! UGHHH! The reason why I have an anger problem is because of people like YOU. I hope somebody fucking shoots you in the head, you arrogant little snotbag," Takada shouted at Munraito.

"Ok then, time to get off the train..." Haruna said, cheerfully, trying to distract from Munraito and Takada.

The train came to a stop near the apartment complex, which overlooked a waterfall cascading down into a fountain at the end of a street. The space colony was truly vast, and life there was nearly indistinguishable from life on a planet. Haruna's apartment complex was situated in one of the more upscale neighborhoods. Her aunt and uncle had set her up in one of the most pristine apartment complexes on the colony, and the Starlight Division was home to many very wealthy people living in the 3,000 square-foot apartments, with Haruna occupying Apartment 127 in block A-12.

As Haruna led the group off the train and through the train station, they passed by several other people looking at an electronic sign displayed on the wall.

"What are those people looking at?" Munraito grumbled, trying to catch a glimpse of the sign.

"Oh my gosh, is it really that time already?" Haruna said, excitedly.

"It's almost time for the Festival of Lights, it happens every year on New Berlin to celebrate the coming of spring!" Haruna cheered, like a little girl on Christmas morning.

"There's a spring festival here?" Munraito asked, quietly.

"It's probably nothing like the festival on Oumi that I just gave the invocation at less than two days ago," Munraito continued.

"You're right, Munraito-kun, it's nothing like Sakura Matsuri. It's brilliant, dazzling, wonderful and happy all at once, and there's no bugs biting you, no threat of bad weather and not a care in the world, oh my God, it is going to be so much fun doing this with you!" Haruna continued, ecstatically.

"Wow Haruna, you certainly seem enthusiastic about this," Munraito remarked.

"Forgive me, but this is my favorite time of year on the space colony and I still act like a small child when it comes," Haruna joked.

"It's perfectly all right. Let's go inside and get ready," Munraito replied.

"Oh, the festival isn't tonight. It's tomorrow night. We still have important work to do here on station regarding the Sangresaara's recent attempts to contact us. Let's go into the apartment. We'll discuss it further from there," Haruna explained, leading the group into the apartment lobby.

"That festival does sound fun. It seems like a great way to meet my fans and promote my brand," Takada thought, calming down from earlier.

"Welcome back, Haruna. I see your group is still in order, with an additional face," the AI personality acting as a receptionist said, looking at Munraito.

"Yes. I am here with Haruna to further her development as a young woman and in her mission," Munraito replied, confidently.

"Oh, how sweet, you make the cutest couple. I'll unlock the apartment for you," the AI personality responded, activating a few switches and unlocking Haruna's apartment.

"Enjoy your day," the AI personality said as Munraito and Haruna led the small crowd of individuals traveling with them into the elevator. Takada, Gwenlynn, Koda, Sei, her Elohim guards, the Troika and Munraito and Haruna crammed into the elevator and pressed the button for the 15th floor. Obviously, having so many individuals crammed into an elevator was less than comfortable.

"Well, this is awkward," Munraito said, sandwiched between Takada and Gwenlynn.

"Oh, lighten up, Munraito. Most men would kill to be in your position right now," Takada joked.

"Well, Gwenlynn's outfit is kind of fuzzy and warm," Munraito remarked.

"That's because I'm always cold. I dress warmly all the time," Gwenlynn replied.

"Takada, your outfit leaves very little to the imagination, and my face is pressing up against your belly. This is really uncomfortable for me," Munraito said, awkwardly.

"Why? Do I make you uncomfortable? Are you attracted to me? Is that the reason you've been such a jerk to me since you met me?" Takada asked, frankly.

"No. Not at all, you just annoy me," Munraito said, very unconvincingly.

"Oh...alright then, tell me when you're okay with telling me the truth, sometime when Haruna isn't around," Takada said, taunting Munraito.

"Excuse me, I'm standing right here!" Haruna protested.

"What are you trying to imply?!" Takada yelled.

"Ai, calm down, now, we can't keep bickering like this," Munraito interjected, trying to defuse Takada's explosive personality.

The elevator doors opened as the lift reached the 15th floor, into a long hallway lined with apartment doors.

"Alright, my apartment is at the end of the hallway. We're almost there," Haruna said, cheerfully.

The group made its way down the hallway past many other apartment doors before coming to door 127. Haruna simply opened the door after having it unlocked by the AI personality in the front lobby, revealing a deluxe apartment suite with an amazing view of the colony outside the windows. The ceilings were more than 12 feet high, creating a very wide, open atmosphere.

"Wow...this place is amazing," Munraito said, looking around.

"Yep, this is where I live," Haruna said, sitting down on the queen-sized bed.

"Denise, show my guests the itinerary for tonight," Haruna asked.

In an instant, a computerized voice echoed throughout the apartment. 'Denise' was Haruna's home AI, and it quickly showed a holographic image of Haruna's schedule for the night ahead on the apartment wall, which contained thousands of intelligent smartchips.

"Haruna, do you seriously have a schedule for everything?" Munraito asked.

"I already told you this on Oumi, yes, I do." Haruna responded.

"Don't you think that's a little obsessive?" Munraito continued

"No, absolutely not, I'm a very organized person," Haruna replied.

Munraito looked at the list of things Haruna wanted to accomplish between now and going to bed, and the list was a long one, to say the least.

"You aren't going to make us stay up and do all this with you, are you?" Takada asked, still a bit annoyed.

"Oh no, this is just work for me. We may have to leave for Shinaeal by morning, however. Warmaster Lumen Ash is getting a bit jittery, according to the Republic Department of State. Something is definitely disturbing him and the rest of the Sangresaara empire, and I don't think it's the usual grievances the Sangresaara have against humans," Haruna explained.

"What would those be, I'm not exactly well-versed in exopolitics," Takada asked.

"Well, the Sangresaara, also referred to by many humans as the Reptiloids, are a very ancient race that evolved more than a billion years ago on a planet in the Orion Nebula called Aldebaran II, orbiting a star much like our own Sun on Earth, called Aldebaran. The Sangresaara lived on Aldebaran for millions of years, until their Sun began to age and make the conditions on Aldebaran far too hot to support life, which forced them to colonize the stars and search for other Earth-like planets. Over the past 10 million years they have colonized the entire Orion Spur of the Milky Way Galaxy and absorbed multiple races of extraterrestrials into their society. However, the bone of contention between the Sangresaara and the Republic, the Elohim and the Astari is ownership of Earth, as the Sangresaara claim that they found the Earth first and that Earth rightfully belongs to them. The Elohim, Republic and Astari claim the same thing, and this dispute between the interstellar superpowers has brought the galaxy to the brink of war on many occasions, something that Lumen Ash still refuses to back down from. The entire purpose of my mission is to iron out these differences and bring the Sangresaara to some form of agreement on terms with the Republic and its allies. A blueprint for a deal was worked out only a few weeks ago, but this continuation of Sangresaara uneasiness about the whole thing is what strikes me as strange. I'll conduct some further communications with the State Department on Earth and Stronghold," Haruna explained.

"Ok, you do that Haruna. I'll be in the other bedroom meditating. Feel free to join me if you wish," Munraito replied, getting up from the bed and walking into the other room, kissing her forehead.

Munraito entered the guest bedroom and closed the door, standing in the utter silence...it was perfect. Munraito closed his eyes, letting his black hair cover his left eye and immediately became immersed in thought. his primary goal was protecting Haruna at all costs, and out of all the people he had met that day, no one struck him as more suspicious than that strange man Takada said she knew from high school, James Cartwright.

"James Cartwright...this is very interesting, very interesting indeed," Munraito thought to himself.

"Denise," Munraito asked.

"Yes, Munraito, what can I assist you with?" The AI's voice responded.

"Search the GalaxyNet for the name James Cartwright," Munraito ordered.

"Is he a friend of yours?" Denise asked.

"Not exactly, he's a man I met on the train over here, Takada said she knew him from high school and wasn't too fond of him. I just want to know more about him," Munraito responded.

"Ooh, a mystery. I'm searching right now," Denise affirmed.

"Wow...there's a lot on him. He was born on Arcana II more than 40 years ago, and uses a standard avatar body. However, he has a rather shady past over the past two decades. The records indicate that he was pursuing a career in archeology when he mysteriously quit his job and became an interstellar vagabond, traveling from planet to planet, as if he was looking for something. He seems like a very interesting character," Denise revealed.

"Yes, and a very suspicious one as well. In case you haven't realized, Denise, my homeworld of Oumi has suffered a rash of attacks by a group of individuals using ancient technology. I fear that James may be somehow involved," Munraito explained.

"You really think so?" Denise asked.

"Yes, Denise. Now, if you'll excuse me, I require complete silence for what I am about to do," Munraito requested.

"All right then," Denise replied.

Denise deactivated and left Munraito in peace, who promptly sat on the bed and closed his eyes. Entering Hyperspace Meditation, his consciousness streamed out into the quantum field across space and time, permeating every corner, every thought and every mind on the New

Berlin Space Colony. Munraito was reading every thought and every

conversation being made on the entire colony...for a few minutes,

Munraito pored through the data he was collecting, and immediately

pinpointed James, sitting in his apartment on the opposite end of the

colony. He was sitting at a desk, surfing the GalaxyNet. Immediately,

Munraito looked through James' eyes and watched the same screen he

was looking at.

"Perfect," Munraito thought.

The GalaxyNet page was a site dedicated to an organization called

"Societas Polyphilae," which was, on paper, an independent archeological

society dedicated to uncovering the mysteries of human antiquity, like the

work that Gwenlynn was doing for the Republic. However, the site

contained particularly inappropriate and distracting content for a

scholarly organization. Interspersed with some of the organizations

findings were disturbing, bizarre images such as a medieval knight fighting

a giant snail, strange, demonic creatures torturing women in sickening

ways, killer rabbits chopping people's heads off with knives and a man

viciously attacking a butterfly with a plasma caster. Munraito recognized

many of the images as being from an ancient religious text written in the

13th century, a text that many had claimed was written while the author was under demonic possession.

Munraito didn't see this as that suspicious, as there were many scholarly organizations that specialized in different areas of human history. However, Munraito had never heard of the Societas Polyphilae before, and it was worth investigating further, to say the least. Munraito exited the Hyperspace trance and recalled Denise into the room.

"Denise, look up the Societas Polyphilae. I believe James Cartwright may be a member of this organization," Munraito directed.

"Coming right up, I'm fetching the information now," Denise said, searching the GalaxyNet for all available data on this bizarre group of people.

"All right, here they are. It doesn't seem very suspicious to me, Munraito. It looks like it's an organization dedicated to studying ancient technology," Denise explained.

"That is precisely why I believe we should investigate it further. The attacks on Oumi were made using ancient technology, apparently built by people related to the ancient Egyptians, Sumerians and Norse. If this society knows something about the attacks on Oumi, I believe it is worth pursuing. Denise, I need to find James Cartwright, and fast. Thank you for the assistance, Denise. I will return shortly," Munraito responded, standing up and walking back into the room with all the others.

"Koda, come with me. There's something we need to do. Lightbringer business, don't mind us. Haruna, we will be back shortly," Munraito reassured to the others as Koda stood up and took his Master's side.

Munraito and Koda walked out of the apartment without a word, leaving the others with confused looks on their faces.

As Munraito and Koda walked down the hallway towards the elevator, Munraito briefed Koda on the situation.

"Koda, I found some interesting details on that man we met on the train earlier, James Cartwright. He's a member of an organization called the Societas Polyphilae, and I believe that they are somehow involved with the attacks on Oumi. We need to find him and get him to tell us what he knows...by any means necessary. Takada was right about him. I have the distinct feeling that this man is a creep, to say the least," Munraito explained, stepping into the elevator.

"Munraito-san, we have no weapons. What if he's armed?" Koda asked.

"We have the Talisman of Uehara. That is more than enough," Munraito reassured, with a very stern tone in his voice.

"I'm sure Takada will be pleased with us for dealing with him," Koda responded.

"I do not care what Takada thinks. She is the source of all dysfunction in our group and if it were up to me, I would cut her off like a gangrenous limb. We cannot focus on that now. We need to move, and fast," Munraito ordered as the elevator reached the bottom of the shaft, and the doors opened. To their immediate shock, there was James Cartwright, standing in front of the elevator, holding a pulse rifle.

"Why hello there good sir, how are you doing today?!" Munraito said, promptly raising his hand and sending James careening backwards into the wall with a telekinetic push from the Universal Energy.

Munraito and Koda ran over to James, crumpled on the floor.

"Why did you just try to kill us? Please, tell us," Munraito ordered.

"Idiots...the Countess ordered it. The Lightbringers are the mortal enemies of our goals..." James sputtered.

"A Countess, eh, who is that?!" Koda yelled, grabbing the pulse rifle and pressing it to James' head.

"She is...beyond your comprehension. She is the Departed God...and the supreme enemy of the Republic. We are her soldiers, and we will not stop until her goals are realized...she's building a dark army to hunt you down, Lightbringers. You cannot stop her...only the Man against Time can. She is trans-dimensional and all powerful. You can't do shit against her," James gagged.

"Was she responsible for the attacks on Oumi?" Munraito asked, using intense mental pressure to coerce the truth from James.

"Yes, she was, and there will be more, I can assure you of that. You haven't seen anything yet. You're all dead. Every last one of you, the time of her ascendancy is near. Our numbers will darken the skies of every world in the galaxy," James gloated. Koda had heard enough. He grabbed the pulse rifle and fired three rounds of plasma directly into James' cranium, killing him instantly.

Just then, two Republic security officers came rushing into the lobby after hearing the commotion, finding Koda holding the rifle in his hands.

"Put your hands in the air, now! Drop the weapon!" The two police officers screamed, pointing their pistols at Koda.

"Officers, this man tried to kill us. We're Lightbringers." Koda responded in his own defense.

The two police officers lowered their weapons.

"Alright...do you mind telling us what happened here?" the officers asked.

"This man, James Cartwright, was employed by the terrorist organization known only as Societas Polyphilae. He tried to kill us as we stepped out of the elevator. Coincidentally, we were actually on our way to apprehend him when the attack happened. He must have known we were coming for him, which means there are probably others on this colony affiliated with the terrorist group as well. He called the Lightbringers a mortal enemy of his organization's goals, and he claimed that the attacks on Oumi and the corrupt police officers were the responsibility of the group's leader, an individual that was only identified as the Countess. He said there was much worse to come as well," Munraito explained.

"Really...that's bad news. If there are terrorists on station, then they might be planning to attack the festival in a few days. We need to be ready for anything," the police officer responded.

"We need to contact the Republic for assistance. Whoever this Countess is, she's after us specifically. If this colony is attacked, we are utterly defenseless," Munraito warned.

"You do know what this means, right?" the police officers asked, somberly.

"Yes. Officer, we are preparing for war," Munraito replied.

"You're right, Master Lightbringer. The Republic must be warned. I will request a fleet escort for the space colony until after the upcoming festival is complete. This threat will be broadcast on the GalaxyNet news channels tomorrow morning. Thank you for your service, Master Lightbringer. Sorry about pulling our weapons on you," the officer apologized.

"It's all right. Keep up the good work," Munraito encouraged.

Just then, Takada, Sei and Gwenlynn stepped out of the elevator and encountered Munraito, Koda, the limp body of James Cartwright and the two police officers.

"Munraito, what happened, I sensed a commotion down here...is that the man we saw on the train?" Sei asked, seeing James' body lying on the ground.

"Yes, unfortunately it is. Takada, you were right after all. That man James was more than a stalker, he was a terrorist, a member of the organization known as Societas Polyphilae. We believe they are planning an attack on the space colony, probably coinciding with the Festival tomorrow night," Munraito explained.

"Excuse me...what organization did you say he was part of?" Takada asked, a tone of concern in her voice.

"Societas Polyphilae. They use archeology as a front for their real purpose. They are not just responsible for this; they are responsible for the ongoing Oumi crisis as well. Just before Koda shot him, he said something about a Countess being responsible for the corrupt police officers and Haruna's parents' murder," Munraito confirmed.

"Oh...dear Lord..." Takada said to herself.

"I know who this 'Countess' is, and I also know what this organization is, as well. I just never thought she would ever take it this far," Takada sighed.

"What in the name of...You know this woman?!" Munraito shouted.

"Know her? I went to high school with her! Her name is Toni, Toni Medici-Feccheira, she's a lot like me, just considerably crazier and more violent. She's also a master at Hyperspace Meditation and interdimensional channeling, able to use her Hyperborean Avatar body to bend space-time and summon beings from other dimensions and universes to do her dirty work. She is one of the acting royals of Serenna, and extraordinarily powerful and influential as well," Takada explained.

"That's bad. James told me that she can do those things, she is the Departed God that we have been looking for. The good news is that we know who the enemy is now, and we know someone who knows the enemy personally: you, Takada," Munraito responded.

"Well, well, well...you've certainly changed your tune," Takada mused, smiling.

"At first, you couldn't stand me, but the moment I have information that could be of use to you, you start treating me nicer. You are probably the most Machiavellian individual I have ever met...fortunately for you, I like that in a man," Takada whispered.

"However, Toni is a very dangerous, unpredictable individual. There are a lot of very sick rumors about her and what she does to people, and I honestly wouldn't doubt that any of those are true. She will not be an easy enemy to defeat," Takada warned.

"I think Koda and I can handle it," Munraito replied, confidently.

"All right then, just don't say I didn't warn you..." Takada cautioned.

"If she's after you, then you have an extremely dangerous enemy. Even I never suspected that she'd go this far," Takada advised.

"Can you tell me a little about her?" Munraito asked.

"Yes, I can. Let's just go back up to Haruna's apartment. We will be safer there," Takada instructed.

Munraito, Koda and the others boarded the elevator and promptly returned to Haruna's apartment, knowing very well what might happen in the next 24 standard hours. All Munraito could hope is that the Republic forces arrived in a timely manner, because if Countess Toni was as brutal as Takada said she was, the New Berlin Space Colony didn't have a chance.

"Countess Toni is more than a mere woman. She is, indeed, a god among men. She is a master of Hyperspace Meditation, interdimensional channeling, molecular manipulation, and many, many other profound feats of technology and energy weilding. She has become one of the most powerful individuals in the galaxy by her mastery of these abilities, and these are only matched by her cunning, intelligence and iron will. Her organization, Societas Polyphilae, is built from most of her followers that she had from her high school and university days...a bit of history, if you don't mind," Takada began.

I went to a very prestigious high school on Arcana II, where Toni and I were among the most powerful and respected individuals in the school. We were both interested in some of the same things, but Toni's personality was even more ambitious, and many would say more sinister. After our junior year at school, Toni began researching ancient history, namely the histories of Ancient Egypt, the Harrapan civilization, the ancient Norse and the ancient Sumerians, and began making claims that these societies possessed highly advanced technologies, far in excess of anything the Republic used. She presented evidence to her friends and many admirers, and used her family's fortune to organize expeditions to locate these technologies on Earth and various other Republic worlds while she attended University. She sent her many followers on these expeditions, paying them hefty sums of money to do so. It was at University that she perfected her manipulation and Hyperspace Meditation techniques, as well as attained her Hyperborean Avatar body, which some would consider the most fantastic in the galaxy. Apparently, she must have found the ancient technology that she had long suspected existed, and she has now set her sights on the biggest prize of all...the Republic itself. However, the Defenders and the might of the Republic Navy and its allies presents a formidable obstacle to her ambitions. Knowing her, however, she'll find a way around it," Takada explained, as they made their way back to the apartment.

"Wow...that does sound imposing. What sorts of technologies are we up against if Countess Toni does have access to this hardware?" Munraito asked.

"Oh, this technology is among the most advanced in the entire galaxy. The good news is that the Republic warships seemed to hold their own against it during the skirmish over Oumi, however, the damage to the Hannibal was significant. The ship, according to the GalaxyNet news, is currently being assessed after the attack on Oumi," Takada replied.

Just then, Munraito had a revelation.

"You knew this all along, didn't you? That's why you joined Haruna's mission, just so that you could get a better idea on what your old high school rival was up to!" Munraito accused.

"So you finally figured it out," Takada said, smugly.

"You are correct. The only reason I'm here is because I knew what was about to happen on Oumi, and who was responsible for it, however, you were so determined to solve the crisis yourself that you didn't bother to seek my help when you had the chance, Munraito. So, let's stop bickering and agree to work together already," Takada reminded.

Munraito looked at Takada with a disgusted look on his face. She was unbelievable. She knew that Toni was responsible for everything that had happened on Oumi over the past 14 years but had said nothing, simply because she believed that Countess Toni was her battle and nobody else's. She felt that even if it meant that people had to die for her to play the hero, it was worth all the suffering and death. However, Takada was now Munraito's only real chance at stopping Countess Toni's ambitions, ambitions that would soon strike again, possibly on the very same space colony where they now stood.

"Well, there's not much we can do for the rest of the night. The colony's going to switch off the lights soon to simulate nighttime and keep our circadian rhythms in working order. Let's get ready for bed. We've got a big day tomorrow," Haruna reminded, deciding the sleeping arrangements for everyone.

"Haruna, who knows if we'll be going anywhere tomorrow? We were just attacked by terrorists on station, the colony may be put on lockdown," Munraito responded.

"If so, we'll cross that bridge when we get to it. For now, let's just assume our plans for tomorrow will hold up," Haruna replied, preparing the bed for the night.

"Alright everyone, Munraito-kun is sleeping with me, and everyone else can have the guest rooms and couches. I'm sorry I don't have beds for everyone. We're just going to have to make this work," Haruna said, already changed into her sleeping attire, which consisted of a set of red silk pajamas that looked very warm.

"You're right. It is getting late." Takada responded, yawning.

Just then the huge lights that simulated the light of the Sun slowly began to dim, creating an artificial sunset that played out over the course of about 30 seconds before the colony became immersed in darkness, letting the vast panorama of space shine in across New Berlin. The city lights winked on, as a brilliant beacon in the vast abyss of space-time. The colony had exited warp space by this point, and was now approaching a Republic colony world called Amane in the Cygnus Constellation, about 156 light-years from Earth. The world was a pale, blue-green sphere with two silver moons; a world completely covered in water, with huge floating cities built on the vast global ocean. Only a few small islands, the peaks of the tallest underwater mountains, protruded from the surface of the ocean, each island with its own unique wildlife. Amane was known as one of the most diverse planets in the Republic, thanks to its oceans and the extreme isolation of all of its land-dwelling creatures. Looking at the day-lit side of the planet, there were several enormous space stations orbiting the world, with several Republic Navy warships in orbit, including 4 destroyers, 6 heavy cruisers, 3 frigates, 2 massive assault ships and one enormous supercarrier, the UHR Agincourt.

"Well, that's certainly reassuring. It's going to be difficult for Countess Toni to penetrate those defenses, for sure," Munraito observed.

"Why are there so many ships here?" Munraito asked.

"Amane is a critical world to the Republic, as the floating cities contain processing plants for the Republic's supplies of healing gel, a substance used to heal wounds effortlessly without leaving any scars. Countess Toni would have to be extremely bold or extremely foolish to attack here," Haruna said, getting into bed.

"We'll go down to the surface tomorrow. I have been here before. I'll show you around," Haruna offered.

Munraito and Haruna climbed into bed and pulled the blankets over themselves, as everyone else prepared for a good night's rest. Sei Ikkiku and her Elohim guards did not need sleep, their artificial bodies were far more advanced than humanity's. Sei and her three guards simply digitized themselves and became small orbs of light, surrounded by small metallic plates, spinning around the light like electrons orbiting the nucleus of an atom. They would remain on watch throughout the night for any signs of terrorist activity, a welcome advantage that they had over their adversaries. The Elohim were not a group that was easily challenged. Munraito turned out the lights and closed his eyes, letting the dull white light emanating from the Elohim' digitized forms illuminate the apartment. It was a nervous time for everyone, however. Munraito was confident that he held the upper hand with his group of allies in hand.

Somehow he knew that he was about to find out far more than he bargained for.

5. The Gathering Storm

"Rise and shine everyone! Wake up, out of bed, let's get ready for the day!" Haruna announced, awake before everyone else. Gwenlynn was already awake, and had changed into a new, far less gaudy outfit, but Takada wanted to sleep in and grumbled slightly when Haruna tried to wake her up. Munraito climbed out of bed and looked out the window at the rest of the space colony, and out at the stars on the far end of the city. Munraito noticed that three additional Republic heavy cruisers had arrived to escort the space colony in response to the terrorist threats. The Olympus-class heavy cruisers used by the Republic were truly massive warships, each more than three kilometers long and armed with some of the most lethal weaponry in the galaxy. However, even these ships were smaller than the Infinity-class assault ships and the Ares-class supercarriers, both of which were present at Amane. Amane was a a critical world for the government located in the Republic's Deep Core, thanks to its production of healing gel.

"We are just surrounded by military hardware out here...look, that's the Hannibal, the ship that repelled the attack on Oumi, I guess it wasn't that badly damaged after all," Haruna observed.

"I doubted it. Those ships are a mixture of human and Naruhol Ihr technology reverse-engineered during the war. No man-made technology could possibly defeat those ships on their own," Munraito responded.

"Well, I certainly feel safer now, to say the least," Haruna sighed, relieved by the presence of the Republic.

Just then, a message came over the colony's PA system, stating that contingents of Republic Marines and Defender fireteams would be boarding the colony to deter terrorist attacks at the upcoming Spring Festival, because of the threats facing the colony.

"Maybe Fireteams Isis and Odin will be here again," Munraito wondered.

"They probably will, they're stationed aboard the Hannibal, right?" Haruna asked.

"Yes, they are, and they have first-hand experience at fighting the Societas Polyphilae from the crisis on Oumi," Munraito replied.

Haruna and Munraito had witnessed what the Defenders were capable of after watching them in combat on Oumi, first during the police uprising, and again during the discovery of the ancient technology under Muranahe. Their 'super' abilities were some of the most powerful weapons in the galaxy, and a major reason why the Republic won the war against the Naruhol Ihr. Now, the Defenders were bringing those abilities to bear on the Societas Polyphilae, possibly the biggest threat the Republic faced since the end of the war.

Munraito turned and walked towards the door to Haruna's apartment, calling Koda to his side.

"Haruna, we need to go. We have business we need to take care of. Stay here, you'll be safe here," Munraito directed, stepping towards the door.

"Koda, come with me," Munraito instructed.

Koda stood up and took his Master's side, opening the door and walking out into the hallway.

"Munraito-san, where are we going?" Koda asked.

"We're going to meet with Fireteam Isis about their encounter with the Societas Polyphilae soldiers. I'd like to know what their forces are capable of," Munraito replied.

"Where are they?" Koda asked, curious as to where they would find these individuals aboard a huge space colony.

"We're going to the main hangar bay again. Fireteam Isis is aboard the heavy cruiser Hannibal. I'm certain they will be open to working with us again," Munraito concluded.

"With all due respect, Munraito-san, I've seen enough combat to last a lifetime after our experience underneath Muranahe, and I cannot stomach the thought of fighting with them again," Koda complained.

"Koda, we will not go through this exercise again. Sometimes to protect, you must fight. This is for Haruna's safety. I hope you remember how to use a firearm," Munraito instructed, sternly.

As Munraito and Koda reached the bottom of the elevator, they checked the lobby carefully, making sure no one was waiting for them. Satisfied with the scene, they exited the apartment complex and walked towards the monorail station, past crowds of people going about their daily activities. Most of the people seemed aware that a threat to the colony existed, but they felt that the Republic military presence was enough to deter any sort of attack. The first few companies of Republic Marines were arriving in the colony's main hangar, and were working with the Republic Security Forces to try and hunt down any embedded terrorists on station. The Spring Festival was later that night, and the Republic was preparing for any eventuality in case Societas Polyphilae decided to make its presence known.

Munraito and Koda boarded the monorail at the station, bound for the main hangar bay, where the Republic troops were unloading military hardware onto the space colony. Munraito hoped that he would be able to intercept Fireteam Isis as they disembarked the Hannibal. He had to gather as much information on his enemies as he could if the possibility existed that they would attack.

"You seem nervous...calm yourself. Nothing is going to happen that we can't handle," Munraito said, reassuring Koda.

"Munraito-san, how do you know that? You heard Takada back in the apartment, what if Countess Toni really is as dangerous as Takada says she is? She may have weapons that we might not even be able to conceive of, never mind fight against. What makes you think that the Talisman of Uehara will be enough?" Koda asked, worried.

"Koda, do you not trust the wisdom and faith of our forebears, those that settled Oumi and brought the Heaven's Gate Galaxy under Republic control? This Talisman is imbued with the collective wisdom and power of a million lifetimes of Lightbringers and their disciples. it is the greatest single force in the entire Universe, and I am its sole possessor. I am the one thing in this Universe that stands as a match for Countess Toni and her organization, which is why she seeks to destroy the Order of Lightbringers. I am a righteous, holy man, anointed by the Radiant Sun, the Book of the Laws and the Holy Light of Purity. I am the Sixth Moon, the Morning and the Evening Star, anointed directly by Uehara to judge the wicked and the righteous. Why should I not destroy my enemies? The Radiant Sun is Light and Wisdom, whereas our enemies are darkness and ignorance," Munraito recited.

"Munraito-san, sometimes I think your faith blinds you to reality," Koda responded.

Munraito said nothing, and continued to face forward as the train sped towards the main hangar bay.

As the train continued towards the hangar, Munraito noticed a growing number of Republic soldiers on station, from all three branches of the military, the Army, Navy and Marines.

"It seems like the Republic is leaving nothing to chance on this...New Berlin is just too big a target," Koda remarked.

"That's good to see...apparently the Republic takes the threat as seriously as we do," Munraito responded.

As the train approached the station near the main hangar bay, the doors opened into a crowd of ordinary citizens and Republic military forces, including several Marines in full armor, carrying heavy plasma carbines.

"Don't mind us, Lightbringers. We're just doing our job," one of the Marines said to Koda, who seemed alarmed at the soldier's huge gun. Koda and Munraito said nothing as they stepped off the train and made their way through the crowd, past the lines of shops on the main avenue and towards the massive bay windows overlooking the main hangar. Sure enough, on the hangar floor far below, he spotted Fireteams Isis and Odin, gathered around a contingent of Navy personnel from one of the heavy cruisers, presumably the Hannibal. The Defenders were part of their own independent Order, but one that was directly under the control of Republic Senate. During times of war, however, the Defenders traditionally served as Generals, in addition to the commissioned officers within the Republic military.

Munraito and Koda stepped into the elevator to the hangar floor to meet with the Defenders once more, hopefully to learn more about Countess Toni and her organization from those who had experience fighting against them. As the elevator reached the bottom of the shaft, Munraito and Koda signaled to the Defenders that they were there and ready to assist.

"Oh, so we meet again, Master Lightbringer," Alnair greeted, from behind his helmet's white face mask.

"So it seems. What can you tell me about Societas Polyphilae?" Munraito asked, his Talisman of Uehara glowing radiantly.

"A pressing subject that is, as we have only limited experience fighting them, but the intel we gathered at Oumi was extraordinarily revealing to the organization. They are a paramilitary group using ancient technology that we didn't even know existed, we had all heard the rumors and the conspiracy theories about civilizations like Ancient China, Mohenjo-Daro, Egypt, Sumeria, the Norse and others, but we never dreamed that those rumors would turn out to be true. Never did we anticipate that we'd have to face the might of those ancient Empires on a modern battlefield. Societas Polyphilae seeks to revive the glory of those ancient societies under a unified government, ruled by Countess Toni and the Cult of Mithras, which we believe is a revival of an ancient pagan religion practiced in ancient Rome and other authoritarian societies. Her beliefs revolve around sexual catharsis and liberation, and her followers perform various, hideously depraved acts in various locations across the galaxy. However, for all their power, we know that they can be beaten," Alnair explained.

"So I've heard. From what I understand, Countess Toni attacked Oumi because she believes the Lightbringers are a threat to her...she believes that the Man against Time and the Lightbringers are somehow connected," Munraito replied.

"That cannot be right...the Lightbringers are pragmatic bearers of power, not reckless terrorists. They would never commit such acts of wanton murder and destruction," Alnair believed, the rest of his Fireteam assembling behind him.

"For many centuries have I defended the Republic with honor and distinction. I have watched the Order of the Defenders rise into full flower under my careful guidance. It was our intervention alone that stopped the Naruhol Ihr in their tracks, and these miscreants shall not trouble us for long," Alnair reassured.

"He's right. Alnair is a living legend, one of the Republic's greatest heroes. His team of three other Defenders, Josephine the Indomitable, Frederic the Radiant, and Lucian the Moonraiser bear the strongest Light of us all, and they continue to shine it into the darkness, wherever it may creep into our lives," Starhunter said, holding his rifle.

"Alnair was one of the only humans that the Naruhol Ihr truly feared," Starhunter added.

"Interesting...you'll have to tell me about your exploits on the battlefield at a better time, because there's work to do. We need to find out as much about Societas Polyphilae as we can. I know a few things about Countess Toni that you probably don't. One of my companions was a high school classmate of hers...Ai Takada," Munraito informed.

"Wait...Takada is with you?" Alnair asked.

"Yes she is," Munraito affirmed.

"Take us to her. If she knows anything about Countess Toni, we can gain an advantage over our enemies before they have a chance to strike,"Alnair instructed, gathering Fireteam Odin and following Munraito and Koda back towards the elevator.

As the six of them climbed into the elevator, Munraito pressed the button taking them up to the main concourse, towards the monorail station.

"I have to warn you, Alnair, my companions will be a bit shocked to see a fully-armored and armed Defender fireteam entering the apartment, let alone Fireteam Odin, the Republic's greatest heroes during the war against the Naruhol Ihr," Munraito cautioned.

"Don't worry, we're used to it. We get the celebrity treatment everywhere we try to go, even when we're just trying to do our jobs," Alnair replied, holding his huge Bipolar Rifle in his hands. The Bipolar Rifle was a highly-advanced weapon designed from recovered Naruhol Ihr technology. Using a binary-charge plasma core to fire a tremendous beam of red-orange energy, it was capable of incinerating an enemy to burning cinders with a single shot. In addition to his Sorcerer abilities, Alnair could perform the impossible on the battlefield, something that even the Naruhol Ihr had no counter for. Sorcerers, focusing more on their telekinetic abilities in the

Universal Energy than brute strength and weapons skills, were the most esoteric of the three Defender classes, and Alnair had achieved the highest rank available for a Defender Sorcerer, the Stormwielder rank. Thanks to their abilities, Sorcerers learned marksmanship before anything else, and Alnair was probably the best shot in the entire Defender Order with the Bipolar Rifle. If anyone could stop Countess Toni, it was Fireteam Odin.

As Munraito and Koda led the squad onto the monorail, several bystanders stood on and gawked as Fireteam Odin walked past and boarded the train, following the two Lightbringers.

"The Lightbringers are here with Fireteam Odin, no way! We're going to be all right after all," some of the bystanders exclaimed as the train doors closed.

"Everyone here is very happy to see you and your squad, Alnair," Munraito observed.

"It's nothing new. People know our history; we bring a certain sense of security that nothing else can." Alnair responded.

As the train pulled away from the station, Fireteam Odin kept a close eye on the situation, both on the train and off it. Their weapons, armor, gear and equipment were some of the most sophisticated in the galaxy, and all of it helped enhance their natural abilities and talents. Everything from the helmets on their heads to the gauntlets on their hands was tailored to assist them with their missions, and no two loadouts were alike.

Frederic toyed with a combat knife as Alnair made sure his Bipolar Rifle was in perfect working order. The weapon was extremely powerful, but the technology was so sensitive that it needed to be maintained perfectly constantly, keeping the weapon ready for combat whenever it was needed.

Munraito observed the four Defenders as they watched the colony pass by the windows. Alnair was the only Sorcerer in the group, Frederic and Lucian were both Olympian-class Defenders, focusing on heavy armor, raw strength and skills with weapons before Universal Energy powers, and Josephine was a Sentinel-class, focusing on marksmanship, stealth and cunning in combat to dominate the enemy. All four of them had reached the pinnacle of their warrior classes, and had achieved some of the highest accolades in the Republic military, as well as the Order of Defenders.

In the Republic, the Defenders were more than soldiers. They considered themselves keepers of the peace in the galaxy, in the same echelon as the Elohim and Astari. They were cunning diplomats, skillful ambassadors, humanitarians and, above all, relentless warriors, yet they never considered themselves more than mere human beings. Alnair's fireteam was one of the most legendary in the galaxy, a force that all living beings respected and gravitated to. Even Munraito was a bit intimidated by their presence. Thanks to their helmets, they were the faceless, almighty guardians of peace.

"Are we almost there? I'm getting bored," Josephine groaned, holding her Overseer particle beam rifle in her hands.

"Master Lightbringer, I sincerely hope we arrive at our destination soon...Josephine has this...issue when she gets bored," Alnair cautioned.

"My trigger finger itches..." Josephine grumbled, ominously.

"She's not really going to shoot someone on the train, is she?" Koda asked.

"A lifetime of war causes some mild sociopathic tendencies, so I can't rule anything out," Alnair responded, nonchalantly.

Munraito felt panic rising in his chest as he silently prayed for the train to reach the apartment block soon...the thought of having four complete killing machines aboard the train just itching to shoot at something was disturbing, to say the least. Thankfully, the train arrived at the Starlight Division quickly.

"Alright, everyone off...here we are. Takada's right inside," Munraito said, stepping off the train with Fireteam Odin and Koda following close behind. Munraito signaled to the AI attendant at the front desk to unlock Haruna's apartment as the two Lightbringers and the Defenders stepped into the elevator.

"We're going up," Lucian said, pressing the button on the elevator.

"Haruna's going to be glad to see you again, Alnair," Munraito remarked.

"I figured as much," Alnair replied.

Munraito and Koda led the Defender team to Haruna's apartment and knocked on the door.

"Haruna, Takada, I have a few people that need to speak with you," Munraito said, politely.

Haruna opened the door and saw the four Defenders standing behind Munraito and Koda.

"Oh, ok...they're back. Takada, over here, Fireteam Odin wants to have a word with you about something," Haruna called.

Takada came walking over to Fireteam Odin, again wearing a very different, unique outfit. She liked to wear something unique every day. This outfit was less revealing, but every bit as exotic-looking as the one she had worn the day before.

"Oh, hello there, what can I do for the Republic's finest heroes?" Takada offered, with her usual tone.

"Do you have a personal history with Countess Toni-Medici Fecchiera?" Alnair inquired.

"Yes, I do. come in, I'll discuss it with you," Takada responded.

The four Defenders walked into the apartment, shouldering their weapons for the moment.

"Nice place..." Josephine complemented.

"Thank you." Haruna said, enthusiastically.

"Now, about this Countess...from the intel we have on her, she's a very dangerous character," Frederic told Takada.

"Yes, indeed...I was the only person she ever called a friend in high school. Other than the people that worshiped the very ground she walked on, I was the only one with any intimate knowledge of her 'inner enigma,' at least that's what she called it. We both had the same views on sex and sexuality, but she took her interests in a much darker, more extreme direction than I did. 'Polyphilae' means 'many loves,' but what she believes in is not love at all. It's about power and domination, the Darwinian struggle, the strong over the weak. She sees sex as a way to exert power and dominance over another, a highly unusual trait for a woman. Countess Toni is unlike any other woman you have ever encountered, and is probably more powerful than any enemy you have ever faced. Her abilities rival even yours, Alnair. If you plan on apprehending her, good luck...you're going to need it," Takada explained.

"That's bad news. When we fought the Societas at Oumi, their soldiers didn't look right. They were pale, grayish, and looked sick, almost possessed. They did not surrender, they did not show mercy and they did not flinch, even after taking multiple plasma rounds to the chest. It's almost as if they were machines, as well as the Architect constructs they use to fight as well," Alnair replied.

"Countess Toni has many strange, almost supernatural abilities...one of the most fantastic being interdimensional channeling," Takada added.

"If that's true, then she may have weapons that we might not even be able to conceive of. This situation could get very hairy very quickly if nothing is done to quickly secure the colony," Lucian cautioned.

"We may not even be able to fight against what she throws at us," Josephine added.

"That's where I come in..." Munraito interjected.

"The Talisman of Uehara is imbued with the wisdom and power of a million lifetimes of Lightbringers. What you cannot defeat, I certainly can," Munraito stated, placing his hand over the Talisman.

"Very well then, we will alert the rest of the fleet to the threat, and prepare for any eventuality here on station. In the meantime, we request that all of you remain on-station until this crisis has passed," Alnair replied.

"Looks like our plans just went out the window," Koda told Haruna.

"I guess so. I'll have to contact Earth and Stronghold that the mission has hit a slight delay, thanks to the ongoing Oumi Crisis," Haruna said, standing up and walking towards the communications console in the guest room.

"It's been a pleasure seeing you, Fireteam Odin. Now, if you'll excuse us, we have other matters to attend to," Munraito said, politely bidding Fireteam Odin adieu.

"Alright then, squad, our work here is done. Let's get moving," Alnair ordered, as Fireteam Odin stood up and walked towards the door to the apartment. As Fireteam Odin left, Takada mumbled something under her breath.

"What was that about, Ai?" Haruna probed.

"Nothing...it's just that this whole resurgence of Countess Toni has me a bit worried. I know her better than anyone in the galaxy, and I know that she'll stop at nothing to achieve her own ends," Takada responded.

"Well, in the meantime, we should get ready for the festival tonight," Haruna added.

"Haruna, you don't plan on actually going to that festival, do you? You just heard Fireteam Odin, it's extremely dangerous, given the threat level at this point." Munraito warned.

"Oh, calm down, Munraito-kun. Just because a threat exists doesn't mean we should stop living our lives like we normally do," Haruna explained.

"I guess...well, as long as I'm there, we should be safe," Munraito said.

"Besides, with the Republic fleet presence around Amane, this is one of the safest places in the galaxy for us right now," Haruna added.

"I guess you're right..." Munraito worried.

"The Festival is in Center City tonight, the center of New Berlin. We should get there at around 7:00 P.M Galactic Standard Time if we want to see the opening ceremonies. I usually play a role in these ceremonies by ringing the bells to open the festival," Haruna responded.

"Very well then, in that case, we have some time to kill before then," Munraito added.

"Ooh, I'd like to do some shopping on the Concourse, there were a few things I had my eye on earlier that I didn't get a chance to buy," Takada suggested.

"Well, that's one vote…" Munraito replied.

"I prefer we just stay here until the festival…" Gwenlynn added.

"I agree…we should stay put," Sei concurred.

"What about the Troika? Where are they, anyway?"

Koda asked, not seeing Anteon, Marduk or Arditi anywhere.

"They are currently elsewhere, presumably gathering intelligence on

Countess Toni. They come and go as they please," Sei explained.

"The Astari are the most ancient and powerful society in the known

Universe. They can do things that we can't even begin to fathom. When

they get back, they will likely have this whole mess completely figured

out," Haruna explained.

Koda nodded his head in acknowledgement.

"So it seems that the majority of us want to stay in the apartment, but

Takada wants to leave. I guess you're on your own, Ai," Haruna said.

"I guess so." Takada said, standing up and gathering her things.

"I'll be back," Takada announced, walking out the apartment door

towards the elevator.

"You know, I worry about her..." Haruna said.

"Who doesn't?" Munraito responded.

"I guess...she's definitely the type to take risks in life," Haruna added.

"It runs much deeper than that. Takada has a systemic and pervasive desire to push the boundaries of her own existence, much like Countess Toni does...the only difference is that Takada didn't take her desires nearly as far as Toni did. Something about Takada and Toni's dynamic disturbs me...perhaps Takada is capable of the same depravities that Toni stands accused of committing," Munraito wondered.

"I doubt it. Takada's more of the submissive type, she's into the same sorts of philosophies, but she's never the dominant one in any of those scenarios. Countess Toni seems like an extremely unusual case as far as women are concerned, I honestly can't think of any woman in human history that behaved the way Countess Toni appears to. It seems as if her entire Empire is based around a cult of personality, something that is almost exclusively reserved for men throughout most of history... for example, she refers to herself as a semi-divine being, a God of sorts, something that all her followers blindly worship. I guess times have changed." Haruna continued.

"From what I can gauge about her, she seems to behave in a way almost identical to that of a 20th-century totalitarian dictator, like a female Hitler. She believes in the same Darwinian struggle between people that Hitler did, she demands total loyalty to her cause, and she follows a similar mythos that the Nazi Party once did. Just how dangerous she is remains to be seen, but if she has access to the Architect technology, then she may be a ticking time bomb waiting to explode," Munraito explained.

"I just hope the Republic knows what it is getting itself into," Munraito continued.

"What are you suggesting?" Haruna asked.

"I'm saying that these events could be the run-up to the greatest war since the Naruhol Ihr. Keep in mind what Sei said earlier. Countess Toni is not the true Inheritor, only the Man against Time can truly control the Architects' technology. This means that Toni, though she can operate it, cannot fully unlock its true power. Any war that results will be costly, but eminently winnable by the Republic. This is still a human enemy using human technology, not an extraterrestrial one using weapons that we could scarcely conceive of. If we had this Architect technology during the

Naruhol Ihr war, we would have had them beaten in a heartbeat," Munraito explained.

"I just hope the Man against Time reveals himself soon," Munraito concluded.

"What about the Guardians...those huge Architect constructs like the one we saw in Muranahe?" Haruna asked.

"They are our allies in this, working to stop Countess Toni as well. We just need to find as many of them as we can," Munraito responded.

"Well then, what are we waiting for? Let's get ready for the Festival later, but in the meantime, we need to do more research on these constructs...I'm sure the Republic managed to collect a lot of data from the events on Oumi," Haruna suggested, walking over to the computer console on the wall, activating the apartment's computer systems.

"Well then, let's proceed while we wait for Takada to come back," Haruna continued, scrolling through the various search results on the screen.

"Well, the news sources are still lighting up the GalaxyNet about this...not to mention the news of the New Berlin Colony taking refuge at

Amane...that's probably not smart to announce that online," Haruna worried.

"At least the Republic fleet is acting as a deterrent to any all-out attack," Gwenlynn replied.

"I honestly don't see how Societas Polyphilae could manage a direct assault on Amane with this large a Republic presence. That would be tantamount to suicide," Sei added.

"Unless that's not what Countess Toni has planned," Munraito responded.

"Haruna, look at that,"Munraito pointed out.

"Wow...it appears to be some sort of manifesto published online...relating to the Man against Time and Countess Toni. It's called 'Sad Woman.' Haruna read.

"Go ahead, open it!" Koda replied.

Haruna moved her hand over the link, and to their surprise, the file opened not a text screen, but a virtual world. However, it became very clear that this was not a normal virtual sim. The sim displayed nothing but a dark, 3-D abyss filled with strange multicolored lights and eerie shadows, it was as if the group had been transported into this dark world.

The sim had no real plot and no gameplay, there was nothing to touch, and nothing to interact with. It was also very confusing and chaotic, with random sequences and strange, very nightmarish noises. These sounds ranged from what sounded like a woman begging her abusive husband to spare her life, children howling in pain from being tortured, sounds suggesting rape, murder and pedophilia, as well as very occasional static images of nightmarish scenes, such as three children lying on the ground naked and covered with animal blood, with three men wearing black robes surrounding them, sex dungeons and images of necrophilia.

"What the hell is this?! Get me out!!" Haruna screamed.

"Calm down! It's not real! This has something to do with Countess Toni...pay attention or we might miss something!" Munraito yelled.

As the disturbing sim continued, Munraito noticed a very small thumbnail image that kept flickering into view. It was a picture of two young girls, being locked in a basement by a tall, imposing man.

"Stop...right there, something related to Countess Toni," Munraito said, pausing the sim.

"Those two girls...run an image scan on them, try and find any matches anywhere on the Net." Munraito directed, as Haruna moved her hand over the images of the two terrified girls.

"Running a scan of these two images...searching...wow...this is heartbreaking..." Haruna said, collecting the results.

"These two girls are Toni and her sister as 8-year olds...they were forced into sex work by their own father..." Haruna gasped, staring in horror at the screen.

"Let me see this..." Munraito asked. His eyes widened when he saw the depths of the depravity that was displayed on screen.

On the Net were hundreds and hundreds of pages with images of Toni and her sister, often naked or wearing extremely revealing outfits and smothered in elaborate makeup with hundreds of comments on the explicit photos and video, many truly disgusting. On one page, there was a brief description of Toni and her sister's history, as written by one of the clients:

"My good friend always had a strange liking for his girls; they both were raised with a lot of sexuality at home, and he taught them to obey his commands and wishes, a few nights locked in the cold and dark basement and other small punishments had been very effective. The two girls, Toni and Tina, grew up as his private little sex toys, always ready to please. Once he had me over to his house on Arcana II, and he made some comments about Toni's nice ass. He offered me to touch her in exchange for some money, and a new idea was born of that. Afterward, their father regularly invited people from all over Serenna to come visit Toni and Tina, and the family became even wealthier off of this business, as it were. By the time the girls were 10 years old, they were already millionaires, and were allowed to keep their share of it. However, as the girls grew older, Toni began to show that she was unusually gifted intellectually, and used her intelligence and her fame to get anything she wanted from anyone...at first, this pleased her father, as his share of the business was only growing now that his daughter was taking a larger role in it...however, even he could not fathom what Toni had become. One day some years ago, Toni attacked her father and sister to hide the truth, torturing them and killing them in some of the worst possible ways, some say with medieval torture tactics, and took the money for herself...she hasn't been seen since."

The text read like a court transcript from a trial, one where someone accused of horrific crimes was being read the evidence against him or her, the trial of an individual who was probably the most dangerous individual in the Local Group.

"Oh My God..." Haruna gasped.

"This is who we're up against. A cunning, Machiavellian tyrant who has lived a life spent in Hell," Munraito confirmed.

"This is a nightmare. After what was done to this woman, there is no telling what she is capable of..." Koda worried.

Just then, the lights throughout the colony flickered, causing the entire ship to shake a bit. A wave of digital messages swept over the colony, casting a gold shimmer across every surface aboard the ship.

"What was that?!" Haruna yelled.

"Something's in the system! Purge it now!" Munraito ordered.

As Munraito yelled, a devilish laughter was heard over the GalaxyNet channel.

"Why, hello there, Munraito...Master Lightbringer. And who are these people you brought with you? The Elohim Queen, the Astari Troika and...my old high school friend, Ha! This is incredible...Wow!" The nagging, sarcastic female voice screeched.

Munraito quickly realized who he was talking to.

"Why did you do it? WHAT DID YOU DO?!" Munraito barked, immediately bringing up the Oumi crisis to Toni.

"Oh, that...well, little Haruna's parents were planning to expose me, so I did away with them and corrupted the entire police force in Muranahe to do my dirty work, and were it not for your eavesdropping on my operations and alerted the Guardians to my presence, I would have succeeded! Do you honestly have any idea what I am, Munraito?" Toni asked, mocking him.

"From these descriptions online, I think I know enough." Munraito replied, angrily.

"Oh please...those are just anecdotal records of my previous life, floating around on the Deep Net and luring people in, curious as to what happened to Toni and Tina...when they find me, they quickly realize the truth...and then I suck them in. Do you know what it is I do?" Toni asked.

"No...do enlighten us, though."

Munraito asked, holding back his rage to learn about his enemy.

"Mithras is real, Munraito, it is an interdimensional entity from another Universe, and using spatial and temporal warps, I rip these curious fools from our dimension, plunge them into Mithras' grip and imbue them with the power of Mithras itself, creating the ultimate soldiers. They stand united, fighting as one body, one mind and one soul. My channeling replaces their mortal, deprived condition with one of true immortality and fearlessness, and combined with the recovered Architect technology, we are building a truly unstoppable force. There is a realm of existence so far beyond your own, you cannot even imagine it. I am beyond your comprehension, Munraito. I am the Countess. Rudimentary creatures of consciousness and Avatar bodies, you stumble, tumble and fall. I am a child of the Gods, and I walk upright. The soldiers that fight for me and my ideals, they are the Departed, and I am their God.

Long have I awaited this day, Lightbringer. Long have I waited in the shadows, like a terrified little girl hiding from her sex-crazed father and his disgusting, vile friends...but now, I embrace it. The time of the Republic will soon be over. Yesterday I ordered the attack on Oumi to hopefully finish what I started fifty years ago...but you...YOU, Munraito, had to get involved. Let me make a few things clear to you. I'm like a little girl playing games, and I won't stop until I win...it does not matter who you are, or where you go, I will find you. That is a promise. The Inheritance has begun. The Inheritor's numbers will darken the skies of every world, and I AM the instrument! Now I am the Master!" Toni screamed, as more computer code streamed across the colony. By this point, many of the authorities on New Berlin began to realize what was happening and were preparing for the worst. Alarms began blaring throughout the city as a sickening feeling began to rise in Munraito's gut. This was it. They were about to get hit.

"Lock the apartment down. Try to get Takada back inside, the Republic needs to be warned," Munraito ordered, his palms beginning to sweat.

"You will not stop me. The shroud of darkness has fallen. Your era of peace is over. Soon you will all suffer the pain I have endured, and these are my spears." Countess Toni hissed, her digital presence disappearing. However, the nightmare for New Berlin was just beginning. In an instant, small, localized spatial and temporal distortions began appearing all over the city, popping like firecrackers as time and space aboard the colony began bubbling and warping, like water in a boiling pot. People in the streets screamed as they ran for cover, the distortions were powerful enough to buckle streets, damage homes and buildings, shatter windows and knock vehicles from their places...and then, it began. From various warp bubbles emerged fleets of dropships which began landing all over the city. This was not a terrorist attack. This was all-out urban warfare. The Republic Marines and Defenders, however, had prepared for just such a scenario. Their intel and tactics were spot-on. The armored Marines and Defenders immediately began firing at the dropships, blowing a few of them clean out of the sky before they could even land in New Berlin. Even at this point, Munraito had to admire Toni's element of surprise. The last place the Republic was expecting an invasion was from inside the colony itself.

The dropships returned fire in a blaze of crimson-red plasma. The ships were clearly of Architect design and they used the same weaponry that the Architect capital ships used. The Marines, whose shielded, pressurized battle armor afforded them more protection than any soldiers in human history used their heightened abilities from their exoskeletons to evade the incoming fire, ducking behind cover and using heavy weapons to bring the dropships crashing down. Unfortunately, a large percentage of the dropships didn't go straight down, causing a lot of collateral damage to nearby structures on board the colony.

Munraito watched as the scene unfolded from Haruna's window. People in the hallways outside were clamoring, panicking as several of the dropships made it past the Marines and Defenders and began setting down on some of the empty streets, and disgorging their armies of ground troops. Munraito caught a glimpse of some of the soldiers emerging from the dropships. They looked like inhuman monsters. They still walked like humans and fought like humans, but these men and women were no longer human. Imbued with the energies of a thousand star-beings of immense age and power, they were tormented, anguished and had their wills completely broken. They existed for one reason and one reason only: to kill, and kill they did. To Munraito, the Marines' and the Defender's horror, these ravaged souls completely ignored the Marines and Defenders firing upon them. They didn't return fire at all. Instead, they turned their weapons directly on the civilian population.

"This isn't a war, it's genocide!" Munraito screamed as he watched the anguished soldiers round up a crowd of civilians before searing the flesh from their bones with merciless streams of plasma.

"They're just massacring civilians! Take them out!" Alnair yelled as his squad fought alongside battle-hardened Marines and Army as they fired their weapons, destroying enemy after enemy. As the Marines and Defenders advanced through the chaotic city streets, they protected civilians where they found them, taking positions and destroying the rampaging Departed soldiers, who completely ignored the Marines and Defenders standing right in front of them. If Alnair and his squad would have allowed it, some of the Departed would have simply pushed them aside to get to the civilians hiding inside the building behind them.

"This is like an endurance match. These guys don't fight back, they just try to kill civilians. Why won't they shoot at us?" Josephine wondered, firing her long-range particle beam rifle at Departed trying to cross the street.

"Heads up, new contacts warping in, this isn't over!" Alnair barked, raising his Bipolar Rifle at the new warp bubbles popping up. Suddenly, three more dropships appeared, deploying three massive units, clad in full armor plating and carrying enormous repeating plasma cannons. Instantly, the huge bipeds raised their plasma cannons and began firing murderous salvos, this time at the Marines and Defenders facing them.

"Jo, Lucian, flank left, hit them from behind! Everyone else take defensive positions!" Alnair ordered, taking cover from the searing heat of the plasma blasts.

"Their armor is weak around their neck! Aim for their heads!" Josephine yelled, firing her particle beam rifle at precisely the right spot, sending the beam of plasma directly through the lumbering beast's cranium, felling it the ground with a sickening crash as more than five tons of heavy armor crumpled to the floor.

"What the hell is that thing?!" one of the Marines yelled.

"It's Departed, but it's not human. Countess Toni's abilities must work on aliens too. They look like Juggernauts."Alnair said, referring to a race of giant, hairy, ape-like humanoid creatures that inhabited the planet Exar about 500 light-years from Earth.

"Juggernauts are a Type-0 civilization, though. They've barely invented the wheel," one of the Marines replied.

"Well Countess Toni's apparently taught them a few things, that's for sure,"Alnair said as the other two Juggernauts were quickly defeated, their armored forms crashing to the ground, scattering some of the Marines out of the way.

"Juggernauts down, move up!"Alnair yelled as the Marines stayed behind to protect the civilians hiding in the building.

Fireteam Odin progressed through the streets near the Starlight apartment blocks. Alnair knew that Munraito and his companions were sheltered inside that building, and the odds were good that Countess Toni knew where they were as well. Alnair just had to beat her to them. Fortunately, the Defenders had some very special talents that would give them a decisive advantage over their enemies.

"Alright squad, engage Supercharge abilities on my mark...3...2...1...GO!" Alnair ordered.

In an instant, Fireteam Odin became cloaked in energy. Lucian and Frederic enveloped themselves in a burning, flame-like energy, radiating as much light as the Sun itself. Alnair began hovering in the air, cloaked in electrical energy, and Josephine conjured a radiant blue light, blessing her with superhuman speed and agility.

"Let's move!"Alnair ordered as Fireteam Odin dashed forward with their drastically-enhanced abilities, with Alnair leading the way, hovering high above the streets, looking for more Departed as they progressed towards the Starlight Apartment complex.

"Hostiles sighted!" Alnair announced, swooping in like a ghost and launching a tremendous blast of electricity at the crowd of Departed, instantly frying them and vaporizing them in a cloud of blue cinders. Three more Juggernauts appeared and began firing their colossal plasma cannons at Fireteam Odin, but Josephine promptly used her superhuman speed to overwhelm the Juggernauts' abilities, leaping over and around the lumbering beasts and putting plasma rounds directly through their skulls, toppling the massive creatures to the ground with sickening thuds.

"All hostiles down, keep moving forward!" Alnair urged, hovering forwards, electricity coursing from his body. They were approaching the Starlight Apartment complex, the apartment towers looming high over the city streets. Alnair breathed a silent sigh of relief as he saw that a contingent of Marines had made it to the apartment complex first, securing a perimeter and locking the area down with heavy weaponry.

"This is Defender Fireteam Odin to Platoons Alpha through September, we are approaching the Starlight Apartment Complex, are the Lightbringers secured?" Alnair barked into his communications suite.

"Affirmative, however, one of their companions is still missing. Takada, I believe," one of the Marines responded.

"That's bad news. Takada is very important to us in this scenario. We need to find her before we do anything. Keep eliminating hostiles and protect the civilians at all costs," Alnair replied as he destroyed another platoon of Departed with a blast of lightning.

"Alright team, mission priority change. We need to find Takada and bring her back to the apartment complex," Alnair ordered, satisfied with the Marines' defense of the Starlight Apartment complex.

"Platoon Charlie, this is Alnair of Fireteam Odin. Where did the Lightbringers say that Takada was going?"

"She was headed to the main concourse to shop before the festival. It's safe to say that probably won't be happening tonight," the Marine replied.

"Understood, the main concourse is completely locked down with Defender teams and Republic troops. Takada should be safe," Alnair responded.

"Good. I'll contact some of the platoons up on the main concourse to notify the Lightbringers that she's alright," The Marine continued.

"Continue with your duties, soldier. We've got a job to do down here," Alnair replied.

"Haruna, Takada is in the main concourse, under the protection of Republic forces. She's alright, and the Marines are telling her that we're alright too,"

Munraito announced, waiting inside Haruna's apartment as the battle raged outside. Thanks to Munraito's warning after his encounter with James Cartwright, the Republic was prepared for the attack, and the casualties were minimal. However, Munraito knew that this would not be the last time they heard from Countess Toni. She would surely up the ante after this, and Munraito had a sickening feeling that they had only seen the minimum of what Countess Toni was capable of.

Just then, Haruna heard a knock at the apartment door. Standing up and opening it, she saw three armored Marines standing outside, clad in full armor and standing nearly seven feet tall.

"Miss Otohime, Miss Takada is safe. She is with Platoon September on the main concourse, and waiting for the situation to improve," the Marine said, holding his Pulse Rifle in his massive, armored hands.

"That's a relief...I was worried those things got to her," Haruna replied, relieved that everything was going to be alright.

"Thankfully, this attack could have been a lot worse. Had Munraito not tipped the police off that this attack was coming, we could have been looking at a true tragedy here on New Berlin," the Marine said.

"Takada was right about James Cartwright, for sure. Maybe I was a little harsh on her,"Munraito added, reconsidering his opinions of Takada.

"Very well then, the Defenders are mopping up the remaining Departed in the city, we just got off the horn with Fireteam Odin. They have the situation under control in this sector. We're just waiting on the all-clear signal from the other Fireteams," the Marine reported.

"Alright then, that's good,"Munraito responded.

"However, we believe that it is no longer safe for you to remain on this colony for the time being. Countess Toni sees you and the Lightbringers as the greatest threat to whatever she has planned, Master Munraito. She's going to keep coming for you at any chance she gets, and your allies are not safe either. You need to move, and stay on the move for as long as possible. The Republic can handle this on its own," the Marine instructed.

"Understood, once Takada gets back, I will confer this with her," Munraito responded.

"Very well then, just sit tight. We're almost through this," the Marine replied, closing the door and returning to his duty.

"Alright then, you heard him. We need to go. For the moment, let's stick with our original plan and head for Shinaeal, we need to figure out what had Warmaster Lumen Ash so concerned, and I've got a disturbing feeling that it has something to do with Countess Toni," Munraito suggested

"I agree. If we could sway the Sangresaara to our cause against Countess Toni, they would be a powerful ally," Haruna explained.

Munraito knew just what the Sangresaara were capable of when the need arose. The last time the Republic and the Sangresaara had been allies was during the conflict with the Naruhol Ihr, and without their help, the Republic would not have won the war. If Lumen Ash could be swayed to the Republic's side, Countess Toni wouldn't have a chance.

Munraito watched out the apartment window as the Marines stood guard and watched for any Departed trying to attack the apartment building. The sounds of plasma fire were beginning to die down across the city as the enemies' numbers began to dwindle. Apparently, Countess Toni did not have adequate intel on the Republic's preparedness to her threats, in addition to gravely underestimating Munraito and his intuition. Countess Toni was dangerous, yes, but the bottom line was that she had no military training or experience whatsoever. Her strategy was to simply overwhelm the Republic with sheer brute force and superior technology, which was very powerful, but not foolproof.

"I wonder what's going on out there..." Haruna asked.

"It's going to be all right. The Republic's just tying up loose ends right now," Munraito reassured.

"I'm still scared," Haruna said, concerned.

"Don't be...the situation is under control," Gronveld replied, standing near Sei Ikkiku, prepared to fight if necessary.

Just then, the Astari Troika suddenly reappeared in the apartment, appearing out of a plasma orb entering the room through the windows, much like ball lightning.

"We are very much aware of the situation facing the Republic, and have conferred with the Astari Galactic Command. We are pledged to assist you in any way we can during this time of crisis," Anteon announced.

"Very well then, I shall confer this with the Elohim Council on Belisaria after this crisis has abated," Sei replied.

"It looks like we're pulling out all the stops to end this threat, Haruna. Just remember, whatever happens, I will assure your safety," Munraito ensured.

"But...what about Countess Toni..."

"She does not frighten me. She appears to be trapped in a perpetual state of childhood, she seems to think she's a doll, nothing more than a scared, tormented child trapped in a woman's body. Just trust me. You will be safe, as long as you learn to stand on your own. I will help you with that, for I see great potential in you," Munraito replied.

"The next step is to see if we can't get the Sangresaara on board with us." Haruna explained.

"That's going to be easier said than done. The Sangresaara's trust is not easily won. The only way to truly earn the respect of the Sangresaara civilization is to prove your strength on the field of battle, or in singular combat with one of their greatest warriors," Gwenlynn explained.

"We are prepared to go to war if the situation mandates it," Marduk added.

"As are we, we shall fight to the end if necessary," Sei replied.

"We shall not allow this monster to destroy everything we hold dear out of a psychotic revenge complex from a childhood robbed," Sei declared, stalwartly.

"Haruna, I will do all I can to protect you. You have my word. With my guidance, I will protect you, by teaching you to protect yourself," Munraito ensured, looking Haruna tenderly in the eye.

Suddenly, another knock came at the door. Munraito walked towards it and opened it...sure enough Takada was standing there, surrounded by three Marines. Takada was a chatty as usual, entertaining the soldiers with stories about her life and excerpts from her tell-all book that she had already shown Munraito.

"There you are! You had me worried sick!" Haruna exclaimed.

"Why, I told you I'd be back. You honestly didn't think any of those freakish things that my old high school buddy sent after you were going to get me, did you?" Takada responded.

"I actually found her attempt quite laughable, actually. She has no knowledge of military strategy or tactics whatsoever, and simply relies on technology and sheer numbers to overwhelm her targets. It's pretty basic," Takada explained.

"She's right. Takada told us everything on the way over here. She knows Countess Toni better than anyone else, and from what we've heard, she's just a tortured woman with an enormous ego," the Marines said.

"Yes, but as we have seen, her revenge mechanisms are a little more serious than we thought," Munraito responded.

"But, truth be told, when it gets right down to it, she's just your typical deep-Net dreg on a power trip," Haruna continued.

"Dealing with her will take some time, but the Republic will eventually win. I guarantee it," Munraito smiled.

"One can only hope," the Marines replied.

"Anyway, the all-clear's been given. Now it's just a matter of tallying the toll, unfortunately. We did lose a few people," The Marines added, solemnly.

"What exactly triggered the attack?" the Marines asked.

"We found a sim on the Deep Net related to Countess Toni. Apparently, she's able to enter the system and travel directly to the colony through the computer networks via the online Universe," Munraito responded.

"Munraito, didn't your parents ever tell you to NEVER go on the Deep Net?" the Marine said, sarcastically.

"I don't even really remember my birth parents, to be honest. I was essentially raised by the Lightbringers. Master Iori is the only father I have ever known," Munraito responded.

"Alright then," the Marine replied.

"Either way, the colony will remain on lockdown until tomorrow, until the full extent of the damage can be assessed by Republic survey teams. We dodged a plasma blast today, that's for sure. Were it not for Munraito, the death toll would have been astronomical," the Marines said.

"It was my pleasure to be of service," Munraito replied.

"Now, if you'll excuse us, we have other matters to attend to. Carry on with your business," Munraito told the Marines, who promptly left them in peace.

"Alright, now that we're all back together again, we need a plan," Munraito said.

"Haruna suggests that we stick with our original formula and head to Shinaeal to meet with Warmaster Lumen Ash about a matter that has been troubling him. Does anyone have any better ideas?" Munraito asked.

"I would recommend we go to Belisaria first. I have information regarding the Architects that would be of vital use to us and the Republic," Sei suggested.

"I still think the issue with the Sangresaara takes precedent. If Countess Toni does plan to attack them, we need to protect as many lives as possible," Haruna replied.

"Very well then, I agree that Sei's point is valid, however, we cannot risk another attack, especially against a civilization known to be extremely warlike. An attack on Shinaeal or any Sangresaara-held world would put the entire galaxy at risk, and we simply cannot allow that to happen. I vote that we go to Shinaeal first, and then travel to Belisaria to see what Sei has to offer about the Architect technology," Munraito responded.

"I guess it's safe to say that there won't be any Festival tonight," Haruna said, disappointed.

"I would have to agree with you on that," Munraito replied.

"Still, I'm happy that we're all still alive. Casualties would have been much higher were it not for Koda's and my efforts to investigate James Cartwright, perhaps I didn't give you enough credit, Takada. Maybe I should listen to you a little more often," Munraito mumbled, somewhat begrudgingly.

"You're absolutely right, Munraito. I may not be as smart or powerful as you are, but if you've survived for as long as I have, you learn a thing to two that you can't learn in a book or a holographic data file. I'll have you know that I grew up in Holy City, one of the more urbanized neighborhoods in Nox Aeterna, the largest city on Arcana II, one of the wealthiest planets in the Republic. That neighborhood is tough to grow up in, and you do what you can to survive. I got out and made it big, but many of my friends growing up were not so lucky. I was discovered and mentored by a truly special individual, one that saw my true potential and allowed me to flourish." Takada informed.

"I guess there are many different types of intelligence..." Munraito replied.

"I will meditate on this. Allow me to excuse myself. Haruna, I will be right back," Munraito continued.

"All right then." Takada responded, letting Munraito stand up and walk into the empty guest room.

"He's certainly opening up," Takada said to Haruna.

"I guess he just needed to be around people other than the Lightbringers for once. Being cooped up in that castle for so long does things to your mind, I guess," Haruna replied.

"I think you're doing a great job with him, Haruna. He needs someone like you in his life," Takada responded.

Munraito, however, was already out of earshot. He was in the next room, sitting perfectly still on the bed, mumbling something to himself.

"Well, well, well, Miss Toni, what do we have here? I see your face...I know your name...let's play a little game, shall we?" Munraito mumbled, entering his Hyperspace trance, his consciousness streaming out of his body. In an instant, it had reached one of Countess Toni's seedy hideaways on an unidentified Republic world. Meeting inside were nine men, each one of them radiating the same Mithraic energy that the Departed soldiers were imbued with. These people were no longer men; however, they were still just as vulnerable to Hyperspace Meditation as anyone else.

Munraito consciousness entered their minds one by one and shut them down, killing each man instantly. Soon, all nine of them lay dead.

"Excellent...now for more..." Munraito whispered.

Munraito's focus shifted from the nine Societas members to Countess Toni herself...it was at this moment that Munraito first saw the Countess for what she was. She was 12 feet, 5 inches tall, due to her Hyperborean Avatar, but looked a good bit taller than she was because of her outfit. Her face was chalk-white because of 4 layers of makeup, much like the bizarre adornments she had worn as a child. She possessed thick black eyeshadow that formed the Eye of Ra symbol around her eyes. One eye was green, and the other was blue, but they were cold, unblinking and staring. She had her pupils dilated specifically to look like cold, eerie shark eyes, like blue and green iridescent lumps of coal. The blank, empty expression on her face never changed, no matter what her mood was. Munraito couldn't tell if she was feeling anything at that point.

Her hair was brown, but styled like a Qing Dynasty empress, with diamond, platinum and gold-encrusted hairpieces that kept her hair in 6 pigtails. Three of them sat on each side of her head, each covered in diamond, platinum and gold-encrusted armor that also kept the braid from becoming frizzy. The adornments made her hair look like insect legs, especially when she moved, causing the 6 pigtails to move like the legs of a spider.

She also possessed a crown made of solid crystal in shape of a three-headed crane with six wings on her head, adding 2 feet to her already impressive height. Behind that sat a huge peacock-fan headdress that changed color based on her mood. Munraito saw that it was the only way to tell her emotions, as she had become so powerful with the interdimensional forces that she was able to disable her physical reactions to emotion. Maybe it was the years of abuse, or maybe it was her extraordinarily heightened senses, but Countess Toni was completely without emotion, except for rage.

The peacock feather eyes changed expression and color in place of Toni's real ones. She possessed a huge feather ruff around her neck made of Supreme Featherwing plumes as a scarf, with pennants and silky cloth scarves that resembled the Twelve-Wired Flutterfinger and Crested Salamandra plumage at the same time, and a train-like veil and cape made of Kyliesian silk dyed with what looked like human blood.

Her dress was woven from spider silk infused with silkworm silk, and woven on a microscopic level so that the border of the dress behaved like a living organism, symbolizing every known organism in the Local Group.

Covering the dress were hundreds of iridescent precious stones, each one reflecting light in such a way that viewed from a certain angle, it made her look almost invisible. She appeared as a shimmering outline, barely visible in standard lighting.

The dress itself was red and black, with huge, yellow eyespots in the black parts of the dress and black eyespots in the red parts of the dress that seemed to blink when sunlight hit it at certain angles or shine with an ethereal, calming glow when the moonlight shined upon it.

The whole dress glowed an eerie, Halloween haunted house-like purple in ultraviolet light, and had large roaring dragon designs embroidered on it. The dress was enormous and supported by the bones of her Mithras ritual sacrifice victims, much like whalebones were used to make a corset.

The part of the dress that covered her torso and chest was the most heavily decorated, with huge dragonfly wings made of woven yarn and glittered with sea salt dust and sand coming out of her back, these were folded under her cape and veil and could be spread at will, even though

Toni couldn't fly. Her necklace was more like an Egyptian queen's brooch, made of solid gold with a huge sapphire in the center, just visible under the bird-of-paradise feather scarves. Her gloves, lacy white dress gloves that were veiled by delicate, red silken sleeves from her dress. Each had a 56-karat gemstone covering every one of her fingernails. Sharpened into a dagger-like claw; these gemstone gauntlet gloves were used to carve enemies like a tiger slashing its prey, and the rest of the glove's surface was covered in razor-sharp, solid diamond blades that could slice through almost any surface.

She also wore a tiara of autumn leaves on her head, on the crown of the three-headed crane helmet, whose three heads are arranged in such a way that they defied the Euclidean geometric form, therefore making her dress impossible to create without immense, physics-bending telekinesis. Her shoes were huge black-velvet Gothic Lolita platform shoes, with razor-sharp dagger-high heels, but these were not visible under her huge dress.

Munraito was a bit shocked upon seeing the Countess, standing motionlessly in a room alone...however, as he immediately tried to penetrate her mind, he was brutally repulsed by a wall of demented, tormented images of rape, torture, murder, child pornography and incest.

"I should have known…" Munraito mumbled.

"Insanity is a powerful shield against mind probing. It is impossible to get a clear reading on someone like this…" Munraito whispered.

Munraito decided to leave Countess Toni alone, and moved on to easier targets. One by one, Munraito's consciousness killed its way through scores of Societas members, each one dying instantaneously. However, he knew that this type of purging was pointless. He could kill as many of Countess Toni's soldiers as he wanted, but it wouldn't solve the overall problem. As long as Countess Toni lived, Haruna was not safe, even if he trained her as a Lightbringer.

Within 15 minutes, Munraito had killed more than 500 Societas members and sympathizers, many of which had profiles on the Deep Net forums. His role as the Man against Time was going to have to grow exponentially if the war against Countess Toni was to succeed. After all, he was the only man who could truly harness the power of the Architects' technology. HE was the true Inheritor, not Countess Toni, and only he could truly understand its power. Munraito relished the thought of going to Belisaria and learning about the wondrous Architect technology, and possibly unlocking its true power. As Munraito continued his silent rampage against the Societas, visions of a glorious victory filled his head...dreams of creating a world where he, Haruna, his companions and all Mankind could live in perfect harmony with one another, and the galaxy would be forever molded into a perfect utopia. At that moment, Munraito breathed a silent vow to Haruna:

"Haruna Otohime...hear my prayer. Give me the strength to accomplish my goals, lay your arms around me and embrace me for what I am, for wherever you go, I will follow, and wherever you fall, I will catch you. Though we face an incredible test, we are strong, and we will prevail. As the unjust fall around me, and the galaxy begins to change, we will never change. We are each a piece of a whole person...and the galaxy is ours for the taking,"

CPSIA information can be obtained
at www.ICGtesting.com
Printed in the USA
BVOW06s1513191117
500800BV00012B/473/P

9 781977 882035